FORTUNA

The Roll of the Dice in the
Throes of History

James Leslie-Melville

The
Book
Guild

First published in Great Britain in 2025 by
The Book Guild Ltd
Unit E2 Airfield Business Park,
Harrison Road, Market Harborough,
Leicestershire, LE16 7UL
Tel: 0116 2792299
www.bookguild.co.uk
Email: info@bookguild.co.uk

The manufacturer's authorised representative in the EU
for product safety is Authorised Rep Compliance Ltd,
71 Lower Baggot Street, Dublin D02 P593 Ireland (www.arccompliance.com)

Fortuna is a work of fiction. The events portrayed in it, while based on
historical figures, are the product of the author's imagination.

Typeset in 12pt Adobe Jenson Pro

Printed and bound by CPI Group (UK) Ltd, Croydon, CR0 4YY

ISBN 978 1835742 631

British Library Cataloguing in Publication Data.
A catalogue record for this book is available from the British Library.

To Clare, and the equally lovely Bev.

'Fate, Time, Occasion, Chance and Change? To these
All things are subject but eternal Love'

Prometheus Unbound, Percy Bysshe Shelley

Contents

Prologue

The Dawn of Chance

The war was over, his father Kronos banished to the infinity of time, his other great adversary Atlas doomed to bear the weight of the heavens on his shoulders for evermore. Zeus reigned supreme over all creation: he had elected himself king of the gods; he had appointed a host of minor deities to serve under him. Now there was one final task to complete. With his younger brothers Poseidon and Hades coveting his throne, he needed to thwart their ambition without turning them against him. And in the battle-hardened palm of his hand and the restless cogs of his brain lay the key.

High on Mount Olympus, Zeus inspected the two small ivory cubes, carved from the mammoth tusk he had found buried in the floodplain of the mighty Indus River.[1] He had marked the surfaces of each cube with black dots numbering from one to six, an easy enough job, and had calculated that he could use them to offer each of his siblings sovereignty over a share of his kingdom. What could be fairer than that?

Summoned to his court, Poseidon and Hades listened impatiently as Zeus set out his proposal on the terrace of the palace, fists clenched behind his back. 'Brothers, you have fought valiantly alongside me in our struggle against the Titans, and it is only right that we share the rewards evenly between us. As you know, I have delegated responsibility for various lesser matters, and now we three must split the fabric of the universe itself. One of us shall rule the sea, another shall hold sway over the earth and sky above and the third shall be master of the underworld. After much thought, I have devised a way of allocating these dominions impartially between us, using these.' He held out his arms, unfurled his fingers and offered a cube to each of them.

'You will see that both have six sides, each one marked with a different number of dots. Thrown down together, their uppermost surfaces will produce a combined total of anywhere between two and twelve. If we ignore the numbers two and twelve, we are left with nine possible outcomes, that is, three for each of us.' He looked at the brothers in turn. 'I suggest that you, Poseidon, take the numbers three, four and five; I will take six to eight; and nine to eleven will fall to you, Hades.' He paused, briefly, then pressed on.

'We will each throw, and if any of us gets one of their allocated numbers, they will receive the dominion of their choice. If there's not a clear result after all three of us have thrown, those for whom it remains undecided will start afresh.' He smiled broadly. 'We will throw in order of age, and may we each get what we wish for.'

Poseidon and Hades glanced at each other, brows creased in suspicion. They had not expected their brother to be so generous in dividing the spoils of war and felt sure there was a catch to his scheme. But it seemed simple enough – three possible outcomes split across the nine numbers, and an even chance for any of them to win the biggest prize of all, command of sky and earth and all life within. Warily they nodded their agreement and passed the cubes to Zeus, as the eldest amongst them.[2]

And so the contest for all the world began. Zeus tossed the cubes onto the olive-wood table between them with a casual flick of the wrist, and the three siblings peered down. Seven black dots gleamed in the bright sunlight flooding the terrace. Zeus splayed his hands in a gesture of commiseration. 'I choose the earth and sky. You next, Poseidon.'

Poseidon swept up the cubes in exasperation, shook them between cupped fingers and let them fall onto the table. Hades and he counted the dots for a second time, Zeus standing by with his arms folded, apparently unconcerned by the continuing duel. Eleven. No clear result. Hades scooped the cubes off the edge of the table into an open palm, juggled them briskly and threw them back down. Four. He and Poseidon glared at each other in silence, their equal disappointment at having lost the greatest prize to Zeus eclipsed by the play-off still to come.

Zeus collected the cubes and presented them to Poseidon with a consoling expression. Poseidon threw again, letting out a bellow of excitement as the cubes rolled to a halt, revealing five dots. 'The sea,' he shouted at the others, as if that had been his first choice all along. Hades strode away, speechless with rage, consigned to the underworld in perpetuity.

The king of the gods examined the retreating back of his youngest brother and turned to Poseidon. 'The sea it is for you, brother, fair and square, I hope you agree.' Then he too left the terrace, adding airily over his shoulder, 'Keep the cubes, if you want them.' Out of sight, in the shade of the palace banqueting hall, he could at last afford to grin with pleasure at a job well done.

Later that evening, Zeus hurled a thunderbolt across the sky in celebration of his triumph. He had taken a risk, but a measured risk, having calculated that the likelihood of scoring six, seven or eight was significantly higher than drawing one of the other numbers.[3] He had given his brothers no time to work out the odds, and he had hustled them into allowing him to throw first. In any case, if the cubes had failed him, he would merely have ignored them. He reigned supreme, did he not?!

The concept of chance, the lure of a gamble, the fateful roll of the dice, had been unleashed on the world. And so, in their wake, as night follows day, had the art of cheating.

Notes

1   *The precise origins of dice are unclear. Preceded by the use of animal 'knuckle' bones, they appear to have emerged in both the Tigris/Euphrates plains of Sumeria (southern Iraq) and the Indus Valley (Pakistan) in the early/mid third millennium BCE. Around the same time the ancient Egyptians were using marked two-sided shapes to play a game similar to backgammon called 'Senet', with cubical dice found in Egyptian tombs dating to c. 2000 BCE. Trade in ivory goods (including dice) is known to have been underway in cities such as Mohenjo Daro during the Indus/Harappan civilisations of the late third/early second millennia BCE.*

2   *Kronos's wife Rhea gave birth to six children in the following order: Hestia, Hades, Demeter, Poseidon, Hera and Zeus. After Kronos had eaten the first five in an attempt to frustrate the prophecy that he would be overthrown by his children, Rhea brought up Zeus in secret and encouraged him to exact revenge on his father on her behalf. Zeus tricked Kronos into swallowing a potion that forced him to vomit up the five children in the reverse order that he had consumed them. From that point on Zeus was regarded not only as the king of the gods, given his role in resurrecting his siblings, but as the firstborn. Of the other five children, Hera was considered the next eldest, and so on, with Hades being the youngest son.*

3   *The likelihood of a particular result using dice is expressed in the formula 'Probability = number of desired outcomes ÷ number of*

possible outcomes.' With two six-sided dice, the odds of throwing a total between two and twelve are:

Score	2 or 12	3 or 11	4 or 10	5 or 9	6 or 8	7
Odds	1/36 (2.8%)	2/36 (5.6%)	3/36 (8.3%)	4/36 (11.1%)	5/36 (13.9%)	6/36 (16.7%)

N.B. In Homer's Iliad, *the division of power between Zeus, Poseidon and Hades is achieved by the drawing of lots, rather than by dice, with no indication of foul play by Zeus.*

The Trojan War

c. 1200 BCE – Greece

Palamedes had almost stopped listening, as the council of war droned on into a third hour and the sun began to dip towards the western horizon. The Greek generals, led by the undisputed commander-in-chief, King Agamemnon of Mycenae, had reviewed the updated numbers of vessels and troops now assembled; they had debated the merits of a diplomatic mission to the enemy's King Priam before launching the fleet; they had argued amongst themselves as to who should spearhead the first attack on Troy's city walls. But the glaring flaw in their plans remained unresolved – where was Odysseus, son of King Laertes, without whose strategic and military prowess the army was sorely ill-prepared for a campaign of this scale? After all, it was he who had created the call to arms.

Amid a swirl of competition for the hand in marriage of Zeus's daughter Helen, said to be the most beautiful maiden in all Greece, Odysseus had offered to stand back from the crowd. In doing so he had suggested that all those seeking to wed her be bound by an oath pledging support to the lucky winner in the event of any challenge to the couple's union. King

Menelaus of Sparta had emerged victorious and when, shortly after their marriage, Helen was abducted by the Trojan prince Paris, the mobilisation of an army to avenge her husband had begun immediately. Ships captained by disappointed suitors, laden with soldiers and supplies, had been pouring into the Aulis harbour for weeks now, yet Odysseus had still not made an appearance, despite a series of messengers being dispatched to his island stronghold, Ithaca, to summon him.

As elder brother to Menelaus, Agamemnon felt particularly aggrieved at this failure to support his family and growled with irritation when the door to the council chamber was flung open to admit an envoy from Laertes. 'Why am I being expected to read a message from the father, when I should be receiving the homage of the son?' he barked. The envoy met the stony gaze of the generals seated round the great oak table and presented a scroll in silence. Agamemnon glanced through it, eyes widening in disbelief, and threw it down on the table before him in disgust.

'Apparently our brilliant soldier Odysseus, the man who devised the trigger for the army to gather in the first place, is not going to grace us with his presence.' He stood, glowering at his colleagues, and picked up the scroll again to shake it at the offending courier. His voice rose. 'Lost his mind, you say? How can this be possible? What proof can you offer?' Every face in the room swivelled towards the bearer of such unwelcome news, and even Palamedes listened attentively for the answer.

'King Laertes has instructed me to assure you it is true, Your Highness. I can offer no proof, as such, except to say that I myself have seen my master's son, incapable of speech and totally deranged. He recognises no one, not even his wife and baby, and is unable to dress or feed himself. How this has come about is a mystery to the physicians, but there is no doubting it.' The envoy paused, and as the silence lengthened, added, 'The king appreciates that it is a severe loss to your plans and asks you to accept his family's apology.'

Agamemnon slumped into his chair, exhaling noisily, any sympathy for Odysseus overridden by frustration at this setback to his arrangements. 'Fifty ships, that's what we'll lose from this. Fifty ships and about five thousand men.' He surveyed his audience and continued more calmly. 'Still, we will manage without him, however experienced or clever he might be. We have plenty of accomplished warriors to captain the troops, and he wasn't the only one with a brain. We will wait one more week for the final stragglers to arrive, and then the fleet can sail. Does anyone have anything to add?'

The generals shifted uneasily in their seats, all too aware of the implications of this report from Laertes. To declare that going to war without one man was perilous would be a sign of defeatism, and no one was going to do that in front of his peers. But they all knew what they would be lacking. Like him or loathe him, and there were plenty of the latter, it was widely conceded that Odysseus brought with him a mix of leadership, bravery and cunning that would be much missed on the Trojan plain.

The silence was broken by the most junior member of the council. Despite his lineage as a grandson of the mighty sea-god Poseidon, Palamedes was a minor prince amongst those sitting at the table, and untested in war. Compared to the fame of heroes such as Ajax and Diomedes, and the authority of kings such as Menelaus and Nestor, he had little martial contribution to offer. His attendance was due instead to his administration skills, on which Agamemnon and the others had come to rely as an ever-increasing body of troops mustered on the shores of the eastern Greek mainland. His marshalling of supplies, his control of costs and his grasp of logistical detail had rapidly become a key talent for the council, and he was now quartermaster to the army in all but name. To the commander-in-chief, his ability to take the sting out of the generals' competing demands for attention within the hastily assembled alliance of regional forces was even more valuable.

'Sire, I'm sure I speak for all of us when I say what disturbing news this is. Of course, we have no cause to doubt King Laertes, and I understand your eagerness to put the fleet to sea. But I wonder if, for the sake of just a short delay, we might check for ourselves the severity of Lord Odysseus's condition.' He hesitated, conscious that to infer Odysseus or his father were lying would also be an accusation of cowardice, linked as it was to the pledge concerning Menelaus and Helen.

'The mind is a capricious beast,' he went on, 'and it can play tricks on the sturdiest of men. Equally, such a disorder can disappear as swiftly as it flares up. Perhaps one of the council should visit Ithaca to see if, by some miracle, the general can be cured. It is less than a week's journey each way, so you would be losing no more than a few days in your timetable for the fleet's launch – a negligible cost if Lord Odysseus can be delivered back to us.'

Agamemnon nodded approvingly at the logic of the argument. Coming from the lowly Palamedes, it was a credible proposal, whereas he would have judged any such intervention from a leading general as a potential threat to his self-appointed position at the head of the army.

'Agreed,' he said brusquely. 'You can go, Palamedes, and Diomedes with you. He is well known to Odysseus – they have fought together in the past – and if anyone can knock some sense into our mad friend, he will. Let us reconvene here in two weeks' time for a final council before embarkation for Troy, with or without the Ithacans.' He stood once again, signalling the closure of the meeting, and the generals followed him out of the room. Only Palamedes and Diomedes remained, to discuss the trip ahead, and Palamedes was careful not to betray his true thoughts on the matter.

Six days later, the two men stood in a field bordering Ithaca's shoreline, accompanied by a woman carrying a baby. A savage heat bore down on them from the midday sun, with neither shade nor breeze to ease their discomfort. Nobody but an imbecile would be out tilling the land in such conditions at this time of day, and there indeed he was, oblivious to everything around him. Lord Odysseus, one of the most intelligent people alive, reduced to a raving lunatic, hobbling crab-like behind a mismatched team of horse and ox, and sowing salt in the chaotic furrows dug by the meandering ploughshare. As he passed Palamedes and Diomedes, they could hear him muttering incoherently, his eyes rolling in their sockets and phlegm drooling from his lips. The woman let out an involuntary sob and Diomedes shook his head in despair, appalled to see his comrade-in-arms brought to such a state. He gestured to Palamedes to stay where he was and began to walk with the Ithacan, addressing him in a loud voice. Any hope that his words would spark a wave of recognition, or at the very least, a return to more normal conduct, proved useless. Odysseus ploughed on regardless, insensible to the outside world.

Palamedes observed the performance with interest. Although he acknowledged the skills Odysseus would bring to Agamemnon's army, he had not liked him on the few occasions they had met. More than that, he had always found the Ithacan's ingenuity and quick wits mildly irksome, his silken tongue and artful manner too smooth to be entirely honourable. As soon as the envoy's report of his madness had arrived, a germ of mistrust had taken root in Palamedes' mind. He could not guess at why Odysseus might wish to dodge the draft for the Greek attack on Troy, but he suspected that his crazed behaviour was a bid to do so. It was a dangerous allegation against such an exalted leader. However, he reasoned that if it were true, he would be protected by Agamemnon, and if it were false, Odysseus would be in no position to harm him. His hand closed on a pair of dice in his pocket, seeking reassurance from the fates for what he planned to do.

The dice had been handed down to him by his father Nauplius, who had in turn inherited them from his father Poseidon with the story of how Zeus had shared out sovereignty of the world with Poseidon and Hades, using the dice to his advantage. Poseidon had always nursed the suspicion that he had been cheated in some way but had never worked out how and had kept the dice to remind himself of his brother's duplicity. Tiring of this eventually, he had given them to Nauplius, who had been equally puzzled and was happy to pass them on when Palamedes began to show his mental agility in his early schooling. Unlike his father and grandfather, Palamedes had understood immediately how to use them.

Being highly numerate, Palamedes was capable of weighing up risk and its likely consequences to a fine degree. Nonetheless, he rarely acted on important events without reading the dice for guidance. He knew this was contradictory to his arithmetical talent but considered it a healthy superstition, gratifying the goddess of chance, Tyche, while allowing him scope for manoeuvre where a decision hung in the balance. Unseen by Diomedes, he withdrew his hand from his pocket and peered furtively at the upturned surfaces of the dice in his palm. An even number for the combined dice would support his idea for unmasking Odysseus; an odd number would require a different approach. Eight dots stared back at him.

At the far end of the field, Diomedes had assisted Odysseus in turning the plough and they were beginning to make their way back towards Palamedes and the woman. They made a pathetic sight, Diomedes still talking at the top of his voice, to no avail, and Odysseus gibbering to himself as he threw handfuls of salt into the newly furrowed soil. When they were ten paces away, Palamedes looked his companion square in the face and said in a harsh whisper, 'Lady Penelope, bear with me, and on no account interfere with what I am about to do.' Then he snatched the baby from her grasp and stepped out to place it in the path of the oncoming horse and ox.

Odysseus was the first to react, stopping in his tracks and hauling on the reins to the yoked animals. His body straightened, his eyes focused for the first time since the visitors had arrived in the field and he bellowed, 'Quick, Diomedes, get the boy out of the way.' The seasoned warrior responded instantly, running in front of the plough team and hoisting the baby into his arms, just in time to avoid it being trampled by hooves or mutilated by the metal blade cleaving the earth below. The child's mother watched in stunned horror, her head reeling between the man who had almost killed her son and the husband she had thought demented.

Diomedes handed the baby to Odysseus with a quizzical expression, then grinned at Palamedes. 'A crafty ploy, but it seems to have worked!' Palamedes shrugged and they both looked to Odysseus for an explanation. He walked slowly over to Penelope, kissed her warmly on the lips and patted the baby fondly. Then, with his free arm draped round his wife's shoulders, he turned to the men with a cheerful smile.

'A belated welcome to Ithaca, my friends! Penelope knows I would never harm our son, but she has not been party to the rest. I should probably kill you, Palamedes, for putting Telemachus in danger, but I admit that I owe all three of you an apology. And King Agamemnon too, I daresay. I will gladly eat my humble pie, and I hope you will excuse me if I tell you that I acted out of love for my family rather than fear of the coming war with Troy.'

Palamedes said nothing, and Diomedes broke the awkward silence. 'All well and good, Odysseus, that you are not the deranged fool we had believed. But you need to give us a better reason for your dishonesty. You have lied to all Greece, held up the fleet's departure by several weeks and, worse still, it appears, gravely distressed Penelope. Of course Agamemnon will want you back. Before we permit that, my question is: how can we trust you going forward after this brazen attempt to deceive us?'

'You can trust me, old friend,' the Ithacan replied, 'I swear it on the life of my son. My problem was the word of an oracle. Penelope heard it prophesied that if I went to war, I would not come home for a decade or more. As you can imagine, she was upset by this, not just for her own sake,' he glanced at his wife and hugged her to him, 'but for what it might mean for our estates here. Who would manage the crops, protect the livestock, help her raise Telemachus?' He squeezed the baby's tiny, outstretched hand. 'When she told me about the prophecy, I decided privately to feign madness in order to escape Agamemnon's call-up. Now that you have found me out, I am fully committed.' He bowed with a flourish. 'We can leave for Aulis as soon as you like.'

'That we will,' said Diomedes, leaning forward to offer his hand in acceptance of the explanation provided. Palamedes followed suit, smiling to demonstrate that he bore no hard feelings for the charade he had been able to expose. Behind his smile, however, the seed of doubt still festered, only now it centred not on the Ithacan's mental state, but rather on his readiness to forgive and forget. Palamedes suspected he had made a bitter enemy, against whom Agamemnon's patronage would prove a flimsy shield.

*

Five years on – Troy

The war had reached a stalemate. Five long years since Helen of Sparta had been kidnapped by the love-struck Trojan scoundrel Paris, sparking the launch of King Agamemnon of Mycenae's fleet. And what a mighty armada it was, the greatest ever to have sailed, numbering more than a thousand ships and one hundred thousand men once Odysseus had brought his troops to the muster. They had anchored off the coast of Troy and had wasted no time in engaging the enemy to form a beachhead onto land. After some fierce fighting on the foreshore, the Trojan army had retreated across the open ground separating their capital city from the sea, and the Greeks had set about establishing their camp. It was a rudimentary affair at first, since no one expected the offensive to last for long. A month or so of skirmishing to soften up their foe with feats of unmatched daring and skill, before breaching the city walls, burning the royal palace and putting Paris and his family to the sword. Helen would be reunited with her slighted husband Menelaus; Agamemnon would be lauded as the new ruler of Troy; and stories of the Greek warriors' exploits would pass down into legend. They would be sailing home before the winter set in, their ships laden with Trojan treasure.

It had turned out very differently.

To be fair, the Greeks had emerged victorious in the early encounters, forcing the opposition back behind Troy's walls and keeping them pinned down within. But thereafter the campaign had stuttered to a halt. Company after company had been thrown at the enemy's defences, with nothing to show for it except a mounting body count and a few individual acts of remarkable valour. The celebrated boy-soldier Achilles had justified his reputation in battle, leading from the front and slaying all before him. Others had distinguished themselves too, Odysseus and Diomedes amongst them. But so had many of the Trojans, Paris and his elder brother Hector in particular. With supply lines intact from their territories to the east of the city, they had no reason to surrender and were prepared to wait out the siege indefinitely.

So the Greeks had dug in, their camp developing over the years into a fully fledged township reliant on provisions gleaned from overseas or from raiding parties ravaging the coastal plain in an ever-widening arc. Agamemnon's determination to win back Helen for Menelaus remained undimmed, but neither he nor his generals could hatch a plan to break the impasse. Moreover, it was rumoured that the sun-god Apollo had built the city walls and would do everything in his power to keep them intact.

During this time Palamedes' star had continued to rise. His deft management of resources had proved invaluable as supplies became harder to find, and his position as quartermaster had been duly formalised. Already highly regarded by the Greek leaders, his popularity had extended to the troops as he introduced schemes to keep them occupied within the camp. Besides the usual competitions to test their athletic and martial skills, his inventive brain had devised a variety of board games to keep them alert, some involving the use of dice, others the cunning of pretence and misdirection. His ability to snuff out petty spats between generals and soldiers alike continued to win the praise of the commander-in-chief, and even Odysseus appeared to harbour no grudge for the events in Ithaca prior to the war. Palamedes had no inkling of the storm brewing, therefore, when he was summoned to Agamemnon's tent late one afternoon.

'Explain this!' Agamemnon snapped, brandishing a small twist of parchment. Palamedes reached forward to take the note and read it quickly. 'Sire, it is a poor jest from someone who aims to discredit me. You know me better than this.'

'I certainly thought so,' said Agamemnon, observing his quartermaster coldly, 'but I take accusations of treason very seriously. The note was found on the body of a man we have identified as a Trojan spy, killed by one of my bodyguards when he was caught sneaking around the camp.' He took the parchment back and read it to himself once again. 'Addressed specifically to you, from King Priam of Troy himself, thanking you for information about our defensive weaknesses here and your plan to signal him at an opportune moment for attack. Where is the gold it says they've paid you?'

'Sire, there is no gold,' Palamedes answered in a level voice belying his confusion, 'just as there is no one short of your brother Menelaus who supports the Greek cause more than me. Ask anyone around the army. As far as I'm aware, I have no enemies, but clearly someone is playing a prank,' he laughed in an attempt to emphasise his innocence, 'in very bad taste, I have to say.'

'I hope so, for your sake. Let's find out what the generals think about it.' The king shouted for the two bodyguards outside the tent, instructing one of them to gather the war council, the other to hold Palamedes prisoner in the camp gatehouse for the time being. Palamedes allowed himself to be marched away, a spark of alarm igniting as he realised Odysseus would be one of those consulted. Agamemnon had always been paranoid about security, and any suggestion of collaboration with the enemy had been met with instant execution.

Night had fallen when he was led back to the council, a dozen men studying him with unusual curiosity in the flickering light of the braziers. Agamemnon had evidently described to them both the note and Palamedes' response and now nodded to Diomedes to begin the interrogation. One by one, they stood to question him on his whereabouts over the last few days and his familiarity with the security measures around the camp, testing his motives for supporting the enemy and seeking to catch him out on his replies. One by one they sat down again, satisfied, until it fell to Odysseus to sum up the discussion. Palamedes displayed none of his inner fears, an air of relaxed unconcern on his face as the Ithacan rose to speak.

'It seems that we are of one mind, Agamemnon. Palamedes has been a faithful servant to us all for the last five years, and we have no reason to suspect him of subterfuge. As for the gold, we can hardly accuse him of receiving it if there is no sign of it. For the sake of good order, his quarters ought to be searched, but a man of his intelligence is surely not stupid enough to have hidden it there!' He smiled at the council members, as if sharing a feeble joke, and Palamedes' nerves screamed, despite the knowledge that he had nothing to hide.

'Yes,' said Agamemnon, 'Menelaus, take a couple of men to his tent and have a look around. Report back in an hour's time, and then we can put this ridiculous matter behind us.' The council disbanded, and the commander-in-chief began a detailed discussion with the prisoner about food supplies for the forthcoming months as winter approached.

Sixty minutes later, the reconvened council listened in astonishment as Menelaus reported on the cache of gold he had found buried in the soil under Palamedes' bed. None expressed their surprise more than Odysseus, but even the great general was unable to steer Agamemnon away from pronouncing the inevitable sentence for treason. 'Death by stoning,' he decreed, 'with every council member to participate, as a demonstration of your continuing fidelity.' Palamedes knew that argument was pointless; the dice in his pocket had foretold the outcome, showing him an uneven total, three, when he consulted them in the minutes before Menelaus returned from the search. And his suspicions were confirmed when in the confusion following Agamemnon's decision, Odysseus leant towards him, apparently to convey his regret. 'Five years apart from my wife and son,' the Ithacan hissed in his ear, 'not so clever of you, after all.'

High above them, the sun-god watched the stoning with distaste. No friend of the Greeks, Apollo had nonetheless taken a liking to Palamedes, impressed by the mix of logic and risk in the plot to unmask Odysseus's deception before the war and appreciating more than humble mortals the mathematical talent required to invent the board games enjoyed by the army during their long encampment on the Trojan plain. He had heard the story of the Mount Olympus dice from Poseidon many years before, while the two gods were constructing Troy's walls, and knew that they had made their way to Palamedes. As the quartermaster's body lay abandoned in the dust, surrounded by the blood-stained missiles that had killed him, Apollo took on the form of a burly grave digger and visited the dismal scene. He heaved the corpse over his shoulder, as if to take it to burial, and carried it towards the camp's perimeter, the throng around him blind to his real identity. At the steps of a makeshift temple, constructed by Palamedes the previous year in dedication to the goddess Tyche, he shed his burden and walked calmly away, the dice nestled in his fist. A time would come for revenge on the Greek generals, and the fates would play a fitting part in that.

*

Year nine of the war – Troy

Four more years and still no conclusive victory for either side. The skirmishing between the armies had ground on, with sporadic triumphs for individual combatants, but after almost a decade, no real progress had been made by the Greeks towards their original objectives; Helen remained with her abductor Paris, shielded by Troy's stout defences; the cuckolded King Menelaus had not had the satisfaction of defeating his rival; and neither the generals nor the common soldiers had come even close to the riches promised from the war. As frustration grew to fever pitch, the Greeks seemed to spend more time bickering amongst themselves than fighting their opponents. Without Palamedes to broker peace within the war council, minor squabbles flared up into major feuds, none more so than the stand-off between Agamemnon and his prize warrior Achilles over the use of an enemy slave, Briseis. That had resulted in the unnecessary death of Achilles' childhood friend Patroclus at the hand of the Trojan prince Hector, as the Greek hero lay sulking in his tent. At least his friend's sacrifice to the Greek cause had prompted Achilles to reach for his weapons again. He remained the one man feared by all Troy's army, capable of turning the tide of a battle single-handed through his skill with sword and spear, not to mention his unquenchable bloodlust on the killing field. Now, even if the city could not be sacked, he was going to avenge Patroclus by slaying Hector himself.

Apollo had viewed the Greek campaign floundering on the Trojan grasslands with increasing interest ever since the stoning of Palamedes. His antipathy to the invaders, initially just a mild prejudice based on his work creating the city walls, had been roused by the death of his son Tenes, murdered by Achilles on the fleet's voyage from Aulis towards Troy. Zeus had commanded the gods not to interfere in the war, and it had taken immense restraint for Apollo to comply. More recently, the same Greek warrior had raised the aggravation to a new level, killing a Trojan named Troilus and defiling his body in a temple dedicated to the sun-god, where Troilus had sought refuge from battle. A second personal insult was intolerable; Apollo would have justice, regardless of Zeus.

His first thought was to foil Achilles' efforts to kill Hector, knowing the impotent fury this would induce in the young Greek. Near the end of a frenzied bout of fighting one day, with the sun beginning to sink over the Ionian Sea and soldiers from both armies still falling in droves, he saw Hector come face to face with Achilles for the first time since Patroclus's death. The Trojan prince was quick to hurl his spear, and Apollo watched in horror as Achilles swatted it aside with his shield before planting his feet to cast his own weapon. Even if the spear proved ineffective, Apollo considered it likely that Hector would be the loser in any ensuing swordplay. As Achilles drew back his arm to throw, a brilliant sunbeam dazzled him, allowing Hector to take to his heels with supernatural speed. The Greek spear flew fruitlessly into the ground and by the time Achilles could scan the battlefield, his adversary was nowhere to be seen.

Hector's divine protection could not last indefinitely. Achilles' rage at the loss of Patroclus still burnt bright, his thirst for retribution unslaked even by further relentless slaughter of the enemy's troops. It was simply a matter of time before the two rivals met again, and when they did, Apollo's sister Athena was on hand to intervene before him. With her own reasons for supporting the Greeks in defiance of Zeus's edict to stay out of the war, she blocked Apollo's attempt to save the Trojan with another sunray, and he was forced to look on as Achilles' spear found its mark in Hector's throat. Blood spewed from the fatal wound, and Achilles roared in exultation as he stood over his twitching victim. Even before the death throes had ceased, he had called for a chariot to be brought to him, and he wasted no time in attaching ropes between the axle and the legs of the corpse. Then, with an expression of grim fulfilment, he mounted the chariot and flicked the reins. For three hours, he dragged Hector's body to and fro just beyond arrow shot of Troy's gates, the dead man's head bouncing across the stony earth until it was an unrecognisable pulp of flayed skin and shattered skull. On the battlements of his palace within the city, Hector's aged father, King Priam, followed the whole display, sobbing with grief at such a monstrous act of sacrilege.

Enough, thought Apollo. Even if Zeus would not permit him to influence the outcome of the wider war, he must find a way to punish Achilles for his brutal treatment of Tenes, Troilus and Hector. Undignified death for the great warrior was the only suitable solution and, tracing the sky each day, he searched incessantly for an opportunity to deliver it. Not prone to self-doubt, he nonetheless consulted Palamedes' dice one evening, to reassure himself that such flagrant opposition to the king of the gods was warranted. Like the Greek quartermaster, he took the view that an even score would support his plan of action and was relieved when he saw two sixes gazing up at him from the bottom of his goat-horn gaming cup. Now all he needed was the means of implementation.

With Hector's removal, the Greek assault on Troy's defences had gained fresh impetus, each new day's fighting making headway in the thrust to take the city. At last, a bid to breach the walls themselves was launched, the besiegers led by Achilles darting in with ladders and battering rams. At the zenith of Apollo's daily arc through the heavens, the moment he had been waiting for suddenly presented itself. In the recess of a window high on the gate tower, he spotted Paris raising his bow, an arrow notched and ready. How poetic that the prince of Troy, the man whose provocation of the Greeks had lit the touchpaper for this entire conflict, should bring the downfall of their finest warrior. What sweeter revenge could there be for the departed?

Paris drew back his elbow, and the sun-god nudged the Trojan's aim downwards. Then the arrow was released, its poisoned metal tip glinting ominously as it flew towards its target above the roiling tide of attackers. For half a second, time stood still, before Achilles looked down at the shaft lodged deep in his heel. Struck in the one part of his body that his mother Thetis had been unable to protect as she dangled her newborn son in the magical waters of the River Styx all those years before, he knew immediately that he was doomed. With the arrow's poison coursing through his veins, he staggered on through the melee, his sword flailing in a final, furious burst of aggression, until an unseen spear thumped into his chest-plate, knocking him off his feet. He was dead before his body hit the ground.

Directly above, Apollo glanced at the cubes in his hand, smiling with relief as the two sixes revealed themselves once again – an Olympian seal of approval, if ever there was.

*

And then...

+ Despite Apollo's efforts, the war is ultimately won by the Greeks, after a raiding party is concealed in a massive hollow wooden horse to gain entry to Troy, and the city is put to the torch. The sun-god helps the Trojan warrior Aeneas, King Priam's son-in-law, to escape the carnage with his child Ascanius and gives him the dice to aid his travels towards the foundation of a new civilisation.

+ After a lengthy journey via Crete, Carthage and Sicily, Aeneas makes landfall at the mouth of the central Italian River Tiber, in a region governed by King Latinus. The king grants Aeneas land on the banks of the river, which comes to be known as Alba Longa.

+ Aeneas succeeds Latinus and is duly followed by Ascanius, establishing a line of kings that go on to rule Alba Longa for the next 450 years. The dice are passed down the line of succession, ultimately coming into the possession of King Numitor.

*

Author's Note

The Trojan War, the events leading up to it, its aftermath and the huge list of characters involved are the subject of extensive myth built up by a variety of ancient Greek and Roman writers, notably Homer and Virgil. Thought to have lived in the ninth/ eighth century BCE, Homer is known to us as author of the Iliad, covering the later stages of the war up to the point of Hector's death, and of the Odyssey, recounting the adventures of Odysseus on his voyage home to Ithaca. Virgil was the first century BCE author of the Aeneid, covering the tales of the Trojan Horse, the sacking of the city and the escape of Aeneas to find a new civilisation on the mainland of Italy. Whether or not these epic stories have any basis in fact, the existence of Troy itself does appear to have been established, thanks initially to the excavation works of archaeologist Heinrich Schliemann in the 1870s, with the fall of the city considered to have taken place around 1190 BCE. My description of events is a selective and heavily pared-down version of the wider legend.

Palamedes' role in unmasking Odysseus before the war and, consequently, being framed and executed for treason, is referred to by numerous writers. His position as a lively and intelligent army quartermaster is my addition, based on his actions in Ithaca and the word of Sophocles (writing in the fifth century BCE), who attributed the invention of dice, board games and other useful devices, such as weights and measures, to him. The Greek geographer/author Pausanias (second century CE) also has Palamedes creating the first pair of dice, going on to dedicate them to the goddess of chance, Tyche (linked to the Roman goddess Fortuna), at a temple in Argos on the Peloponnese.

Despite Zeus's command not to interfere in the war, some gods and goddesses aligned themselves with one or other of the protagonists. Apollo was cast as a protector of Troy, having laboured with his uncle Poseidon to build the city walls. I have based his interest in Palamedes and the dice on his status not only as sun-god but overlord of knowledge, reason and truth (amongst other things) as well. He was also known as a gifted archer, causing him to feature in the shooting of Achilles by Paris following the brutal slaughter of Tenes, Troilus and Hector. Achilles' vulnerability at the part of his body where he was held upside down by his mother Thetis and dipped in the River Styx as a baby is the driver for the modern reference to an 'Achilles heel'. There is no mention by poets or playwrights of Palamedes and Apollo consulting dice before taking action, but the ancients were notoriously conscious of the fates and any such search for reassurance would have been understandable to an audience of the time.

Romulus and Remus

770 BCE – Alba Longa, Italy

*L*ife in the last twelve months has become very dull, thought Rhea, as she walked the short distance down the hill to the olive grove, wicker basket in hand. One of six maidens appointed to act as custodians of the eternal fire in the Temple of Vesta, goddess of the hearth, she was consigned to a shrunken world of devotions and purity, loosely translating, in her opinion, to one of intense boredom. The other five girls had been selected as children, offered up to the chief priests by their parents and tricked into believing they were the fortunate few. For Rhea, the tedium of prayer, study and temple rituals was particularly galling given that she had come to it both late and enlightened. She was a princess, who had grown up with a lusty appetite for royal life in all its glory, including the licence to roam her father's kingdom at will, taking lovers as she went. A natural candidate for vestal virginity she most certainly was not.

Dipping her head under the outermost branches of the trees in the grove, her mind wandered to the events of the previous year that had reduced her to this sorry state. The only daughter of King Numitor, she had shared in his fate after his younger brother Amulius had led a revolt to overthrow him. Numitor had been chased from his throne into a cell, and Rhea had been dispatched to the service of Vesta, an alternative but equally effective type of imprisonment. Amulius had let it be known that they were being spared death due to his benevolence, but she had been sceptical of her uncle's claim from the outset. It seemed much more likely that she was being used as a peace offering to the gods in mitigation of the attack on family. Moreover, she was being pressed into a lifetime of chastity so that she could not conceive a son who might one day seek to recover Numitor's kingdom. Worse than all of that, she knew that if she failed in her vestal duties, Amulius would have won the justification to kill both her and her father. Which brought her back to her immediate frustrations, she smiled ruefully, liberty and love.

Beyond the dense wall of foliage forming the perimeter to the olive plantation, the trees thinned out, each one bathed in sunlight and laden with fruits. Rhea walked on to the centre of the grove, marked by a grassy glade with a shallow pond at one end. The pond was fed by a small stream running the length of the clearing, fringed with a rich carpet of wildflowers. It was a favourite spot for Rhea, her only escape from the temple precinct where she lived and worked and a precious chance to relax on the occasions over the last month that she had been sent to harvest the olives for the priests' larder. There was never anyone else there, lending it an other-worldly feeling of tranquillity, and she was relieved to find that she had the place to herself once again.

Setting the basket down on the grass, she knelt to pick a handful of the flowers, a colourful bouquet of reds, yellows and blues. Then she inspected the individual blossoms, marvelling at the fragile petals and savouring their delicate fragrance, before laying them aside and unfastening her gown. It was hot;

a few moments' delay before beginning to gather fruit would do no harm; and lying naked in the sun on a private bed of flowers was too luxurious an opportunity to miss. Rhea stretched out on her back, enjoying the warmth on her skin and listening idly to the water trickling by. She was asleep within seconds.

Some time later, she was woken by the sound of whistling, an exquisite melody dancing above the stream's song. The sun had moved from its midday peak and shadows were beginning to creep across the glade. Drowsily, she sat up, yawning and looking around vaguely for the source of the music, heedless of her lack of clothing. With a start she realised she was being watched, and her hands flew to cover her breasts and lap. Someone was standing at the edge of the trees beyond the pond, continuing to whistle his ethereal tune as he observed her. Not just anybody, either, but the most beautiful young man she had ever laid eyes on. A sheaf of curly blond locks tumbled over his ears and neck; the unblemished skin of his bare chest and legs gleamed with oil; and the muscles beneath rippled with suppressed power as he hefted a golden spear in his right hand.

'Who... who are you?' she stammered, acutely aware of her nakedness, somehow all the more embarrassing in the presence of a man clad in nothing more than a loin cloth.

'I might ask you the same question, considering you are in my grove,' the man answered calmly, before advancing round the pond towards her.

'Your grove...' Rhea frowned, a wisp of memory nudging her. 'I'm sorry, I was sent here by the priests to pick olives. They never told me it belonged to anyone like you.' She stopped, recognising the absurdity of what she had said, and took in the man's features for the first time, now that he was close enough to see in detail. Bright blue eyes under the mop of hair, a strong nose and jawline and full red lips, behind which a dazzling row of teeth peered out. Belatedly, the recollection of how the priests had described the grove came to her. 'The god of war?' she said hesitantly. 'Mars, is it you?'

'Ah, so you do know.' Neither stern nor amused, he gazed down on her, the spear held upright at his flank, its base resting idly on the ground. 'Yes, this place is dedicated to me. I don't come here often, but when I find a pretty girl sunbathing in my flowerbed, I feel it's worth a visit.' Suddenly, his face lit up and he laughed. 'What am I to do with my trespasser?'

Rhea put her arms down and lay back. 'Well, I have an idea,' she said quietly, leaning on her elbows and shifting her hips. 'I have invaded your privacy. I feel obliged to pay you in kind.' Mars flung his spear to one side and knelt between her legs. 'Fair deal, and you can have some olives too,' he muttered, as his lips closed on hers. He was used to getting what he wanted, but it was good not to have to wield his divine power.

Five months later, as a wintry squall swirled round Alba Longa, Rhea was led into the palace by one of Vesta's priests and presented to King Amulius. 'I beseech you, Uncle, to let me visit my father. It's been the best part of two years since he was imprisoned, and I hear his health is fading. I would dearly like to see him before he dies.' She drew her cloak around her against the cold draught sweeping through the building and added, 'I have given myself to the goddess Vesta, as you demanded, and have worked hard to honour her. A few minutes with my father is all I crave.' She put on what she hoped was a demure expression and held her breath.

'An hour,' the king grunted, 'until nightfall, when the priest will return to collect you for the evening rituals.' He nodded brusquely at the priest and Rhea was escorted across the palace courtyard to the gaol beyond the privies. Gasping at the stench of raw sewage leaching over the rough earthen floor, she was ushered into her father's cell.

'Leave us,' Numitor commanded the priest, and to his surprise the man did so, turning the key in the door's lock as he departed. Father and daughter examined each other in silence, before Numitor stepped forward and hugged her to him.

'My darling girl,' he mumbled into her hair, his voice thick with emotion, 'I thought I'd never see you again.' He stood back and looked her up and down. 'You seem well, and you have put on weight, so they must be feeding you. More than me anyway.'

Rhea studied him in turn, taking in his emaciated frame for the first time. 'You are skin and bone, Father. But still alive, which neither of us had any right to expect from your wicked brother.' She kissed him on the cheek. 'Life at the vestal temple is dull, but it smells better than here, that's for sure.'

It was the first time they had been together since the palace revolt, and they spent several minutes discussing it, Rhea relating what had happened to her father's household and why she suspected they had not been murdered by Amulius. She asked about the conditions in the gaol, and Numitor assured her that, despite his appearance, the rumours from the priests about his failing health were false. Then her tone changed, and she broached the real subject of her visit.

'Father, I have something to confess.' She faltered, conscious that what she was about to say would upset him but desperate for his guidance. 'I am having a baby. Not ideal for a vestal virgin, and I don't know what to do. When the priests learn of it, which they will do soon, they're bound to tell Amulius, and we'll both be executed.'

Numitor recoiled in shock, then stared at her with fresh eyes, understanding for the first time the cause of her swelling stomach. 'How?' he rasped, and Rhea embarked on the story of her encounter with Mars in the olive grove, carefully omitting any suggestion of her compliance. 'So he raped you,' her father broke in, more as a statement than a query. 'Well, it's hardly the first time the gods have taken advantage of young maidens, but to defile a vestal virgin...' he tailed off, too appalled at the plunder of his daughter's virtue to continue.

Rhea chose not to admit that the calamity was only half of what he presumed. 'I'm fine, Father, honestly, but we both know what awaits vestals if they become impure. The priests will kill me immediately, and then Amulius will have no reason to spare you either.' She began to cry, her head in her hands.

Numitor leant against the cell door and thought for a long moment. 'If your theory is correct, and my brother has kept us alive thus far as a sop to the gods, then nothing has altered. In fact, our position is strengthened – your death would mean the loss of the child, and Amulius would surely not dare to kill the spawn of the god of war.' He reached out to grip her by the shoulders. 'It must have been terrible for you, but perhaps we should be celebrating the future rather than grieving for what you have forfeited. I shall be a grandfather after all!' He smiled and wiped a tear from her face, then rummaged in a pocket. 'Whatever happens to me, you need some insurance, and it's just possible these might help you.'

Rhea lifted her head to find her father holding out an arm, palm upturned. On it rested a pair of dice, the ivory stained and dirty and laced with miniscule cracks but otherwise intact. He gestured to her, and she took the cubes from him. 'You will not have seen these before, my dear,' Numitor went on, 'but they belonged to my father before me, and his before that. They have passed down the royal line for centuries, right back to King Aeneas, and it is said that he was given them as a token of good fortune by no less than the sun-god Apollo. They are the sole trapping of sovereignty I was able to hide when Amulius attacked. One of the benefits of looking and smelling like I do is that the guards never search me, and playing with the dice has been a welcome diversion during my time in here. Now you should have them. Who knows, they might save your life, and if so, you must pledge to hand them on to your child.' He folded her fingers over the dice and wrapped his bony hands round hers, as if to conclude the transfer of inheritance.

Outside the cell, they could hear the priest calling to the guards as he came to retrieve his charge. 'Time to go, my princess,' Numitor murmured. Rhea embraced him without speaking and put her hand into a pocket as the door swung open. Then she gave him one last glance of enquiry and received a wink of affirmation in response. Following the priest across the courtyard, she wondered whether she would ever see her father again. If not, at least she had a memento of him to cherish on her precarious journey into motherhood. As she walked, she felt the baby within her kicking, and not for the first time she was astonished how vigorous it seemed to be.

That astonishment was nothing compared to the disbelief of childbirth. Four months after visiting her father, Rhea's confinement began, alone in the quarters she had been assigned once the news of her condition had been revealed at the temple. She had been reviled by the other vestal girls, cast out by the priests and forced to beg her uncle for his support in overriding the call to execute her. She had appealed to him in the name of her abuser, Mars, hoping that since Amulius had spared her once in supplication to the gods, he might do so again. Even though she had been raped, she pleaded, the god of war was not to be provoked. It had worked, not just on her account, but her father's too, and the king had grudgingly agreed to house her amongst the servants at the palace. She had been granted entry with no more than the shift she wore and a basket of insignificant personal belongings. Now, at the end of an interminable labour, the old hag attending her had held up the baby and solemnly announced that another one was on the way. Twenty minutes later, the second child slithered out of her in a rush of blood. Twin boys – as healthy and beautiful as their father had been in that flower-strewn entanglement at the olive grove, but how long would they be permitted to survive?

The answer from Amulius was swift, and hideous. As males, the infants must be killed at once, by drowning in the River Tiber. While he was prepared to let his brother and niece live on, the king's goodwill did not extend to potential rivals from a third generation. Rhea wept uncontrollably when the decree was relayed to her the morning after the birth, clinging to the babies as two servants sought to remove them and releasing them only when the men threatened to smother them in front of her. 'Wait,' she shouted at them, 'wait until I find a keepsake for their crossing into the underworld.' The men nodded reluctantly, turning away in embarrassment at their part in such a dreadful enterprise, and Rhea reached for her basket, the same basket she had used to gather olives in nine months previously. Padding it with a pair of cloths, she settled the twins gently into it and then went to a small box by her bed. She extracted a pair of dice and placed them, one after the other, in a plump pink fist belonging to each child. 'Now, take them if you must, and may the gods be with them.' She lapsed back into tears, and the servants fled from the room with their burden.

Standing on the riverbank, the men looked at each other and then around them to check that they were not being watched. No words were required. Neither one could bring himself to hold a newborn baby under the water's rippling surface and wait for it to drown, even if the king's orders had been explicit. There was a different way of meeting their master's objective, without having to bear the guilt of a double murder. They launched the wicker basket into the current and listened to the twins grizzling as wavelets splashed onto their unprotected faces. Somehow or other, the children would die of natural causes as they floated away, and the servants could report to the palace that they had done their duty.

An hour's journey downstream, the heavily laden basket bumped against a rock at a bend in the river and was edged sideways into a minor channel. Seconds later it was caught amongst the branches of a rotting tree trunk that had washed up on a semi-submerged mud-bank in a winter storm. Unaware of the deadly edict they had escaped, the babies slept contentedly in the warm spring sun, their arms folded over their stomachs, their fists closed. The basket bobbed gently in the crux of the tree's limbs, hidden from the riverbank, and passers-by throughout that afternoon were oblivious to its presence.

As dusk approached, the temperature dropped, and the babies awoke. With their muted gurgles lost in the noise of the river, only a fox was able to find them, catching their scent as it nosed its way upwind in the twilight. Tentatively, it padded across the web of branches, suspicious of the unfamiliar smell and careful to avoid toppling into the water. Just as it was mustering its courage to pounce on the basket, one of the children let out a squeal of hunger, and the fox retreated in alarm. Whatever the curious prey was, the combined hazard of the river and the commotion was not worth risking. The second baby began to cry, and together the twins bawled in fury at the absence of their mother's milk, punching the air with tiny, clenched hands. It was more than two hours before their keening dwindled into exhausted whimpers.

Around midnight another animal came prowling down the riverbank, stronger than the fox, and more desperate as well. Two days earlier, the she-wolf had been nursing her litter of five pups in the low hills lining the eastern bank of the river's course when a pack of wild dogs had found her lair. Her mate had been scouring the scrubland on a distant ridge for food, and by the time he heard her call the dogs had goaded her into the open. As some of them snapped at her heels and throat, others had been able to dart behind her into the den. One by one, they had plucked the pups out, tearing them to pieces between them until only one remained. Taking advantage of the dogs' distraction over the spoils of their raid, the she-wolf had finally succeeded in fighting them off, and as they sped away into the darkness, she had limped back to her single surviving whelp. Now her maternal instincts were racing, her teats bulging with unused milk, as she took her turn to search for quarry to restore her scarred body.

The she-wolf recognised the babies' odour immediately. More importantly, she recognised the bleat of a distressed infant, and the impulse to protect overrode her embedded wariness of humans, built up amongst her species over countless millennia. Too heavy to slink across the branches, but powerful enough to brave the current, she waded into the river and paddled round to the far side of the fallen tree trunk. Using her nose, she was able to dislodge the wedged basket and push it into the shallows. Then she scrambled up the bank, the basket's handle between her teeth, as the squirming infants looked up at her in surprise. This was not the mother they remembered from their brief time at the palace, but she did not appear to be dangerous, and it seemed they had not been deserted after all. For her part, the wolf had come to a decision. Rather than devour the humans, she would suckle them in place of her lost pups, and she started to howl for her mate so that the two of them could carry the babies to safety in their mouths.

Over the next six weeks, the twins lay in the dark of the animals' den, wriggling and mewling and sleeping alongside the single pup. All three thrived on the she-wolf's milk, and as the weeks wore on, the pup became sturdy enough to walk, venturing out to explore the world. The twins, in contrast, remained immobile and defenceless, even when they were carried into the daylight. They were spotted by an inquisitive woodpecker, which began to feed small berries to them as a supplement to their nourishment, but it was soon evident that this was still not enough to generate any form of independence. The she-wolf realised gradually that humans must follow a different rearing schedule to her family and that once her pup was weaned, she would no longer be able to care for the little pink cubs. She had grown fond of them, but her work in rescuing them was now done and she turned her mind instead to the problem of how to ensure their wellbeing going forward.

On one of her rare excursions from the lair she was crouching in some thin shrubbery, watching a flock of sheep grazing and gauging which of the weaker animals to chase down, when the shepherd came into view. It gave her an idea and she abandoned the hunt. An hour later she had summoned her mate and the two of them had carried the twins onto the open pasture ahead of the path being taken by the sheep. The she-wolf knew that when the flock came to the babies, it would regard them as an uncommon threat and would swerve aside, leaving them in full sight of the shepherd. The man was bound to take pity on his discovery, she thought, and assume responsibility for cubs of his own kind.

The she-wolf looked on with satisfaction as the plan unfolded, tracking the shepherd as he carried the babies to his homestead and making a point of being seen by him before turning away. Faustulus would never know the original source of the twins, but he guessed that the wolf had deliberately spared them for him to find, and he sacrificed a lamb to the gods that night in thanks. His wife Acca Larentia had been unable to have children, so it was nothing short of divine intervention that they were now blessed with a ready-made family. He could not explain the presence of the pair of dice he had also collected from the grassland, but he was a superstitious man and felt certain they were somehow linked to the fate of his new charges. He would raise the babies on the story of their deliverance and on the understanding that the dice belonged to them jointly, and equally.

*

753 BCE – *Alba Longa, Italy*

Acca Larentia surveyed the boys fondly as they jousted over the breakfast table. It had been this way ever since they had learnt to speak, Romulus the more serious of the two, disciplined and self-assured but easily provoked when his word was challenged. And Remus never missed an opportunity to do so, channelling his irrepressible spirit into annoying his brother. More lively, more spontaneous, wilder at heart; more fun, their mother admitted to herself, not that she would ever tell them that. She often wondered which one was older, but it was no use speculating. They had arrived as equals and her husband had been careful to treat them as such throughout their sixteen years with the couple. Now he was dead and the role of peacekeeper had passed to her. 'You will manage the flock together, as your father taught you,' she cut across their shouting match, and they had the grace to stop arguing at the mention of him. 'The sheep have to be moved today. It will need both of you to drive them upriver towards the city for fresh grazing. Now, take your food and waterskins, and don't forget your staffs. I know you think there is nothing to fear from the wolves in the hills, but you should be prepared for them, just in case.'

The boys looked at each other, Romulus nodding gravely and Remus rolling his sparkling blue eyes in amusement. Despite the verbal battles between them, they knew full well that they would have to work together on a day like this, even if Romulus saw himself as the natural leader and Remus instinctively teased him for it. They had also heard their mother's warning about wolves more times than they could count and had seen for themselves the havoc a pack could wreak on a flock of sheep. But they had been raised on the tale of their discovery by Faustulus after being spared, and possibly even cared for, by a she-wolf and took a more benevolent view of these ferocious creatures than most. 'Don't fret, Mother,' said Romulus, brushing a golden coil of hair from his forehead, 'we'll find some good new pasture and be home by sundown. I'll make sure.' He glared imperiously at his twin and, once Acca Larentia's back was turned, Remus made a crude gesture in response.

By early afternoon the boys had rounded up the flock and were herding them upstream, as instructed. They were familiar with the grasslands and knew not to stray too near the city, where King Amulius and his family held court. An old man now, Amulius had been on the throne throughout their lives, and rumours abounded of how he had snatched it from his brother Numitor. He was also said to have imprisoned Numitor's daughter, the rightful heiress to the throne, where she continued to languish even after Numitor's death five years ago. These stories meant little to the twins in their remote rural existence, but they occasionally met shepherds from the palace who were quick to assert the king's authority, insisting that the grazing close to the city was for the royal flocks alone. There was plenty of pasture elsewhere, and despite their irritation at this high-handed behaviour, Faustulus had always warned them not to be tempted into a fight about it.

Today, however, events took a more severe turn. As Romulus and Remus crested a ridge, their flock stretched out in front of them but still a fair distance from the city, they found themselves facing a band of young men accompanied by four sheepdogs. The men were directing the dogs into position between themselves and the twins, evidently intent on flushing the sheep down the long slope ahead. It was plainly an ambush, set up in order to steal the flock. The boys were incensed and launched themselves at the thieves, brandishing their staffs as they ran amongst them. They were each able to land a few forceful blows before being overwhelmed by weight of numbers and clubbed onto their knees. Their assailants crowded round them, some holding their bodies in pain, others shouting suggestions for retaliation. Above the noise, one man, heavily bearded and several years older than the rest, bellowed for quiet.

'You have no right to be here. This is the king's land, and any livestock grazing on it are his. Go back wherever you came from, and consider yourselves lucky we haven't set the dogs on you.' Romulus was too dazed to take in what was being said, but his brother struggled to his feet and swung a fist at the speaker. The man dodged it with ease and his colleagues leapt on Remus, two of them pinning his arms while others punched him repeatedly in the stomach. Yet more kicked Romulus in the ribs, to deter him from attempting a counter-attack of his own. 'You don't seem to have been listening,' said the leader drily. 'You,' he pointed down at Romulus, 'will go home and make sure all your fellow shepherds understand the king's reach. And you,' he switched his gaze to Remus, 'will come with us to learn some manners.' Remus spat a thick gob of blood-flecked phlegm at him, inviting another salvo of punches, before being hurried off behind the flock. Battered and bruised, Romulus could only watch in fury at the loss of the sheep.

Twenty-four hours later, a group of fifty shepherds assembled outside Acca Larentia's house after receiving word from Romulus about the previous day's ambush. He stood on a tree stump to address them, his frustration at the humiliation he had suffered overriding any nervousness in the presence of such a big gathering. 'This was my family's flock, but the message I was given applies to all of us. We cannot stand by and let the king's men steal both our common pastureland and the sheep we seek to graze on it. Remus and I were nowhere near the city and had as much reason to be there as anyone. I need my flock back, and I want to teach those brigands a lesson too. And I ought to rescue Remus,' he added belatedly. 'Who will help me?' The shepherds shouted their support in unison, recognising the threat to their livelihoods and the boy's air of authority, despite his young age. 'Thank you,' he said, 'then let's not waste time. Bring whatever weapons you have got, and we will head for the city immediately.' He waved goodbye to his mother and led his new-found force of troops away.

They entered the city an hour before sunset. Barely a handful of them had visited it in the past, but one man knew enough to guide them to the palace gatehouse, where they barged past the sentries and swarmed into the main courtyard. Spectators scurried clear of them, alarmed at the fierce expression on the face of their commander, and he looked about him in brief hesitation. 'Where now?' he muttered to himself, before choosing at random a low building lining one side of the enclosure. A few of the shepherds followed him through the doorway, the remainder turning to oppose a contingent of the king's guards that had been hastily mustered after the tussle at the gates. What Romulus had envisaged as a simple show of strength in front of Amulius to assert their rights now descended into a full-scale battle, as a rush of palace occupants joined the fray.

Unbeknown to him, Romulus and his followers had entered the servants' sleeping quarters, and as they dashed through the long dormitory, a middle-aged woman emerged from a washroom at the far end, barring their path. Panic flared across her face, before being replaced with gaping astonishment. 'Mars…' she stuttered, 'after all these years! In the name of Jupiter, I can't believe it…'

Romulus halted, his men jostling for position behind him to see who was speaking. 'I am no god, woman, just a shepherd whose flock the king's underlings have stolen. And they took my brother too. Where would they have hidden him? Quickly, it's important.'

'But you look identical to Mars. Surely it's you, my love, come to free me from Amulius?'

'No, lady, just a shepherd, as I said.' Romulus softened his tone, guessing that this was no servant, even if he had found her in the maids' rooms. 'And I really must find my brother.'

At the repetition of the word *brother*, Princess Rhea sank to the floor and tears began to pour down her cheeks. 'You are a twin.' She gasped, and it was Romulus's turn to look confused. 'You must be about sixteen. You've been alive, all this time!' She stared up at him. 'And you are so like your father, so beautiful…' Her voice trailed off, and after a sizeable sniff she rubbed her eyes dry and smiled weakly.

Romulus could hear the din of the brawl outside. 'Please, lady, I've no idea what you're talking about, or how you know I am a twin, but I have to rescue Remus. Come with me, show me where to find him, and in turn I will help you escape from the king, if that is what you want.' He pulled her to her feet and led her to the dormitory's entrance.

The fighting in the courtyard was raging. The shepherds had disarmed a score of guards and were using their weapons to force their way towards what Romulus presumed was the royal apartment. As he was about to plunge into the mass of bodies, a man appeared at its door, yelling for order. Rhea whispered into his ear, 'Amulius', and Romulus shouted at the shepherds to stand down as well. An uneasy hush followed, until Rhea prodded Romulus forward.

'King Amulius, my name is Romulus. I live on the grasslands downriver. Your men stole my flock of sheep yesterday on a false charge of trespassing on royal pasture. I am here to retrieve the flock and my brother Remus, who was arrested.' He paused and was about to explain that he meant no further harm to the king or his supporters, when Rhea stepped forward.

'Uncle, your past has come back to haunt you.' She spoke with the confidence of a princess, not the brow-beaten drudge she had been reduced to in captivity. 'This boy, and his twin that your men are holding, are my sons. The sons of Mars too, as I'm sure you remember. You have not only stolen their flock. You stole my father's throne, my newborn children and sixteen years of my adult life. Release Remus and give them your assurance that they may graze their sheep wherever they choose. And when they leave, I will leave with them.'

The crowd parted as Amulius strode across the open space. 'Never!' he snarled at her. 'You will remain where you belong – a slave girl to serve me. And your bastard offspring, if indeed that is who they are, will meet the fate they deserved as infants.' In a sudden movement he reached across his body with his right hand and drew a dagger from his left sleeve. Romulus reacted instantly, swinging his wooden staff with all his might at the king's head. There was a sharp crack, and

Amulius fell sideways, the dagger under him sliding between his ribs as he slumped onto the ground. There was very little blood, but he was obviously dead.

Silence reigned for ten long seconds, and then a buzz of noise began to swell within the courtyard. Romulus stepped away from the body, his staff at the ready as he braced himself for a fresh attack from the palace guards. It did not come. Slowly, it dawned on him that what he was hearing were not the howls of a mob demanding vengeance for the murder of their king, but cheers of approval instead. Incredibly, he was being applauded by all around him for killing a usurper to the throne, a tyrant against whom the population had been itching to rebel for years.

Romulus swept his gaze over the sea of faces in front of him, suddenly aware of the position he found himself in. King-slayer and rough country boy, yet the grandson of a king himself, and a son of Mars too. There were plenty of questions, but they could wait; this was no time for vacillation. He caught Rhea's eye and took a deep breath. 'Bring my brother to me in the royal apartment,' he shouted at the crowd, 'my mother and I will greet him there.' In the heavens above, the god of war looked on approvingly, delighted to see the villain who had attempted to have his twin sons drowned at birth destroyed by one of them. A fitting end to a memorable encounter in the flowerbeds of his olive grove.

*

Three months later – The Place of the Seven Hills, Alba Longa, Italy

Autumn was in the air as the twins walked up the incline from the riverbank towards their old home. They had been back there just once since the death of Amulius, the morning after that extraordinary day, to explain to Acca Larentia what had happened. Her relief at the sight of Remus had switched to bewilderment at the story of how they had ousted the king, and then to tears on the news of their parentage. After caring for them ever since Faustulus had brought them into the house, the knowledge that they were reunited with their birth mother had been bittersweet, and Acca Larentia had refused the invitation to join them living in the palace. 'I will stay here. The city is no place for a lifelong shepherdess.' Despite their efforts, there had been no persuading her. 'It is quite right that Princess Rhea has you at her side after believing you dead all these years. It would be wrong for me to intrude, and in any case having two mothers under one roof would be asking for trouble. I have already had to share you with a she-wolf!' She had forced a laugh and added, 'Remember to tell her, you were raised as equals, and those dice that you own between you are your witness to it.'

The purpose of the visit this time was very different. As soon as Romulus had taken control of the city, and Remus had been released from the gaol, the two of them had assumed command of the entire kingdom. There had been no resistance from the people of Alba Longa once they learnt that the twins' grandfather had been King Numitor, and the rumour that their father was the war-god Mars had only helped to increase their popularity. But after a few weeks at the palace, both boys had confessed to Rhea that they found it a claustrophobic reminder of their great-uncle's tyranny. 'Then build your own,' she had said, and they had soon identified a worthy location.

'One of the hills above the river where Faustulus discovered us,' Remus had suggested, and Romulus, to his annoyance, had been unable to come up with a better idea. There were seven small hills to choose from, and today's trip was their first attempt to establish where best to build.

After surveying the area from each of the seven summits, they walked down to Acca Larentia's house. She welcomed them in with a mock curtsey and produced some midday food for them. As they sat at the living room table eating together, the twins revived the argument they had been having throughout the morning, and Acca Larentia smiled to herself at how little had changed. Romulus had all the facts, figures, heights and distances at his fingertips; he talked of construction materials, defensive positioning, water supplies and sewage removal; he had no doubt which hill he wanted, and he even had a name for it – the Palatine, herald of the grand palace they would create there. Remus pealed with laughter at this. His hill had better views, better morning and evening sunlight; it was closer to the exact point where Faustulus had found them; and if Romulus was pompous enough to have invented a name, then so could he – the Aventine, in honour of one of the fabled Alban kings that preceded them on their recently acquired throne.

'Oh, for heaven's sake, boys, be quiet,' said Acca Larentia, after listening to them well into the afternoon. 'You will never agree, if you continue going round in circles like this. There's a much easier way to choose a hill, so long as you both accept the outcome. Remember, you are ruling the kingdom together, so it has to be a joint decision.' The twins glanced at her, uncertain where this was leading. 'Get the dice out. I know you carry them with you wherever you go. Whoever throws the highest number can pick the hill. It's very simple.'

Remus leapt up to kiss Acca Larentia on the forehead. 'Sound advice, as always, Mother. Thank you.'

There was a long silence and then Romulus nodded. 'You first,' he said sourly, and they each reached into a pocket.

Remus threw, and the ivory cube rattled across the table before coming to rest against a plate. 'Two,' he said unnecessarily, as his brother stared down alongside him. Then it was Romulus's turn, and one lonely dot showed its face. He snatched up both the offending dice, scowled at Acca Larentia and left the room without a word, as Remus performed a jaunty dance of celebration at having won with such a low score. Rhea had told the twins the story of the dice's origin, as she remembered it from Numitor, and Remus now set great store in their divine powers. Evidently the gods supported his choice of site.

They made their way back to the city separately, and when Remus went looking for his twin the following morning, he was unable to find him. Still chuckling to himself at his good fortune, he decided he would return to the hill, his hill, to begin planning the layout of the new township. He knew Acca Larentia would frown on any effort to start the project without consulting Romulus, but his brother's behaviour the previous day had been childishly surly, and they could pool their ideas once they were on speaking terms again. Approaching the curve of the river below his mother's house, he noticed fresh traces of numerous footprints on the path, but he thought no more about it as he began to climb. It was only as he gained height that he was able to see across to the hill preferred by Romulus, and he stopped in shock. A dozen or more men were at work there, piling rocks into a line for what must be the base of a boundary wall, while Romulus moved amongst them shouting orders. He might have guessed his twin would try to get his own way, but a decision made on the roll of their dice was sacrosanct, and Remus was not going to back down on that. He began to run.

As he came closer to the group of men, he entered a fold of hidden ground, and by the time he emerged he was less than fifty paces away from them. A few looked up at him, but Romulus was on his knees with his back turned and remained unaware of his presence until Remus clambered onto a waist-high section of wall. 'How dare you defy the fates?' he shouted down at his brother. 'You agreed to our mother's scheme. What gives you the right to ignore it?'

Romulus stood and swivelled towards Remus, a large stone in his hands. 'You know very well she is not our mother, so her scheme, as you call it, is of no consequence to me. As for my right? I am the king, not you. I took the throne from Amulius, and as king I will choose where to build.'

'Oh, your high and mighty majesty,' sneered Remus. 'Forgive me for not recognising you in your new stronghold. What I see before me is a liar and a cheat. Faustulus would be ashamed of you.'

Romulus flushed at the jibe. 'My father is a god, not a shepherd, although I often ask myself where you came from. Get off my hill and go back to your hovel with Acca Larentia.'

'You arrogant fool,' Remus continued to taunt him. 'This little wall I'm standing on is as pathetic as you are.' He kicked at a rock on the parapet with his shoe, and it tumbled to the ground in front of him. Romulus exploded with rage and flung the stone he was holding at his brother. It caught Remus obliquely on his shoulder and he staggered sideways, losing his footing and falling forwards. There was a dull thud as his forehead hit the rock he had dislodged, and he lay motionless, face down in the grass.

Fists bunched in readiness for the fight that had been brewing in him since the previous day's dice match, a resentment brought to the boil by the way Remus had addressed him in front of the workers, Romulus waited for his brother to rise to his feet. When nothing happened, he hissed, 'Get up, you clown. Stop play-acting,' and prodded him in the ribs with his toe. Still, there was no movement and, conscious of his audience at the wall, Romulus knelt to shake a response out of him. The body rolled over, limp and passive, and the reason for the inaction was immediately apparent for all to see. Remus had a deep depression in his skull, just below the hairline, and Romulus needed no second opinion on the severity of the wound. He had killed his twin, unintentionally of course, but bystanders might not describe it that way.

'He's dead,' he said in a flat voice, climbing slowly from his knees to face the workers, and they looked at him in horror. Over the last three months they had watched the brothers manage the kingdom together and had been encouraged by Princess Rhea to consider them as co-rulers. The gossip around the city was that Romulus was the more domineering of the two, and that Remus was preferred for his easy manner with underlings, but a display of temper such as this between them had never been reported. Four men began to busy themselves lifting the body away from the wall, while the rest waited for instructions, not daring to comment on what they had witnessed. The king hesitated only a moment before speaking again. The scene in the palace courtyard after Amulius had died flickered through his mind's eye, and once more he knew this was an opportunity not to be missed.

'It was a terrible accident, as you all saw, but my brother brought his fate on himself, by insulting me and undermining my authority. He will receive a prince's burial when we return to the city later, but for now we'll continue to build the wall. Remus and I shared many things, but be in no doubt, the throne was always mine alone.' He felt the pair of dice pressing against his skin through the thin material of his shirt pocket and wondered how he was going to break the news to Rhea. Co-rule would never have worked, he consoled himself, and he would surely have the god of war on his side.

*

And then…

+ Romulus names the new city, Rome, after himself as its first ruler. On his death the throne, and the dice, pass down the line of six further kings. The last of these, Tarquin the Proud, is expelled by the senate in 509 BCE after his son rapes a noblewoman, triggering a popular uprising.

+ The newly formed republic suffers a famine in 508 BCE and enters a treaty with its more powerful neighbour across the Mediterranean Sea, Carthage, which controls the supply of grain between Northern Africa and Italy. The dice are presented to the Carthaginian leaders as a token of the republic's authority to deal on behalf of Rome.

+ Several further treaties are negotiated between the two states over the next three centuries, and the dice become a trophy of command for successive Carthaginian rulers. By the end of the First Punic War (264–241 BCE), in which Rome inflicts a series of defeats on Carthage, they are owned by the general Hamilcar Barca, father to Hannibal.

*

Author's Note

The story of Romulus and Remus, and the founding of Rome, is another myth built up from numerous sources, the earliest written version emerging in the third century BCE. Later writers included Livy, Virgil and Plutarch. Legend places the birth of the city at 753 BCE, but archaeological works indicate that the first settlement (on Palatine Hill) may date back to the late tenth/early ninth century BCE. An ancient bronze sculpture of a she-wolf suckling the twins has served to support the tale of their upbringing and can be viewed in Rome's Capitoline Museums.

Aside from the part played by the dice, I have followed the basic outline and characters of the myth. Relegated from princess to vestal virgin by her uncle Amulius, Rhea is generally described as having been defiled by Mars, although Livy appears to downplay the charge of rape. The infants' unlikely rescue by a wolf and the added provision of food by a woodpecker (a bird associated with the god of war) suggest positive intervention by the fates, if not the power of the dice. As for the contest between Romulus and Remus over who should select the location of a new city, the myth attributes it to an augury (the interpretation of omens based on the study of natural phenomena) rather than a game of chance. The twins compete to spot a flock of birds, with Remus claiming victory as the first to see any, and Romulus disputing this with a count of twelve against his brother's six. Romulus presses ahead with the building of a city wall and kills Remus after the latter has jumped over it to taunt him.

The transfer of power from Romulus down the line of kings over a 250-year period, and the events leading to the ousting of Tarquin the Proud, are considered a blend of myth and fact. The 'And then' sequence of events thereafter is easier to verify. Between the early days of the republic and the Punic Wars of the third century BCE, Rome grew in stature, taking control of adjacent regions within Italy and negotiating a series of treaties with Carthage from a position of increasing strength. Hamilcar Barca died in battle on the Iberian Peninsula in 228 BCE and was succeeded in due course as commander of the Carthaginian army by his son Hannibal.

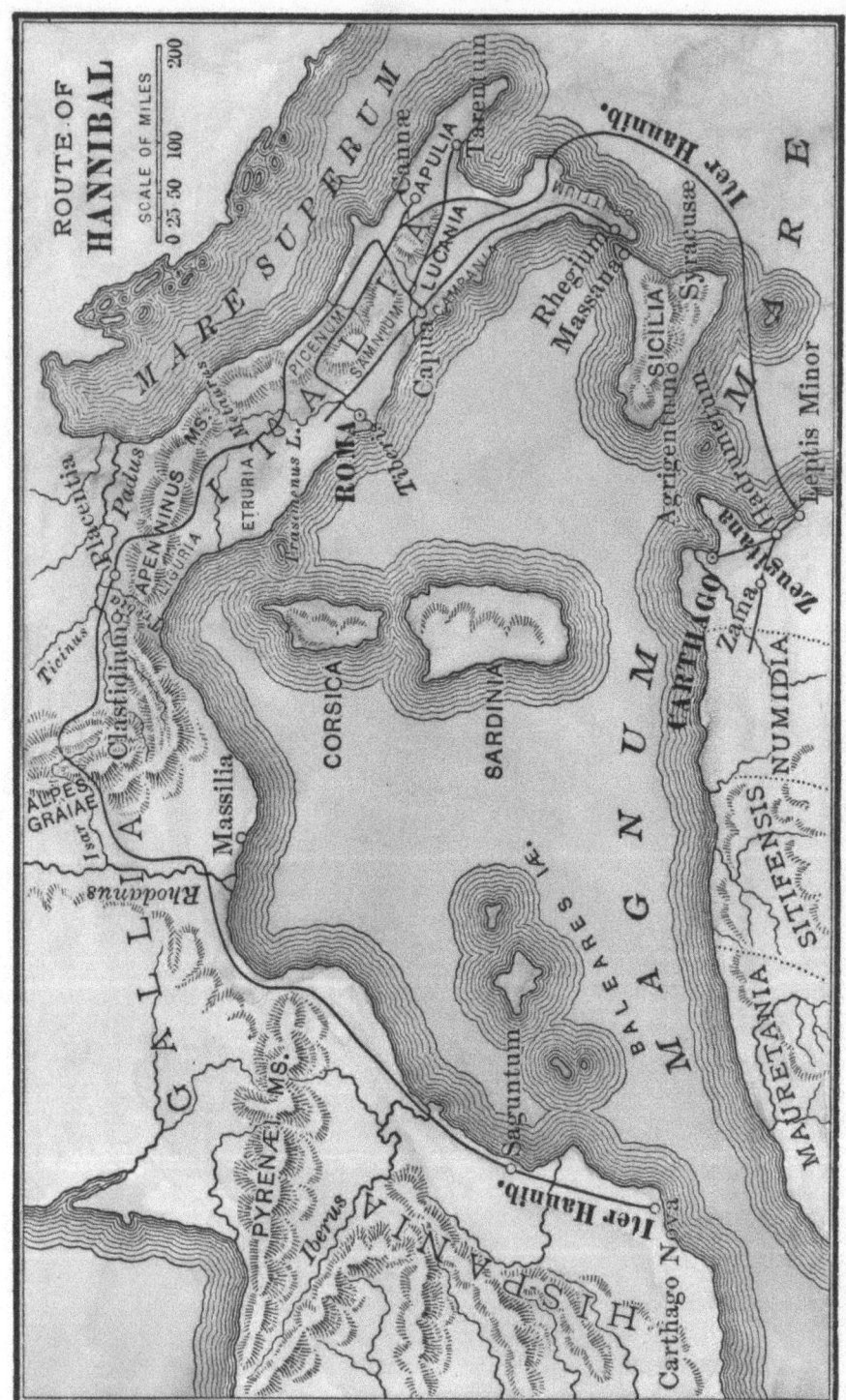

Hannibal

238 BCE – Carthage, North Africa

Preparations for the army's expedition to Hispania were almost complete, now that the politicians sitting at the Suffete had finally authorised the military offensive. The general Hamilcar Barca had been pressing his case for years, his bitterness at the humiliation of his country's loss of domain in Sicily and Sardinia over the last decade only increasing with the passage of time. He would have his revenge against Rome, he had promised himself, and Carthage would be restored as the pre-eminent power in the western Mediterranean. A naval attack on the mainland around Rome was impossible with the upstart Italian republic now ruling the Tyrrhenian Sea, but invasion of the Hispanic peninsula would give Carthage territory, wealth and the springboard for a future land war in Italy.

It had taken all his diplomatic skills to bring the faint-hearted government round to his view, but from then on it had simply been a question of logistics. His infantry and cavalry were ready; transport ships had been commandeered, weaponry commissioned and food stores gathered. The brief voyage along the African coast and across the open waters to Hispania would be over before the enemy knew what was happening, and his spies on the northern shores were primed to seek allies amongst the local tribes there. There was just one last matter to attend to before embarkation, which amused Hamilcar as much as it had annoyed his wife.

The general looked down at his eldest son, Hannibal, as they began walking the short distance from their family house to the high temple dominating the Carthage city skyline. The boy had been badgering his father to be allowed to accompany him to Hispania ever since learning of the invasion plans. At the age of nine he would be of little practical use to the officers, but Hamilcar had admired his enthusiasm for the campaign ahead and his interest in the workings of the army. His younger brothers Hasdrubal and Mago were enough of a handful to occupy their mother, so he would barely be missed at home, and besides, it was never too early to learn how to wage war.

'Understand, boy, that although we will be fighting against the people in Hispania to take control of their lands there, the real reason for it is to stop the Romans from doing the same. And one day, once we have built up our strength, we will be able to launch an attack on Rome itself. We will avenge all the defeats of the last twenty-five years and make Carthage great again.'

'Yes, Father,' said Hannibal breathlessly, as he struggled to keep pace. 'But why are we going to the temple?'

'To get the blessing of the gods for the battles ahead. And something else, as you'll see.' Hamilcar halted abruptly in the street and held up two small ivory cubes between finger and thumb for the boy to inspect. 'You know what these are?' Hannibal frowned in surprise at the change in direction of the conversation. He had watched his father playing dice with his friends in the market square many times over the years.

The general strode on. 'You think they are toys to play games with. But they are much, much more than that. They were given to me when I was put in command of the army, as a symbol of leadership, but also a reminder of my duty to my country. And what is the first duty of a leader?'

Hannibal had no idea, but he knew his stern father would require an answer of some sort. 'To protect the people?'

'Correct. And to do that, you must recognise your enemy.' He patted Hannibal on the back. 'Now, here we are.' He took hold of the boy's arm and pulled him up the temple steps, past the eternal flame burning in the entrance hall and on towards the big, oblong altar at the far end of the main chamber. 'Be quiet, do as you are told and speak only when you're spoken to.'

Alerted by the sound of footsteps amid the tranquillity of the inner temple, a clutch of priests emerged from a door behind the altar. As Hannibal's eyes adjusted to the darkness of the interior after the bright light of the afternoon sun outside, he could see that one of the men was carrying a newborn lamb, the stub of its birth cord still trailing beneath its belly. Despite being parted from its mother, it seemed more bemused than frightened by its surroundings and lay passively against the man's chest. Hannibal had heard enough about offerings to the gods to know what lay in wait for it. 'Welcome, General,' said the priest, 'we have the sacrifice to the great god Baal Hammon ready for you. Do you have any private prayers you wish to make before we start?'

'Later, perhaps,' answered Hamilcar, steering his son by the shoulders to within touching distance of the altar and motioning for the ceremony to begin. Hannibal stood stock still in front of his father, his excitement at being part of such a ritual for the first time mixed with a sneaking dread of the fate in store for the lamb. The priests began to chant softly, and their master raised the animal high above his head. 'Oh, mighty one,' he intoned over his colleagues' incantations, 'take this, our humble gift to you, as a pledge of our faithfulness. Honour with your favour Hamilcar Barca, a distinguished general to Carthage yet a mere mortal in your shadow, and protect him and his army against their enemies across the sea.' He swung his arms forward to hold the lamb over a shallow earthen pot on the altar, and it began to bleat, as if realising at last its part in the proceedings.

In a swift movement the chief priest changed his grip to hold the lamb with one hand by its back legs, while his other hand reached for a knife, hidden from Hannibal until now behind the pot. The chanting grew in volume, and the lamb wriggled in desperation, its bleats turning to a continuous high-pitched squeal. The priest rested the curved blade on the animal's throat, gave Hamilcar a piercing stare and then shouted, 'A tribute to the god of gods,' as he slashed sideways. Blood spurted into the pot, and the singing from the other men ceased instantly. Nobody stirred. Hannibal continued to gaze at the lamb with its half-severed neck, taking in the smell of the blood, the profound stillness in the chamber and the reverence of the adults around him. More than anything he was conscious that the killing had not shocked him as much as he had expected.

Hamilcar was the first to break the silence. 'May Baal go with us,' he said, his stentorian soldier's voice booming round the temple. 'Now my son will take an oath.' He moved alongside Hannibal, as the priests nodded approvingly. 'Dip your right hand in the pot and then place it on the altar.' Hannibal did as his father asked, noting the warmth of the freshly spilled blood as he brought his fingers up and fat scarlet droplets fell onto the grey slate tablet of the altar top. He laid his hand, palm down, on the cool surface and looked up at the priests.

'Do you vow to defend your country?' said Hamilcar.

'Yes,' Hannibal replied firmly.

'And who is your country's enemy?'

'Rome.'

'And what will you do when you have become a man?'

The words welled up unbidden, and the nine-year-old boy did not hesitate. 'I will be an enemy to Rome for as long as I live.'

*

November 218 BCE – The Alps, France

'This is madness, General. Look at us. No supplies, no clear route, half the army lost and the rest of us likely to die of cold if the Gauls don't kill us first. Turn back before it's too late; this is no way to fight the Romans.' The cavalry captain, Maharbal, looked round at the others huddled in the tent, but they avoided his eyes and waited for the inevitable outburst from their leader.

'Maharbal, how many times must we discuss this?' Hannibal's tone was curiously gentle. 'We are so nearly there. The guides tell me we have only four more days' march before we reach the pass. You have been with me all the way from Carthage; surely you are not going to abandon me now?' His voice hardened. 'I never said it would be easy. But when we descend from the mountains into the Po Valley, the Romans will be unprepared, and we will crush any defences they put up. Then the road to Rome itself will be open. You've always known I need your elephants for the battles ahead. And I need your support out there with the troops right now. Just four more days.' He glanced at his brother Mago and the other divisional commander, Gisgo. 'The same goes for you two. There is no question of turning back. Are we all agreed?'

An icy blast of wind shook the tent, and the four Carthaginians hunched forward on their campaign chairs, each wrapping his fleece coat closer to his body in an involuntary movement. Mago was the first to reply. 'Hannibal, I support you in everything you do, I always have. What you have achieved to bring us here is nothing short of miraculous, but on this I am with Maharbal. The men are verging on mutiny. More and more of them are deserting, and the walking wounded from the fighting this last month are dropping like sandflies from disease and exhaustion. Trying to cross the mountains now that winter has come is too much. We should retreat to the Rhone and save the army's strength for another attempt in the spring. I think I speak for Gisgo on this too.' The other man nodded. There was no more to add.

Their situation was atrocious, and in complete contrast to the accomplishments of the expedition over the summer and autumn. Five months previously they had marched from New Carthage on the east coast of Hispania with an army of ninety thousand foot soldiers and twelve thousand cavalry, crossing the Iberus River to the north in violation of a treaty with Rome and sweeping aside resistance from local tribes. At the Pyrenees Hannibal had left ten thousand troops behind him to protect supply lines and had sent a similar number back to his brother Hasdrubal in New Carthage to maintain control of the southern part of the peninsula. By the time they had entered Gaul and identified a suitable crossing place on the River Rhone in the late summer, desertion and disease from the mosquito-infested swamplands of the river's southern delta had accounted for further losses, reducing the army to around fifty thousand infantry and nine thousand horsemen. They also had some forty elephants, under Maharbal's watchful eye.

Crossing the Rhone had been a major feat in itself. With the hostile local Volcae tribe massing on the far side to pick off soldiers as they landed, Hannibal had sent a detachment of cavalry upstream to cross at a different location, while his officers assembled thousands of small boats from the surrounding area and arranged the construction of huge rafts to transport the elephants. As the flotilla was launched, the horsemen had ridden downriver on the eastern bank and caught the Volcae unawares, slaughtering them in their hordes. A more amenable Gaulish chieftain had then been found to provide the troops with fresh footwear and warm clothing for the journey into the mountains, and the army had continued its march eastwards as the autumn days began to shorten.

It had soon become evident that the Rhone and the Volcae would not be the only impediments to their progress through Gaul. In a deep crevice of the alpine foothills, strung out in single file along a perilously narrow cliff path, the Carthaginians had been ambushed at their most vulnerable by another tribe, the Allobroges. Rocks and spears had rained down on them from the heights above, and there had been no escape. Hundreds had died, many plunging into the rushing torrent below them as pack animals stampeded in the confined space. Only once the vanguard had regrouped at the mouth of the gorge had Hannibal been able to organise a counter-attack to disperse the enemy. With the weather turning to rain and the temperature falling rapidly at the higher altitude, it had been a pivotal moment in the general's mission, so successful in the five months to this point. Hispanic and Gaulish troops drafted into the ranks had deserted in droves, and the unaccustomed conditions had begun to take their toll on the African soldiers, already debilitated by the long march from New Carthage. Worse still, suspicion had taken seed that the local guides employed by the general to take the army over the mountains were either lost or leading them into another trap. Maharbal, Mago and Gisgo were worried by the growing dissent and were finding Hannibal's faith in the proposed route increasingly difficult to defend. Now the winter storms had begun in earnest, and moving the exhausted men and animals any significant distance in a day was proving an impossible task.

Maharbal resumed the protest. 'It's even worse than Mago says, Hannibal. By my reckoning, the army is now down to about forty thousand, including my Numidian cavalry, and men and horses are dying at every step. As for the elephants, I am losing at least one a day, either from the wounds they suffered in the ambush or from the freezing cold, and we've had to jettison the siege engines. This high up there's barely any timber to burn for the campfires, and while the men will eat raw horse meat, or even elephant if they must, the animals have virtually no fodder. If we do manage to cross the mountains, we will be totally unfit for battle on the other side. When we left New Carthage, we assumed we would be taking a route along the coast into Italy, or else over one of the lower mountain passes below the summer snowline. How can we be sure the guides are not deliberately—'

'Stop!' barked Hannibal. 'You have a long list of complaints, Maharbal, but I've heard them all before. I need solutions, not problems.' He straightened his back as the wind howled around them and raised his hands in a placatory gesture to his three companions. 'As my senior officers, you know I am sworn to fight the Romans and their allies wherever I can. But we must do so on Italian soil, not Gaul or Hispania, so that when we defeat them and march on the citizens of Rome itself, they will flee in terror. The route along the coast was blocked by their army at Massilia, and the pass we are using over the mountains will take us directly down onto their positions at the head of the River Po. Look at the map.' He reached behind him for a leather satchel, extracted a folded piece of fabric and spread it out on the matted floor between their chairs, a foot on either end to keep the draught from ruffling it. 'We have climbed all this way from the Rhone,' he leant down to trace a wide shaded area on the western side of the ridge between Gaul and Italy, 'and we will cross here.' His index finger moved a little to the right, and then on again to indicate the headwaters of the Po. 'Maybe we could have found a lower pass, but we are committed to this route now, and we will have the element of surprise when we swoop down out of the storm clouds.' He paused as another gust shook the tent, blowing a swirl of snowflakes through the laced entrance onto the makeshift map drawn by the guides.

'We are so close. Four days, that's all. The guides are insistent. They realise their lives depend on it.' He looked up with a grim expression. 'And then we start killing Romans. My spies tell me they have garrisons here, and here.' He lifted a foot to tap at points further east on the Po, and the draught stirred a corner of the map, flicking it into an untidy heap under Mago's chair. 'But they are tiny outposts, and the main army is nowhere near that far north yet. We will have plenty of time to reprovision before the real fighting begins.'

Hannibal gathered up the map and returned it to the satchel on his knees. The silence stretched out, broken only by the noise of the blizzard and the drumming of his fingers on the ice-cold leather. It was clear something more than words was necessary. 'Gisgo, Maharbal, each of you is as much a brother to me as Mago, and the three of you are my dearest friends. I *must* have you with me, both in body and in spirit, so I will offer you this.' He dug into a pocket at his hip and produced two dice in his palm. 'There are three of you. If any of you can throw a three, using both dice, I will order the retreat. If not, we will persevere and you will not question my plan again, even if it takes longer than the guides are telling me.' He looked at each of them in turn, and one by one they nodded their assent. They recognised the dice as the totem of his authority as commander-in-chief and had seen him resolve disputes in this way several times before.

As the principal spokesman, Maharbal took the dice from Hannibal and threw them onto the open space where the map had been. They bounced on the coarse matting and came to a halt, showing a six and a four. Gisgo went next, and a one and a five were displayed. No one spoke, and for a strange moment even the gale outside abated. Then Mago rolled, and the dice settled in the centre of the floor. 'Two threes,' he said in a despondent tone. 'Just when I didn't need them both!' He gave the others a rueful smile. 'It appears we are with you, brother, come what may.'

Hannibal stood, stooping under the low roof of the tent, to embrace him, and then Maharbal and Gisgo. 'So be it. Tell your company captains and the mahouts, and we will not speak of this again.'

It took them eight days and nights, toiling ever higher into the mountains, cutting steps in the snow, slipping and sliding on the sheet ice hidden below, edging their way along precipitous rock faces and stumbling blindly on through the thick cloud. All the while the infernal wind blew without interruption, and the temperature continued to drop. At least there were no tribesmen assailing them – the weather was a much more ferocious enemy – and there were no longer any runaways either; there was nowhere to go amongst the crags except forward with the body of the army. To the hardy Africans, used only to crisp desert nights, the cold was a hell more tormenting than their worst fears. Fingers and toes were lost to frostbite, and as the officers roused their men each morning, the death toll from exposure was unremitting. The suffering of the elephants was greater still, worn out by hunger and utterly ill-equipped for the arctic conditions. One after another, they sank to their knees and refused to move, preferring to die in the snowdrifts rather than plod further into the freezing fog. As predicted by Maharbal, their flesh was hacked out and consumed by the troops, in the absence of alternatives, and their butchered carcasses were abandoned where they lay. By the start of the ninth day, a mere twelve of the massive beasts remained alive.

At dawn that morning Hannibal set off with a guide to explore the way ahead as the army prepared to strike camp. At last, the wind seemed to be abating and the fog thinning slightly. The two men walked in silence for an hour, the Carthaginian wondering what lies he would be told this time about the route and timetable to the top of the ridge. He had been given the same projection on each of the last five days – one last push to the final pass – and his trust in the guides was now sorely tested. They scrambled up a goat path, enormous rock stacks soaring above them to each side, and suddenly he found himself teetering on a crest, the ground falling away steeply below. The guide pointed down, and as if by magic, the clouds parted to reveal trees and then lush farmland on the flats far beneath the snowline. Italy, and Rome, at his mercy, ready for the taking. The great god Baal was with him after all.

*

Midsummer 216 BCE – Cannae, Apulia, Italy

Hannibal watched as the spiral of dust on the far fringe of the plain bloomed into a sprawling haze, indicating that the mass of the Roman army was now following the advance guard into position. He had been waiting for two days, tempting the enemy to descend from their hill camp with a series of skirmishing attacks. His patience had been rewarded, and battle would be joined in full today. It had been a cat-and-mouse affair for several weeks, and it was time to bring the campaign to a head.

In truth, it was a matter of many months rather than a few weeks – over a year and a half since that wondrous day when he had led his depleted forces across the alpine ridge into Italy. Half dead from cold and hunger, they had picked their way down the vertiginous slopes awaiting them, gaining strength with every step and seeing out the rest of the winter on the banks of the River Po. The troops' faith in their commander had been further restored by his delivery of heavy defeats on two Roman armies, firstly at Trebbia on the Po and then to the south on the shores of Lake Trasimene in Etruria. Both victories had been achieved through tactical cunning rather than numerical superiority, a fact the Roman generals had belatedly come to recognise. After the disaster at Lake Trasimene, where some fifteen thousand legionaries had died, the military leaders had deliberately avoided set-piece engagements, choosing instead to harry the flanks and rear of the Carthaginian army from a distance over the following six months. With his siege equipment dumped in the snowdrifts of Gaul, and having failed to attract his enemy's Italian allies to his cause in any meaningful scale, Hannibal had been unable to launch his long-anticipated attack on the city of Rome itself. So he had adopted a different strategy, wintering in the fertile meadows of Apulia, the bread basket of Rome, and then seizing a major storage centre at Cannae close to the Adriatic coast the following spring. In doing so, he had stolen vital supplies and blocked access to the forthcoming harvest in a single manoeuvre. If they were to feed their citizens that autumn, the Roman senators knew they must send an army to meet him in open combat once more. And the host they had assembled was larger than any previously mustered in the three hundred-year history of the republic.

It was time to share his battle plan with his trusted lieutenants. Messengers were dispatched and soon Maharbal, Mago, Gisgo and a small handful of other senior officers had gathered. Hannibal took a step back and drew his sword. Using its tip, he carved out a diagram on the baked earth in front of his audience and explained in a few brief sentences what was expected of each division. One moment the blade was stabbing the ground and the next it was moving in swift arrows and half circles, first on one side of the image, and then on the other. The illustration was brisk and crystal clear, but he concluded nonetheless with an invitation for questions. The officers continued to study the diagram in silence, committing the plan to memory, until Gisgo spoke.

'General, my scouts are reporting the enemy's numbers at around eighty thousand infantry and six thousand horse. That's almost double our own strength. Surely, we will be overwhelmed.' He had proved his worth as one of Carthage's bravest warriors over two decades of conflict, and Hannibal knew it was an observation born of long experience rather than fear.

'Numbers are meaningless, Gisgo. Remember Trebbia and Trasimene. Follow my plan, and we will scythe them down like ripe corn, I promise you. And, in any case, you are forgetting one crucial factor.' The man looked puzzled, and Hannibal smiled. 'In all their thousands, they don't have anybody called Gisgo!' Gisgo began to laugh, and the others joined in. Their renewed confidence was infectious, and the general knew it would be transmitted to their troops when they led their divisions out to face the Romans. He alone would now have the luxury of doubt about his scheme, the ultimate preserve of leadership.

By late morning the two armies were drawn up opposite each other across the Apulian plain, their battle order loosely corresponding with a central, elongated rectangle of infantry flanked by cavalry units on each wing. Only in one visible regard did they vary, the Roman foot soldiers presenting a single flat fighting line whereas the Carthaginians were formed into three separate divisions, the centremost standing slightly forward of the others in the shape of a crescent bulging out at the enemy. Even to the layman's eye it was evident that the invaders were vastly outmatched, and the Roman consul-general, Varro, felt supremely assured as he issued the command for war trumpets to be sounded. The eight Roman legions marched forward, slow and ponderous in their heavy armour, while skirmishers sprinted towards the static Carthaginian columns and the cavalry began to engage.

The minor contrast in presentation was more subtle than it appeared. Taking personal control of the infantry in tandem with his brother Mago, Hannibal had filled the central division with his weakest troops, the Gaulish and Hispanic tribesmen he had bribed, bullied and cajoled to follow him over the Alps. He knew they would not withstand the might of the advancing Roman shield wall for long, but the crescent formation would allow them to absorb the legions' initial charge before falling back and drawing the enemy in behind them. His African veterans in the two supporting divisions would then be in a position to attack the Romans from both sides, and if Maharbal's well-drilled cavalry on the outer flanks could better Varro's smaller mounted force, then they would be able to sweep round and set upon the Romans from the rear as well.

Hannibal watched as the legions' front line smashed into the crescent, the tumult of battle rising into the windless summer air above thousands of men thrusting with spears and then slashing with their short swords. The luckless tribesmen fought

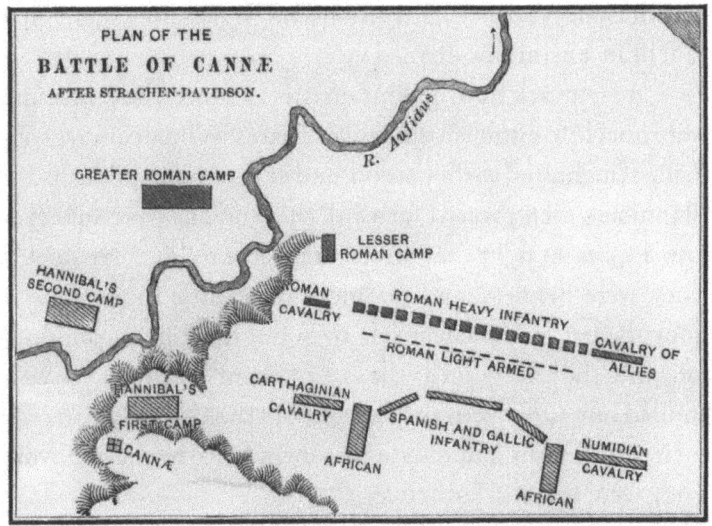

PLAN OF THE
BATTLE OF CANNÆ
AFTER STRACHEN-DAVIDSON.

R. Aufidus

GREATER ROMAN CAMP

LESSER
ROMAN CAMP

HANNIBAL'S
SECOND CAMP

ROMAN
CAVALRY

ROMAN HEAVY INFANTRY

CAVALRY OF
ALLIES

ROMAN LIGHT ARMED

HANNIBAL'S
FIRST CAMP

CANNÆ

CARTHAGINIAN
CAVALRY

SPANISH AND GALLIC
INFANTRY

AFRICAN

NUMIDIAN
CAVALRY

AFRICAN

bravely, but as he had predicted, they were soon beaten back. As the legionaries broke ranks and rushed forward in pursuit, he sprang his trap, directing both of Mago's African divisions to advance at an oblique angle onto the disorganised mob of enemy infantry.

Tired and depleted from the early fighting, the Romans were now under assault from fresh troops on two sides, while Hannibal himself was steadying the retreating Gaulish and Hispanic soldiers into a new front. In the heat and dust and ear-splitting noise of clashing blades and screaming men, the centurions within each legion tried in vain to regroup their units, hoping that if the shield wall could be restored, they might ram their way into open ground and the protective cover of their army's cavalry. They were not to know that, after fierce contests on both wings, Maharbal's horsemen had prevailed and the Roman cavalry were in headlong flight. Although some Africans had been permitted to indulge in the chase, cutting down fleeing riders in their scores, the majority were wheeling in squadron order to frustrate the Roman infantry's withdrawal. Varro's eighty thousand legionaries were now caught in a giant box-shaped vice.

Under attack from all four quarters at once, the centurions were unable to establish defensive squares. Whole cohorts were being slaughtered as they stood, and as the bodies piled up and Hannibal's men pressed forward, the Romans were squeezed into a mass so tight they were barely able to lift their shields. They were helpless, and doomed. After little more than an hour the battle was effectively over, but the killing continued long into the afternoon as the last remnants of resistance were snuffed out. Only with the twilight did the Carthaginians rest their sword arms and offer a prisoners' truce to the survivors. They were few and far between.

It was not until the following day that Hannibal was able to absorb the true scale of the massacre. Returning to the battlefield with his officers, he saw for the first time the success of his tactics, measured in the form of the enemy's losses. There were bodies wherever he looked, lying in a bloody patchwork on the periphery of the main killing zone, then heaped high in dreadful concentric rings within the closing vice of his four-sided assault. In an area no larger than the Carthage barracks parade ground of his childhood, more than sixty thousand legionaries had died, together with about ten thousand of his own infantry. Further out, dead horses and riders from both armies littered the wider area of combat – some five thousand according to Maharbal's estimate – bringing the total death toll to around seventy-five thousand. Set against the outcome, Hannibal's casualties were remarkably modest, the consequence of a plan so perfectly executed, a victory over his lifelong foe so complete, that he was still struggling to take it in as he detached himself from the others and began to walk back towards the Carthaginian camp. Lost in his thoughts, he did not hear the cavalry commander at first.

'General, by tomorrow morning my troops will be ready for the next step.' Maharbal came abreast of him, panting after running to catch up. 'If we ride hard, we can be at the gates of Rome in four days, possibly even before the news of the battle has arrived. We may not be able to force an entry, but we can hunt down any bands of militia in the surrounding area, and your infantry will be marching into the city within a month. Tell me how many horsemen you wish me to leave with you, and I will arrange the rest.'

Hannibal stopped and turned, allowing his gaze to take in the terrible view once again before he replied to his countryman. 'I congratulate you, Maharbal, on your cavalry's triumph. Without them in place to close the door on the legions, the battle might have taken a very different path.'

'My pleasure,' Maharbal grinned, 'and now we need to make the most of it. When do you propose to begin the march west?'

'Look around you, my friend. We have slaughtered more Romans in a day than even I could have imagined. We will march on Rome in the fullness of time, of course we will, but enough blood has been shed for now. Let us simply enjoy this mighty achievement while the army recovers.'

'How can you say this?' Maharbal's voice rose. 'You of all people, Rome's sworn enemy. We should strike immediately, before their senate has time to raise fresh troops and strengthen the city's defences. It would be madness to delay.'

'I seem to remember you accused me of madness once before, in a tent in the mountains of Gaul,' Hannibal retorted sharply. 'You wanted me to retreat and now you want me to attack. Which is it, Maharbal? Will you never trust me to make the right decisions?' He gave a heavy sigh and continued more calmly. 'Despite our success here, we still don't have siege equipment, and we have yet to bring any of the major local tribes across to our side in the war. Until we have both of those, the attack on Rome will have to wait.'

'You have been saying that ever since Trasimene last year. You know how to win, Hannibal, but it appears you have not yet learnt what to do with your victories.' Maharbal made no attempt to hide his exasperation. 'Perhaps you should consult your dice,' he added sarcastically.

'There will be no dice. Siege engines and allies, that's all. We are here to win the war, not just the battles. You would do well to remember it.' Maharbal remained rooted to the spot as the general strode away. It was the first real argument over strategy between them since leaving New Carthage and, much as he respected his commander-in-chief, the cavalryman knew in his heart of hearts that Hannibal was making a serious mistake.

*

182 BCE – Nicomedia, Bithynia, Asia Minor

The summons to Nicomedia's citadel from his host King Prusias had been almost inevitable. The rumours of Roman spies at large in the obscure mountainous state perched on the south-west coast of the Black Sea had been circulating for some weeks, and the fact that Hannibal had been granted asylum in its capital four months previously was surely an open secret amongst the king's subjects. He had no illusions as to the direction the interview would take. His limbs ached from the swift pace through the streets set by the boy sent to collect him, but he steadied himself and followed the lad up the steps onto the palace forecourt, where he was told – not asked, he noted – to wait. The audience would be held in the sweltering heat of the afternoon sun, it seemed, so it would at least be short.

'You look well, Hannibal. Life in Bithynia is obviously suiting you.' The voice came from an unseen doorway in the deep shadows to his left. The old king stepped into the light, and Hannibal bowed, his back twinging in pain. They both knew the compliment was a lie, but it would be ungracious to say so. 'Thank you, Your Majesty. It does indeed, and it is time I started working for you in exchange for your kind hospitality. I have several schemes to suggest, any one of which would be a thorn in the side of Rome.'

'Ah, yes, Rome.' King Prusias grimaced, and if there had been any question of what would happen next, the Carthaginian knew now that it had been answered. 'There has been a development since you first arrived here. I have received a delegation from Rome, proposing attractive trading terms. They wish to enter a treaty, a condition of which is that I cease harbouring you. Somehow,' he began to inspect the weather-bleached paving stones underfoot, unable to look Hannibal in the eye, 'they have learnt of your presence at my court. Regrettably, I must urge you to find a new home. If I do not, they will bring war instead.'

Despite himself, Hannibal swallowed hard in disappointment. 'Beware, Your Majesty. They will promise much and deliver little. Your fine country would be better off forging links with any one of the Greek principalities, or even with the Ptolemys of Egypt. And, as we have discussed before, I can help you raise an army to defend your borders. Rome is your enemy, not your friend.'

The king shook his head wearily. 'My best years are behind me, Hannibal. My sons are still too young to take on the reins of government, and I have neither the energy nor the appetite for war. You are right, we have a fine country, but alas it is built on rock, and we need trading partners if we are to feed ourselves. The Romans are too powerful to ignore. They have always been your enemy, but never mine. I have made my decision, and I will expect you to have gone within one cycle of the moon.' He walked slowly towards the shadows from which he had emerged. 'You are a remarkable man, Hannibal; I'm sorry it has come to this.' Then he passed through the doorway, and it creaked shut behind him. The king's protection had been withdrawn, and there was nothing more to be said.

Early that evening, in the modest low-roofed house on the outskirts of the city that he had been allotted on his arrival in Bithynia, Hannibal sat brooding over the options available to him. After thirteen years in exile, they were sadly limited. During that period, he had continued to honour his childhood oath by offering his services around the east Mediterranean to nations hostile to Rome, but in every capital the threat of betrayal to his enemy's assassins had eventually forced him to move on. More recently, his value as a military advisor had taken a severe knock when, as strategist to King Antiochus of Seleucia, the navy under his command had suffered a mauling from Rome's fleet. He lacked the vitality he used to take for granted and at the age of sixty-five he was bound to admit that, like Prusias, he was getting old, maybe even too old and infirm to keep the flame of hate burning bright. It had been a thirty-six-year campaign since marching the army out of New Carthage into Gaul, and if he was honest with himself, he knew precisely where the turning point had come. Cannae, at once the pinnacle of his extraordinary achievements and the beginning of his descent towards banishment and irrelevance.

Cannae... the words of his friend and comrade-in-arms Maharbal still rang in his ears. He should have attacked Rome when it was at its most vulnerable, but instead he had spent fourteen more years marching his troops the length and breadth of Italy, performing audacious raids against all odds, winning battles whenever the enemy could be teased into confronting him, but never quite finding the momentum to strike at the capital itself. Gradually the balance of the war had begun to shift, as the Roman leaders studied his tactics and learnt how to contain him. And then the consul Scipio had taken the conflict to Africa, obliging Hannibal to follow him across the sea to defend his homeland. In parched semi-desert several days' march south of Carthage city, the two generals had met in person. Scipio had dismissed Hannibal's terms for peace, despite the Roman army being substantially outnumbered, and the great Battle of Zama had taken place the following day. The young consul-general had proved an excellent student, nullifying Hannibal's attempt to repeat the three-sided vice manoeuvre of Cannae by superior use of the Roman cavalry and even turning an elephant charge onto the Carthaginian's own infantry. The result was a rout, leaving twenty thousand of Hannibal's veterans dead and the same again in captivity. Hannibal had slipped away to the coast, and the war between the two countries had finally come to an end.

The seven years after Zama had seen Hannibal shed his military ambitions for Carthage and reinvent himself as a statesman. He had worked hard in the Suffete to meet the peace conditions imposed by Rome, which included a massive reparation payment, and in doing so had exposed a web of corruption amongst the ruling classes alongside him. In Rome Scipio, now bearing the title 'Africanus', had recognised his rival's efforts and had rewarded them by persuading the senate not to press for Carthage's further humiliation. As the years went by, however, his political influence had waned whereas the senators' desire for Hannibal's arrest and deportation to Rome for execution had remained constant. Meanwhile, in Carthage it had become increasingly apparent to Hannibal that he risked betrayal by the aristocracy whose fraudulence he had uncovered. Self-imposed exile had been the only solution, and so had begun his thirteen-year peregrinations amongst Rome's enemies, always one step ahead of her assassins.

Glancing around him, the true extent of his fall from grace was all too evident. His accommodation comprised two small chambers: a cell-like bedroom through the wall facing him; and the living room he sat in equipped with a rough wooden table, a scattering of hard chairs, a window overlooking the dingy lane outside and an open hearth for cooking in one corner. Soot streaked the walls and ceiling above the fire, and with neither cupboard nor travel chest for storage, his few possessions were spread haphazardly across the earthen floor. The privy was a shared experience with innumerable neighbours in the paddock behind the house, and running water had to be drawn from a standpipe fifty paces away. From what he had seen of the more prosperous quarters of the city, standards there were not much better. As a soldier he was long used to tough conditions, but in the years since the end of the war he had begun to appreciate the comforts of a wealthy civilian existence. The poor quality of life in Bithynia, even amongst the relatively rich and powerful, had been an unwelcome surprise. But it was the only state to have offered him asylum after his flight from Seleucia, and he had been in no position to reject the lodgings provided to him.

So what exactly were his choices, as the world closed in on him? He could remain in Nicomedia beyond the king's deadline to test whether Prusias was prepared to call Rome's bluff on the terms of the treaty. But from what he knew of Bithynia, a trade deal would be more important to Prusias than a single, old, discredited Carthaginian general. Alternatively, he could seek shelter in a fresh country opposed to Rome, but after his various moves the list was short, and again he now had little to offer by comparison to the republic's patronage. Moreover, his health was failing and perhaps, after all the bloodshed, the time had finally come to forsake his boyhood oath of enmity. Or, thirdly, he could risk a return to Carthage and the renewed danger of betrayal by his fellow citizens.

He drummed his fingers on the table, unconsciously repeating the gesture that had led to his defining moment on the alpine mountainside all those years ago. To continue this miserable existence in Nicomedia was unacceptable; to go crawling to another country for sanctuary was too humiliating to endure; and he would be signing his own death warrant the day he set foot in Carthage. There was just one other option, and it lay in a battered leather satchel under his mattress in the next-door room.

Hannibal rose and fetched the satchel. In the fading light he peered inside and removed a miniature glass phial, a wax-coated wooden tablet and a stylus. Carefully he set the phial to one end of the table and then reached into his pocket for his dice, the dice that had accompanied him every step of the way from Hispania after his promotion to commander-in-chief of the army as a young man. He turned them over in his hand and then rolled them across the table's surface towards the phial. A score of three... the number that Maharbal and the others had bid for in the Alps to win the argument for retreat. He smiled at the irony of it and picked up the stylus to begin writing on the tablet.

I bequeath these dice to Scipio Africanus, a fine soldier and a worthy adversary on the battlefield of Zama. Three centuries ago, they belonged to his country. He has earned their restoration. Hannibal Barca, son of Carthage and lifelong enemy of Rome.

Then he lifted the phial, pulled out the stopper and drank.

*

And then…

+ Following Hannibal's suicide in 182 BCE, King Prusias sends the tablet and the dice to Scipio Africanus. He in turn gifts the dice to his daughter Cornelia, mother to the Gracchi brothers, reforming politicians in late second-century BCE Rome.

+ In the hands of the Gracchi, and thereafter, the dice revert to their previous function as an instrument of office for successive Roman leaders, passing eventually to the second emperor, Tiberius, great-uncle to Gaius Caesar Augustus Germanicus, a boy more commonly known as Caligula.

*

Author's Note

The heroic deeds of Hannibal Barca are the stuff of legend, but unlike the myths of ancient Greece and the founding of Rome, they are regarded as factual, thanks in particular to two sources, the second-century BCE Greek historian Polybius and the Roman author Livy writing about 150 years later. The expedition across the Alps and Hannibal's brilliant generalship against great odds at the battles of Trebbia, Lake Trasimene and Cannae are well known. Possibly less familiar are his subsequent fourteen-year campaign in Italy, always threatening but never succeeding in his quest to take Rome; his political activities in Carthage after the defeat at Zama in 202 BCE; his long exile; and his death by poison in Asia Minor.

Hannibal's father Hamilcar had deeply resented his country's defeat in the First Punic War and the ensuing loss of prestige around the western Mediterranean. The story of Hannibal pledging, as a boy, to be Rome's lifelong enemy may be apocryphal, but he would certainly have inherited Hamilcar's bitterness, born and raised as he was in the military surroundings of Carthage and then Spain.

His remarkable leadership qualities were clear from the outset, the army giving their overwhelming approval to his appointment as General at the age of twenty-six. Within three years, he had not only won a series of victories against Rome's allies on the Iberian Peninsula, culminating in the successful eight-month siege of Saguntum (in the province of modern-day Valencia), but in doing so had obtained authorisation from his government (the Suffete) to take the army north towards Italy itself.

The precise location for the crossing of the River Rhone has not been established but is likely to have been at or slightly upstream of Arles in Provence. Likewise, the route over the Alps has generated much debate. The cliff-path ambush by the Allobroges tribe is thought to have been in the Col de Grimone, a tributary of the River Drôme near Gap, while the pass into Italy may have been at the Col de la Traversette above Briançon. More obvious alternatives at lower altitudes have been discounted by historians for a variety of reasons, prompting the assumption of treachery amongst Hannibal's local guides. By the time the army arrived in the Po Valley, somewhere close to Turin, its numbers had been reduced to around twenty-three thousand infantry, five thousand cavalry and just a handful of elephants.

The Battle of Cannae is a famous early example of the 'double envelopment' manoeuvre known to military tacticians down the ages. The pincer movement by Hannibal's flanking divisions, and the attack from the rear by Maharbal's cavalry, produced a bloodbath of unimaginable ferocity. Within consul Varro's battalions several of the principal generals (although not Varro himself) were killed, alongside some eighty senators (25–30% of the republic's governing body). Including those slain at Lake Trasimene the previous year, it is estimated that around one in five Roman men of fighting age perished. The total death toll of between sixty to eighty thousand across the two armies at Cannae is probably one of the biggest massacres in a single day *throughout history. Hannibal's ability to motivate and direct his troops in the face of a much larger and well-equipped enemy force was extraordinary, whether or not his speech to Gisgo, reported by Plutarch, actually took place. Equally, his failure to follow his victory with an assault on Rome, whether or not encouraged by Maharbal as told by Livy, was surely a serious strategic error.*

The description of Hannibal's career after the high watermark of 218–216 BCE is accurate but necessarily brief. His conversion from soldier to statesman in Carthage was successful until he became threatened by his corrupt countrymen, and Scipio Africanus's interventions on his behalf in the Roman senate appear to have prolonged his survival. But by the later years of his self-imposed exile, he had lost support amongst Rome's enemies and risked imminent betrayal or assassination. It is unclear whether the poison he drank was at the order of his Bithynian host King Prusias or at his own hand. His bequest of the dice to Scipio, their path over the next two hundred years into the hands of emperor Tiberius and their role in the crossing of the Alps, are all fictitious. However, it seems true to say that Hannibal remained an enemy of Rome to the end.

Caligula and Claudius

37 CE – Capri, Italy

The helmsman ordered the sails to be trimmed as the harbour came into view, and the fresh south-easterly breeze brought the boat neatly round the jagged reef towards the dock. In the mellow golden light of the early evening, Caligula could see a group of men waiting to greet them, and as the gap across the water reduced, he was surprised to find it was the prefect of the Praetorian Guard, Macro, with a handful of soldiers. He was used to being accompanied by members of the Guard wherever he went, and they had inevitably joined him on the brief expedition to the mainland town of Surrentum, but an additional escort awaiting his return seemed unusually overbearing. He gave it little thought; after six years of living with the old emperor Tiberius on the beautiful island of Capri, he was well acquainted with his great-uncle's paranoia. He was effectively under house arrest and there had never been any opportunity to escape. In any case, he had grown accustomed to the pampered existence there. The regular supply of women and wine, falling from the top table, as it were, suited his tastes perfectly. It was definitely a better fate than the death of his mother and brothers, almost certainly at the emperor's bidding.

'Good evening, Macro,' he called out in a jovial voice as the small vessel nudged alongside the wooden wharf. 'What have I done to deserve such a welcome? I can't believe a day trip to Surrentum to see my sisters merits such attention!'

The other man's dour expression did not alter. 'You will come with me,' the Guard prefect said gruffly and beckoned Caligula to step off the boat. Caligula jumped down from the gunnel, landing heavily, his ungainly legs folding beneath him. He picked himself up and scurried across the harbour waterfront after Macro, the squad of soldiers forming up behind him at a respectful distance. 'Not a word, Caligula,' Macro said over his shoulder, 'not until we are in private at the house.'

A few minutes later, a slave closed the double doors to the dining hall at the emperor's villa, and the two men were alone. Caligula was mystified by the reception to his arrival on the island. Nothing untoward had been reported before his voyage to the mainland that morning, and he had seen Tiberius the previous night at the monthly lunar banquet. The old man had been his usual self, gross with overindulgence and obscene commentary about the young boys and girls attending them, but healthy enough, if that was the right term for his bloated, wine-soaked body. There was no reason to suppose he had been taken ill, and Caligula's sources around Capri had given no indication of bad news from Rome. He waited impatiently until Macro ceased pacing the room and stood square in front of him. Then, to his astonishment, the prefect unsheathed the sword at his hip and proffered it, hilt first. 'Hail, Emperor! I give you my allegiance, and that of your Praetorian Guard, on this auspicious day.'

Caligula gaped. 'Explain, Macro. What's happened in my absence? Has Tiberius died?'

'So it would seem.'

'What do you mean? Either he has, or he hasn't. Surely you must know?' Caligula raised his fingers to his temples in exasperation.

'He must have had some sort of seizure last night after the feast. He was found unconscious in bed this morning and has been there ever since. He was still breathing when I checked on him in the middle of the afternoon. But just as your boat was spotted returning from the mainland, I had word from the servants that he had died. I came straight down to the harbour.'

'Why, Prefect?' Caligula asked apprehensively, not convinced he wanted to hear the answer.

'Because Rome needs a swift transfer of power, and Tiberius always led me to believe that you, being descended from the great Emperor Augustus, should succeed him. Your uncle Claudius is not up to the job, and Gemellus is too young.' He looked steadily at Caligula. 'And too far away.' The rest of the message was left unsaid.

It was Caligula's turn to walk, and he moved to the window to gaze across the tiered gardens outside. His heart pounded with excitement and, with his back to the room, he permitted himself a long smile of satisfaction. Unremarkable in appearance and outwardly resigned to the apathy of his enforced detention, he had in fact been waiting for this day ever since Tiberius had appointed Macro to command the Guard. His birthright to the throne was tenuous, but his grasp of history was sufficient to appreciate that whoever the legitimate heir might be, military support had a habit of deciding the result. As grandson to Tiberius, Gemellus would probably have been the senate's natural choice, but he was still a teenager, compared to Caligula's comparative maturity at twenty-five. Hitherto, Macro had never ventured an opinion on the succession, but Caligula had been careful to curry favour with him, calculating that his assistance might prove crucial when the time came. It was convenient that the old man had died while Macro was visiting him on the island, and now the commander had shown his colours.

Thoughts of what he would do as emperor crowded Caligula's mind, and as quickly a host of likely hurdles occurred to him. He pushed them away. What was it that his father, the famous general Germanicus, used to say to his family all those years ago on the campaigns east of the Rhine? 'Never look a gift horse in the mouth...' He could barely remember him, but he recalled the maxim vividly, as he did his childish fury at the teasing he had endured from the legionaries there. They had nicknamed him Caligula after the boots of the little uniform he had been made to wear around the camp, and it had stuck with him ever since. With Macro at his side, that would change now, or people would learn to regret it. He would travel to Rome immediately, with the full weight of the Guard behind him, to see off the boy Gemellus and knock the senators into line. Emperor, at last!

He composed himself and turned back towards the prefect. He was about to speak when there was a knock at the door. 'Enter,' shouted Macro, and Caligula made a mental note to admonish him later. It was for the emperor to invite people into his dining room, not his underling. The two doors eased open, and a middle-aged woman peeped through the gap. She seemed flustered and spoke in a rush. 'Forgive me, Prefect, but the emperor... we thought he had died, but he's breathing again. His eyes are flickering. Come and see. Please, hurry.' Without a word Macro ran to the doors and barged past her. Taking the steps from the hallway three at a time he raced upstairs and out of sight. Caligula followed more slowly, his imagination churning at this unwelcome revelation.

When he arrived in the emperor's sleeping chamber, puffing from the exertion of the unaccustomed exercise, he found the

Guard prefect leaning over Tiberius, flanked by two matrons clutching at each other and sobbing quietly. The women were clearly terrified, though less by the apparent resurrection they were witnessing, Caligula suspected, than by fear of the penalty in store for their previous misdiagnosis. The old man lay immobile, his torso and legs shrouded by bedclothes and his head propped up on several pillows. His face, usually a mottled rash of flaring blood vessels and weeping patches where he had scratched at a long-standing skin complaint, was ashen and his hands, lying on the coverlet over his stomach, a lifeless grey. He looked dead enough, but as Caligula went to the opposite side of the bed from Macro, he saw a spasm shudder through the body and the eyelids twitch.

'It's true!' he exclaimed, and Macro nodded as he straightened up. The two men stood, regarding each other across the supine body, saying nothing. At length Macro turned to the women and spoke, his voice low and harsh in the enclosed space.

'Stop your snivelling. Who knows about this?'

'No one, sir. Only us and Marilla downstairs.' The spokeswoman wiped her nose on the sleeve of her dress. 'The three of us were about to start preparing the body for the coffin, and suddenly...' Fresh tears poured down her cheeks and she gestured feebly at the bed.

'Stop it, I said! Go downstairs, find this Marilla, and the three of you wait in the dining hall. My men are on guard around the villa, so don't try to leave.' His voice lost its edge. 'You did well to call me so fast. Now, leave us, and I will talk to you again later.' He ushered the two women out of the room and watched from the threshold as they began to descend the stairs. Then he shut the door behind him and turned the key in the lock.

'So, Caligula, where do we go from here?'

Caligula stared at him, gauging the situation and realising that a misguided answer could imperil both his ambition and his life. Another of his father's catch phrases – strike while the iron is hot – sprang to mind. Yes, his time had come, and Tiberius's revival was an inconvenience that must be addressed without hesitation. The purpose of the Praetorian Guard was to protect the emperor, and Macro had hailed Caligula as such, so the prefect should perform his duty. Order would be restored, and the twenty-five-year-old's hands would remain clean.

'My great-uncle has suffered enough from his seizure. I have no doubt he would want you to help him on his way.' Caligula reached towards the bed and pulled a pillow out from beneath Tiberius's neck. He tossed it to Macro and paused for a brief moment as the prefect bent to hold it over the old man's mouth and nose. Then he crossed the room to the door, unlocked it and headed down the staircase, the other necessary measures in his ascent to the throne now taking firm shape in his thoughts. The servant women would need to be silenced, which he could rely on Macro to do, and in Rome he would also have the prefect killed, to remove any danger of betrayal going forward. But first and foremost, he required some explicit evidence to support his claim to the senate that Tiberius had nominated him as the next emperor.

Caligula had been in the old man's office on the ground floor many times, listening to him boasting about the power he wielded across the Mediterranean and northwards into Gaul and Germania. During one of those lectures Tiberius had produced a pair of ivory dice from a drawer in his massive desk, declaring that they were the original trappings of Roman command. According to him, they dated back to the founding of Rome, and even the sacking of Troy further off in the mists of history. He who held them, controlled the empire itself. Caligula had been sceptical of their origin, but he had heard the same story more recently from his uncle, Claudius, a gibbering halfwit in most ways and certainly no realistic candidate for the throne, yet an undeniable expert on ancient history. If the dice were a recognised emblem of imperial authority, then the new emperor must find them. He entered Tiberius's office and wondered fleetingly if the pillow upstairs had completed its work.

*

40 CE – Rome, Italy

Watching the emperor weave his way across the Forum towards him, Claudius tried to imagine what guise the humiliation would take on this occasion. He had plenty of time to contemplate the possibilities, as Caligula stopped to exchange words with several groups of senators and army officers thronging the ancient marketplace at the heart of the city. Claudius was not fooled by the hearty laughter and shouts of goodwill marking the emperor's path. In the febrile atmosphere of the last two years, no one dared incur their leader's wrath, and unctuous appeasement was generally accepted as the safest means of dealing with him. His readiness to take up and discard favourites was renowned, and there was no swifter route to the underworld than the mistake of getting his name wrong. Gaius Caesar Augustus Germanicus had made it abundantly clear from the moment he had inherited the imperial throne that he would not tolerate being called Caligula anymore.

Despite the sensitivity over his title, Claudius mused, the new emperor's first few months following the death of Tiberius had been encouraging. He had been a popular alternative to his aged, autocratic predecessor, visible in Rome rather than hidden away on Capri, and winning immediate favour by instigating political reforms, announcing major building projects around the empire, improving the army's pay and laying on lavish entertainments for the masses. But within a year, after a mysterious illness, his behaviour had seemed to change, and the clouds of tyranny, so familiar from Tiberius's last years, had begun to gather. Rumours had circulated that, with the help of the Praetorian Guard, Caligula had seized the throne from under the nose of Tiberius's heir Gemellus, conceivably even triggering the process by assassinating the old emperor himself – rumours supported by the unexplained deaths of both the Guard prefect Macro and Gemellus. Then the extravagance of his early decisions had developed into a severe financial crisis for the exchequer, to which he had responded by raiding the coffers of the patrician class by fines, appropriation of their estates or crude blackmail. With every month he had become more capricious and more fearful of conspiracies against him, resulting in the purge of perceived rivals on unsubstantiated allegations of treason. Whispers of madness had started to ripple through the city, further fuelled in recent weeks by his appearance in the streets dressed as a god and demanding the obeisance of all around him. This morning, evidently, he was a mortal, but sycophancy remained the order of the day for anyone interested in preserving their fortune and their life.

Claudius's position was particularly unenviable. As the emperor's uncle, he ran the constant risk of being seen as a contender to the throne. To date, Caligula had not considered him a threat, due to his hesitant manner and his failure over decades to demonstrate any form of political or military initiative. A limp, an acute stutter and a tendency to shake and drool as he attempted to speak accentuated the perception of stupidity, carrying with it the potential charge of worthlessness and therefore dismissal by execution. The emperor's preference was to torment him, playing practical jokes on him, ridiculing him for his speech impediment and never missing an opportunity to belittle him in public. The most recent instance had been at the Liberalia feast three days previously, where Claudius had been required to hobble to the front of the high table and describe the origins of the annual festival. 'G-g-g-go on, t-t-tell everyone ab-ab-ab-about it,' Caligula had mocked him and had led the diners in pelting him with food as he tried to reply. With so many onlookers nearby, it was fair to assume another shaming lay in store today.

'Good morning, Uncle,' said Caligula as he approached. 'What brings you to the Forum on this fine day?' Claudius was wary of the unusual cordiality, but he took care to maintain a placid expression of welcome. 'Good m-m-m-morning to you, Emperor G-G-Gaius. I am si-simply enj-enj-enjoying the sun.' A bead of phlegm trickled down his chin and he wiped it away with a quivering hand.

'Excellent, although it sounds rather dull to me; I should have thought you would be in the library, writing one of your splendid history books. Well, I'm glad to have found you. I wanted to apologise for our behaviour at the feast the other night and allow you to have your revenge on me.'

Claudius's nerves jangled at the unlikely proposition, and he guessed what might be coming. They had gambled together in the past, at the emperor's insistence, and when Claudius had won, Caligula had refused to pay up. 'Thank you, Emperor, I would be de-de-delighted,' he replied. 'What do you have in m-m-m-mind?'

'I suggest a game of dice. We will play for money, and we can use these.' Caligula opened his hand to reveal a pair of dice. 'You've probably never seen them, but as our illustrious historian I expect you know the tale behind them. They've belonged to kings and emperors of Rome right back to Aeneas. In fact,' he made a pretence of sudden recollection, 'I think it was you who told me about them in the first place!'

Claudius glanced at the palm in front of him and knew instantly what Caligula's plan must be. Long ago Tiberius had shown him the ancient dice and told him of their fabled journey from Troy to modern Rome. He remembered them well, the grey ivory gnarled and pitted and irrefutably cube shaped. Caligula's dice, by contrast, were of black ebony and slightly more oblong than square in structure. Claudius had heard numerous stories in recent months of his nephew challenging people to games of chance and winning large sums off them, time after time. It was happening so regularly, the dice must be weighted, and it was presumably Caligula's latest way of extracting money from the aristocracy. Claudius would be no exception, the stakes would be enormous, and he would inevitably lose. He quashed a sigh of resentment at being taken for a fool with such transparent deception and said, politely, 'How exci-ci-citing! It would be an honour to pl-pl-pl-play with them. What wager do you pro-pro-propose?'

By the end of the morning, Caligula had won three hundred thousand sesterces, a material amount even to a descendant of Augustus, and more than anything Claudius had heard others lose to the young emperor. To anybody else, his persistent success with the dice would have been sufficiently embarrassing to call a halt, if not a clear indication of cheating. But Caligula had pressed on regardless, and so therefore had Claudius, congratulating his opponent on every loaded throw and biting his lip at the injustice of it. Behind his physical limitations lay a studious intelligence, and he was an experienced dicer, with a keen appreciation of the odds at play and an equally strong awareness of his role in this charade. At midday Caligula had finally relented, clapping a hand on his uncle's back and wishing him better luck next time before sauntering off across the Forum's paving stones. Given the amount Claudius had lost, there would be little point playing again, he thought bitterly. But his finances were secondary to his survival, and surely the emperor could not continue to rule in this fashion for much longer. The performance he had just witnessed was that of a cruel and avaricious bully, not a madman – Gaius Caesar Augustus Germanicus had known exactly what he was doing – but Claudius would never be the man to supplant him.

*

50 CE – Rome, Italy

The iron fist of merciless subjugation, or the imperial gift of clemency? As the guard departed to wait outside the room, Emperor Claudius inspected the dishevelled Briton prisoner before him with interest, weighing up who the primary audience for his verdict might ultimately be. The man had impressed the senate with his petition for deliverance from the executioner, and the emperor was always careful to retain the politicians' goodwill. But what message would it send to Rome's enemies if he agreed to spare a barbarian general such as this? The news would find its way across Gaul and over the narrow sea channel to Britannia in a matter of weeks, and the military governor there, Publius Scapula, would have another rebellion on his hands before the year was out.

Seated on his throne in the magnificent reception hall of the palace, Claudius was conscious that the tall, broad-chested prisoner was staring at him, standing in silence with shoulders squared and head held high. His speech to the senators the previous day had been in his mother tongue, intelligible to them only thanks to the efforts of an interpreter, but it was rumoured that he knew some Latin, enough at least to carry on a basic conversation about life or death. More than that, he was said to be a man of many talents, an exceptional leader in the rain and mud of his home country and a brave soldier whose recent capture by the Roman army had arisen through betrayal rather than poor generalship or surrender. It was lucky, Claudius reflected, that they had not met seven years ago; as king of the Catuvellauni tribe in southern Britannia, the man could so easily have led an attack on the emperor as he made his way through the newly acquired province to visit the garrison fort of Camulodunum. Despite the Briton's downfall, and the humiliation of being exhibited in chains to the crowds after his dispatch to Rome by Scapula, he still cut an imposing figure, carrying himself with an air of regal authority. The emperor realised with a start that it was time to assert himself. He stood up from the throne and found, to his annoyance, that he remained well short of the prisoner in height.

'Good day, Caractacus,' he began, taking care to speak slowly in order to control his customary stutter. 'I am told you spoke persuasively at the senate yesterday, but let us not forget you are an enemy of the state. As a prisoner and a king, you should die. Tell me why I should allow you to live.'

Several moments passed as the Briton pondered the question and, Claudius suspected, whether he should disclose his grasp of Latin. Then he gave a shallow bow and began to talk in a thick foreign accent. 'Good day, Emperor Claudius. Seven years ago, when your army invaded my country and you yourself came to besiege our capital, the city your soldiers now call Camulodunum, I had the choice of entering battle or negotiating a peace treaty. Even though my people live in poor conditions, with little wealth to defend, I chose battle, to safeguard their freedom from slavery. We were defeated, but I have no regret at my decision. However, now that I have seen the scale of Rome's empire and the riches of its capital city, I ask myself why you would wish to steal my countrymen's humble homes and barren lands. If you kill me, I will simply be another example of Rome's aggression. But if you spare me, your army's fearsome reputation in warfare will remain untarnished, while you personally will be lauded throughout your realm for your grace in victory. The name Claudius will be the hallmark of wisdom amongst your people and of magnanimity amongst your enemies, for centuries to come. I appeal to you as a fellow king, not an abject prisoner, whatever my appearance may suggest.' He adjusted his stance and the shackles around his legs clanked noisily in the hush of the throne room.

Claudius put a hand to his mouth and furrowed his brow in what he hoped was a display of deep thought, although the principal purpose was to wipe flecks of spittle from around his lips. As well as being taken aback by the king's ability to speak Latin so fluently, he was surprised at the man's measured analysis of his position. It was evident that the barbarians across the Mare Britannicum were more enlightened than their quality of life had indicated to him on his visit there. He recognised the flattery of Caractacus's proposal for what it was, but it struck a chord nonetheless. He stepped past the king, to escape that unsettling stare, and walked to the far side of the room to study an imperial map hanging on the wall.

The fact that he was emperor of such a vast dominion never ceased to amaze him, even after the best part of a decade following the bloody revolt that had brought an end to Caligula's wicked regime. It had been an ignominious beginning, plucked by a Praetorian guardsman from behind a curtain in the Palatine palace where he had hidden in terror as his nephew was being hacked to pieces. The soldier had taken him to the Guard camp where the same group of officers that had led the assassination had immediately declared him emperor, a puppet leader to their treasonous cause. The senate had attempted to block the appointment, but the tribune Cassius Chaerea had forced it through, assisted by a long address from Claudius demonstrating that he was not the idiot his predecessor had believed. His trembling and slobbering had moderated, if not disappeared altogether; his stutter had been curbed and his manifesto for the role ahead well structured. He had been able to refer to numerous events in the history of Rome to support his views, and he had not felt it necessary to explain that his bodily frailties had been deliberately exaggerated in recent years to avoid death under Caligula.

Since his unexpected elevation he had grown steadily in confidence, proving an able administrator and a far-sighted strategist in the development of the empire, both politically and geographically. His decree for the invasion of Britannia eighteen months into his reign had been a calculated risk, and it had been essential to go there himself with reinforcements shortly after the initial attack, to bolster his position with the army. But the new province was now firmly established and there had been other successes as well in the annexation of Thrace, Judaea and Mauretania. Yet even after nine years on the throne there remained an undercurrent of hostility amongst certain factions within the senate, and given the circumstances of his election, the importance of retaining their support was never far from his mind. From what he had heard, the Briton's performance in front of them the previous afternoon had also dwelt on the Roman values of virtue and benevolence, though not, he presumed, in relation to the emperor as an individual. The senate was prepared to let Caractacus live out his life in peace in Italy, and by association Claudius would be celebrated throughout the world as the epitome of judgement and tolerance, Rome's new broom after the chaos and brutality of Caligula. It was very enticing, but was it in reality the sign of weakness his opponents had been waiting to pounce on? An emperor's dilemma, he thought wryly, as he crossed the room again to face the barbarian.

'A com-com-compelling argument, Caractacus. But just words. I already command the respect of my people, and my army are paid to assert my power. Why should I worry about the opinion of those in sl-sl-slavery across my domains?'

'It is said that you are a historian,' the Briton answered, regarding him with a patient expression. 'You will know better than most how difficult it is to retain power without your subjects' goodwill. Benevolent occupation of your enemies' territories will reduce both the threat of uprisings and the cost of quelling them. As for your own position, consider your predecessors – how many in the last hundred years have died in their beds rather than by insurrection and assassination? You can break the mould. Save me and you save yourself.'

So he knew about Julius Caesar and Mark Antony and Caligula, not to mention his own father dying on campaign in Germania, Claudius supposed, and he understood the massive financial burden of maintaining order around the flourishing empire. The lure of the Briton king's case was ever more attractive, yet the emperor's instinctive reservation remained, until suddenly a solution came to him. An imperial dilemma was worthy of consultation with the gods.

'I have no need to spare you, Caractacus, be clear about that. But as an indulgence to a brave man and a fine orator, I will per-permit you to gamble for your life.' Claudius reached for a small box on a side table to the throne and emptied out the ivory dice that he had first seen in the hands of Tiberius thirty years before. 'I take it you are familiar with dice?' The Briton nodded. 'Then you shall roll these, and if you have a score of seven or more you will live. Six or less and you will die. An equal chance, and more than you de-de-deserve as Rome's enemy.' Claudius left it unsaid that, since a score of one from two dice was impossible, the odds were weighted very slightly towards the barbarian's survival and Claudius's legacy.

'Accepted,' said Caractacus calmly, shuffling to the table and picking up the dice. He threw, and the dice skipped across the oak surface. They settled, and both men looked down at them. Five and four. Caractacus raised his head and smiled broadly. 'Congratulations, Emperor. Your place in history is secure.' Then he pointed to his leg irons. 'Now, release me from my bonds and let me go in peace.' Claudius was mildly irritated that he seemed to have lost control of the discussion but secretly delighted at the result. The gods had spoken, although he did wonder if they had voted in favour of him or this remarkable barbarian. The answer lay in the future, and the manner of the emperor's death to come, hopefully a long way off now that the senate's wishes were to be met. He held out his arms, in what he imagined was a gesture of his new-found magnanimity, and called for the guard.

*

And then...

- Caractacus lives out the remainder of his life in peace in Italy. On Claudius's death by poisoning in 54 CE the imperial dice pass to his successor Nero. In the chaos that follows Nero's suicide in 68 CE, they are seized by a young military officer, Agricola, who hands them to

Vespasian in support of the latter's (successful) bid to become emperor.

+ Agricola is appointed governor of Britannia in 77 CE, with orders from Vespasian to quell Caledonia. The emperor returns the dice to Agricola as a talisman for the march into previously uncharted enemy territory. In 84 CE, after a successful campaign in the lowlands the previous year, the Roman army engage the Caledonii tribe in battle at Mons Graupius, north of the River Tay, where the governor is captured. The outcome of the battle itself is inconclusive, and as part of a negotiated agreement for his release and the army's withdrawal, Agricola gifts the dice to his opposing general.

+ The dice remain with the general's family for the next four hundred years, ultimately coming into the ownership of King Lot of Orkney towards the end of the fifth century CE. On his death they pass to his wife Morgause, a half-sister to England's King Arthur of Camelot.

*

Author's Note

Caligula's reputation for cruelty, sexual perversion and capriciousness verging on insanity is long established but largely unsupported by impartial historical sources. Little survives from contemporaneous authors and those writing in later centuries (principally Suetonius and Cassius Dio) are considered heavily biased, possibly reflecting Caligula's increasingly repressive rule and undoubted financial mismanagement of the empire. The details of his path to the imperial throne are unclear, but it was rumoured that the Praetorian Guard prefect, Macro, helped him smother Emperor Tiberius on the island of Capri after the old man had been pronounced dead and then mysteriously revived. Certainly, the young contender Gemellus was assassinated shortly afterwards, and Macro seems either to have committed suicide or been murdered around the same time.

The origin of Caligula's nickname, his detention in Capri, the early months of his reign, his dramatic change in behaviour after an unexplained illness (maybe epilepsy), his extravagance and his aggressive efforts to raise money to bolster the exchequer are regarded as accurate. His concerns about conspiracy were well founded, and he was assassinated in Rome's Palatine palace in January 41 CE by a group of Praetorian Guard officers and senators. The familiar story (initiated by Suetonius) that he planned to nominate his horse Incitatus as a consul appears to have no basis in fact.

Claudius was well into middle age when he was discovered hiding from Caligula's assassins and promoted by the leaders of the Praetorian Guard as a successor to the throne. Until that time he had been overlooked for public office and had made a career as a historian author instead. His physical afflictions, present since childhood, are said to have diminished once he became emperor, supporting the theory that he embellished them in front of Tiberius and Caligula as a means of survival. During his reign he proved an able administrator, restoring the imperial finances and expanding the empire, including the formation of a province in England and a visit to Camulodunum (Colchester in Essex) in late 43 CE. The capture of the Catuvellauni chieftain Caractacus seven years later, his plea to the senate for clemency and Claudius's readiness to spare his life are all thought to be true. Claudius faced opposition from some senators throughout his thirteen years on the throne and was continually seeking ways to retain their goodwill.

Both Caligula and Claudius were known to be keen gamblers, the latter's preference being games of dice, whose shape in Rome *tended to be rectangular. According to Suetonius, Claudius wrote a book entitled* On the Art of Dice, *although neither this nor any of his historical writing survives. The journey of the dice in the 'And then' section is of course fictitious, although the details around the deaths of Claudius and Nero, Agricola's role as governor of Britain and his march into Scotland in 83/84 CE are correct. The Battle of Mons Graupius marked the northernmost point of Rome's invasion of Britain, but the outcome and the precise site of the engagement (probably somewhere in Aberdeenshire) remain subject to debate. There is no evidence to suggest that Agricola was captured, nor that he negotiated an agreement to retreat.*

Family Tree of the Arthurian Legend

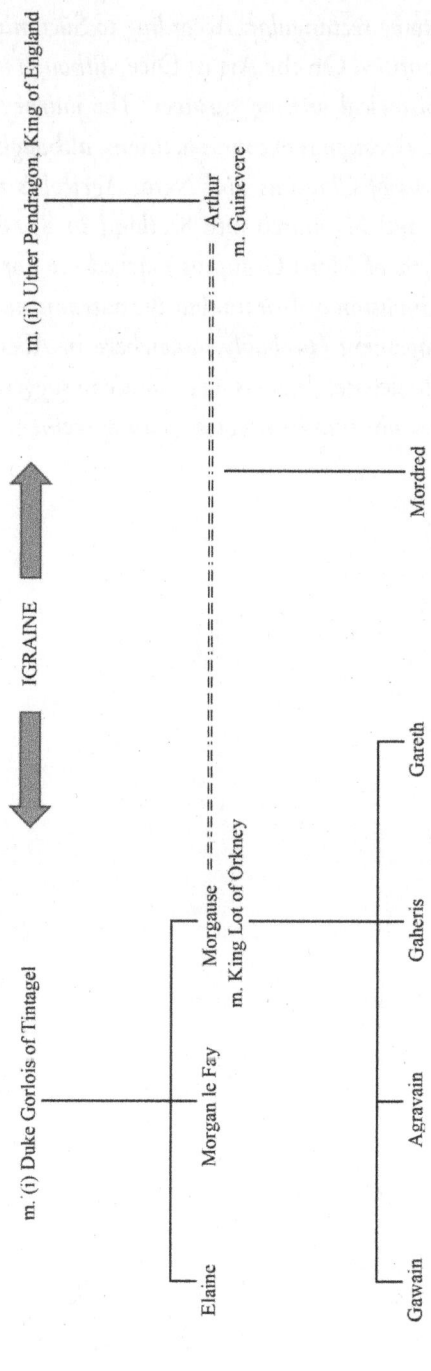

The Knights of the Round Table

c. 500 – Camelot, England

Gawain could hardly bear to watch, as his friend and brother-in-arms persisted in making a fool of himself at the top table. Even from the gallery at the far end of the dining hall, where he was supervising the minstrels who would shortly begin their performance, he could see Lancelot fawning over the queen, commanding her attention to the exclusion of all around, simpering at her pleasantries and ignoring completely the knight sitting on his other side. He was acting like a love-struck teenager, apparently incapable of rational thought and oblivious to the proper etiquette of the Round Table that he and Gawain had been so instrumental in establishing. The epitome of chivalry, Lancelot seemed to have abandoned all his own principles for a silly infatuation, and he had been behaving like this for several weeks now, long enough for the knights around him to begin taking notice. It would not have mattered, Gawain reckoned, if he had chosen to do so over a simple maiden, but Queen Guinevere? Was he out of his mind?

The only good thing to be said for it all was that, by some miracle, the king did not appear to have realised what was going on. Gawain could see Arthur, sitting on the far side of Guinevere from Lancelot, smiling benevolently at her on the few occasions she leant back to include him in her conversation with the besotted knight. Within seconds, however, she would turn away from her husband and renew her private discussion with Lancelot, and the king would be left staring into the distance until one of the other knights around the table began to speak to him. This had happened increasingly over the previous weeks, and repeatedly during this evening's banquet. If King Arthur was unable to recognise what it signified, then he must have an even more inflated opinion of his favourite knight than people already believed, Gawain thought sourly. He dragged his gaze away from the scene playing out at the end of the hall and shouted to the musicians to prepare themselves. As the opening chords of their melody rang out, and the diners fell silent, he climbed down the gallery's spiral staircase and slipped through the shadows below the wall-mounted oil lamps to the back of the top table. He tapped Lancelot on the shoulder and bent to mutter, 'A word in your ear, if I may, outside,' then waited as Lancelot made his whispered excuses to the queen. No such courtesy was offered to the king, Gawain observed. The two men left the hall through a servants' door to the kitchens and walked quickly out into the courtyard beyond. Gawain looked around them to ensure there were no eavesdroppers and spoke in a low, insistent voice.

'I should have talked to you about this weeks ago, Lancelot, but I was giving you the benefit of the doubt. How can you continue behaving like this with the queen? Have you taken leave of your senses?'

'And good evening to you too, dear friend!' Lancelot laughed amiably. 'Whatever are you on about? You've interrupted my conversation with a lady and deserted your minstrels just as they were tuning up. It seems to me your behaviour is more questionable than mine.'

'You know very well what I mean. Your obsession with Queen Guinevere. It's there for all to see. You only have eyes for her; you can barely string two words together with others when she's in the room, and you act like a lovelorn boy when she's not. This is not the standard of conduct our king expects from a Knight of the Round Table. The court is awash with rumours that you aim to bed her.' He paused and then put into words for the first time the notion he felt ashamed even to consider. 'Or maybe you already have? By all the saints, what's got into you, Camelot's great pillar of gallantry?'

'I have not,' Lancelot answered tartly, frowning with irritation. 'Be careful, Gawain, you take your role of court steward too far. I have no desire to fall out with you, but I will not stand here to be abused with false accusations. I am the queen's champion, remember, appointed by the king, so of course I have a close relationship with her. If Arthur has a problem with my conduct, then I daresay he will tell me. But I can assure you Guinevere's honour is intact, and so is mine.' He reached out to grasp Gawain by the wrists and said in a lighter tone, 'Come now, we've been through too many battles to squabble like this. Where is the companion I've shared my life with these past few years? Cheer up, and let's return to your fine minstrels.' Without waiting, he led the way back into the kitchens and the opportunity for any further discussion was drowned out by the music swelling from the hall.

Gawain slumped into an empty seat at the end of the top table and eyed his fellow knight moodily, as Lancelot resumed his position next to Guinevere. The first men to be created knights in Arthur's fledgling kingdom, they had known each other for the best part of a decade, fighting shoulder to shoulder in countless clashes with Camelot's enemies and leading the way in forging the ethos of the Round Table as Arthur had recruited additional knights to join them. Lancelot had saved Gawain more than once from almost certain death and had supported him in his family feud against his father's murderer, the odious Pellinore. Gawain could not help feeling disappointed at his friend's lapse in judgement over Guinevere, but perhaps he was overreacting to what was indeed an innocent rapport between the queen and her champion. It was an accolade Lancelot had won after rescuing her from abduction by one of her husband's most villainous opponents, an act that was bound to induce a heightened level of familiarity between them. And if Gawain required his friend to live by the code of behaviour that they had built up between them, then he was compelled to do the same himself and take Lancelot's avowal of honour on trust. Anyway, if the king was unconcerned, then what business was it of his? Gawain decided to put the matter behind him and beckoned to a servant for a jar of ale. He took a deep draught and turned to speak to his neighbour at the table, the Cornish knight Tristan. Out of the corner of his eye he spotted Lancelot's hand on the queen's, in full view of Arthur. Not his business, he reminded himself, but the image was seared onto his brain.

Over the following month, he looked on at the couple with rising frustration, torn between his wish to believe in his friend's virtue and his distaste at the breach of manners being so freely displayed. He found himself having to refute the allegations of adultery that were now rife throughout Camelot and dreaded being drawn into conversation with the king in case he should be challenged on the nature of Lancelot's attention to the queen. Meetings at the Round Table were particularly agonising, as he worried that a loose comment would be made alerting Arthur to the affair – for that was the name for it on everyone's lips. Yet the king remained blind, and Lancelot blithely unabashed. Honour and trust, Gawain repeated to himself at the end of each day, cornerstones to the knighthood standards that he and Lancelot had initiated, but now under attack at the very heart of the royal court. His patience with his friend was wearing very thin, but he was unsure how to raise the subject after the blunt rebuff received on his previous attempt.

The issue was taken out of his hands late one evening, when his brothers Agravain and Mordred burst into his quarters and flushed the servants out of the room where Gawain was sitting. 'What are you doing?' he exclaimed.

Agravain could barely contain his excitement, blurting out, 'Wait till you hear this!' and motioning Mordred to continue.

'We left the dining hall a few minutes ago and went to Lancelot's apartment to talk to him about tomorrow afternoon's hunting party. As we approached the main door we could hear his voice inside, and because you had already left the dinner, we assumed it was you in there with him. So, we went straight in without knocking, and guess what we found?' A malicious grin spread across Mordred's face. 'Guinevere! The door to his bedchamber was open, and the two of them were in there. Not just chatting either!'

Agravain let out a yelp of laughter and took up the story. 'They were naked, and going strong,' he said gleefully. 'Lancelot didn't even have the grace to be embarrassed, although the queen looked like she wanted the mattress to swallow her up. It's hardly a surprise, but the question is, before we denounce him at the Round Table, who should tell the king? We thought it should be you, as the model of propriety.'

Gawain ignored the jibe. He had always tolerated Agravain, the eldest after him of his three full brothers, and had learnt to live with the boy's clamorous tongue and outsized sense of entitlement. He often wondered why Arthur had agreed to knight him, given Agravain's dim wits and evident indifference to the chivalric code, but his ability to cause trouble was limited by his general incompetence. Their half-brother Mordred was an altogether more dangerous character, possessed of a razor-sharp intellect and a capacity for mischief unrivalled at the Round Table. Gawain knew they both regarded him as a pious bore and gave him no credit for trying to protect the standards they had all sworn to uphold. From their tale, he suspected that, far from walking in on the couple by chance, they had been skulking outside Lancelot's rooms waiting to catch the queen in the compromising position they had been gossiping about for so long.

'I will not be party to this,' he said primly. 'There may well be some innocent explanation for what you saw…' Agravain snorted with amusement and Mordred's smile broadened still further. 'But even if it is true, think about the repercussions of making such news public. You will be impugning the queen's honour and accusing the king not only of being a cuckold, which no man takes kindly to, but also a fool for failing to see it for himself.' He looked from one sibling to the other. 'No, I cannot believe Lancelot would stoop to this, and I will not be the one to raise it with Arthur. You can, if you dare, but I warn you against it.'

'You're the fool, Gawain,' Mordred replied. 'We saw them with our own eyes, and neither one made any attempt to conceal their filthy union. Even if we don't tell him, the king will find out one way or another, and it would be better coming from you, as his most loyal knight besides the worthy Lancelot.' His last two words were laden with contempt, and he turned to his accomplice. 'Let's go, Agravain, we're wasting our time here. Leave your brother to stew on it. We can discuss it with him again tomorrow before we ride out to the hunt.' He nodded brusquely to Gawain and ushered Agravain from the room.

Gawain lay awake all that night, tormenting himself on what to do. It was his duty to the king to share the news, but he owed his friend the opportunity to defend himself, however implausible it was likely to sound. Which was the greater obligation? At breakfast the following morning he sat alone, miserable in the knowledge that whichever route he chose, his relationship with Lancelot would be irreparably damaged. He was not to know that his dilemma was about to be solved for him at the Round Table, from a most improbable direction.

Far to the north, over the wild Scottish sea, his mother Queen Morgause of Orkney had been considering the matter on the same evening that Gawain had spoken to Lancelot outside Camelot's dining hall. The news of Lancelot's infatuation with Guinevere had reached her through her web of spies, built up across Arthur's kingdom after he had invaded Orkney and stolen her husband's lands. Unlike Gawain, she had not given the amorous knight the benefit of the doubt as to his virtue, nor that of Guinevere. Morgause had loathed the young queen ever since Guinevere had accepted King Arthur's hand in marriage. It was an irrational emotion, for Morgause had never met her, and it owed more to her association with Arthur than to the unfortunate girl, an entanglement dating back many years.

Morgause had been born in Cornwall, the daughter of Duke Gorlois of Tintagel and his wife Igraine. She had two sisters but, as far as she knew, no brothers. The duke had married her off as a teenager to King Lot of Orkney, to whom she had borne Gawain, Agravain and two younger children, Gaheris and Gareth. When the boy king Arthur had brought his army to Orkney, his initial proposal to her husband Lot had been the olive branch of an alliance between the two kingdoms. Morgause had been suspicious and, unbeknown to Lot, she had inveigled her way into Arthur's bed to learn more of his real intentions. The liaison had resulted in a baby, Mordred, an outcome bad enough in itself but made much worse when she discovered who Arthur's mother was. After Duke Gorlois' early death, Igraine had married the King of England, Uther Pendragon, and given birth to a son, Arthur. Morgause was Arthur's half-sister, and their offspring, Mordred, was the spawn of incest. She could never forgive Arthur, however unintentional the act, and when he went on to breach his promise of peace, sacking the main township of Orkney and having her husband killed, her hate for him was sealed.

Since that time, she had spent many dark nights scheming on how to get back at Arthur. She had encouraged her sons to seek their fortune in Camelot, where each of them, to her delight, had been offered a place as a knight of the celebrated Round Table. Despite her concern that the eldest, Gawain, was too principled for his own good, she had secretly hoped that, thanks to the bloodline, he might be adopted as Arthur's heir. That possibility had taken real root as Guinevere failed to bear Arthur any children, although Morgause had worried that, from what her spies reported, Lancelot appeared to be positioning himself as the royal favourite. So, when she had heard of his passion for the young queen, her immediate thought had been not so much that Lancelot would dishonour Guinevere, but rather that Guinevere would willingly bed him in the pretence of conceiving a son by the king. Morgause needed to stop that happening, and a means of doing so, which would aggravate Arthur and dislodge Lancelot in the process, had occurred to her.

Many years previously, during a rare visit to the Scottish mainland, she had encountered a wandering sage called Merlin. She had offered him shelter on Orkney, should he ever want it, and he had later spent several months at her castle. More than merely wise in the ways of the world, she had seen in him the mystic gifts of second sight and magical touch. Acting as his apprentice on a few occasions, Morgause had watched and learnt, and some of his sorcerer's skills had rubbed off on her. On the night of Gawain's conversation with Lancelot in the Camelot courtyard she had sat at her writing desk, the desk she had inherited from her husband Lot, and rummaged through its drawers. She had found the box she was looking for and had tipped its contents onto the desktop. Two ivory dice had tumbled out, grey and streaked with age, and she had studied them carefully. Lot had shown them to her when they were first married, explaining that they were the relic of a long-forgotten battle between Rome and Caledonia, the symbol of power from many centuries back. If that were true, the hour had come to use them in securing Gawain's future claim to the throne. At the stroke of midnight, she had hunched over the desk, holding the dice tightly in her clasped hands, and shouted out a terrible curse. Then she had taken up a writing quill and begun to draft a message for King Arthur. The following morning, she had summoned her steward and instructed him to have a small package delivered to Camelot with all speed. Four weeks later it had arrived, the morning after Mordred and Agravain's revelation to Gawain, in time for Arthur to open it in front of the knights assembled at the Round Table. The king shook the dice from the package and then extracted a single sheet of parchment on which a brief verse had been written:

The queen that throws an even score is honoured by her champion knight.

The queen that throws an odd amount belies her virtue in plain sight.

Loving wife or cuckold king? Roll the dice and shed the light.

King Arthur read the rhyme to himself, then lifted the dice and examined them with an air of bewilderment. The knights looked on in silence, unaware of the content of the letter and the potential severity of the moment. At length Lancelot, sitting to the king's right, spoke.

'What is it, Your Majesty? What does the letter have to do with the dice?'

'It seems that is a question for you, Lancelot, rather than me. Listen to this and tell me what you make of it.' The king read out the verse, and there were muted gasps from several round the table.

'Your Majesty,' Lancelot smiled politely, 'this is a feeble attack from an enemy of Camelot who dares not show himself. I am the queen's champion, and I serve to protect her. What more can I say?'

'I trust you,' said Arthur, 'as I trust everyone here, and since I have no secrets from you all, I expect the same in exchange. But it is a vile slur on my wife, and I cannot simply disregard it.'

Lancelot interjected again, before anyone else had the chance to speak. 'We can prove its falsehood very quickly, Your Majesty, by getting the queen to throw the dice.'

'Half prove it, you mean. But that is certainly the first step.' Arthur stood and walked slowly round the great table to the door, surveying each of the knights in turn. 'If you have anything to say, gentlemen, then this is the time.' No one answered and he unlatched the door to shout for a servant. 'Find the queen and ask her to join us here.'

Desultory conversations rose up between clusters of knights, as the king resumed his seat and waited silently for his wife to appear. After a few minutes, there was a commotion in the hall beyond the door, and Queen Guinevere entered the room. It was uncommon for her to attend the Round Table, and each man stood to welcome her. She looked enquiringly at her husband. 'Guinevere,' Arthur said, 'we have an unusual situation. A missive has been received accusing you of a liaison with Sir Lancelot here. It is anonymous, and absurd of course, but I must beg your indulgence in rebutting such an appalling insult. Roll these,' he pointed to the dice lying on the table, 'and depending on the score you throw, we will know for sure that it is nonsense.'

The queen blanched and moved towards the king on the far side of the room. 'How strange,' she said mildly, avoiding eye contact with Lancelot. 'Both dice, I assume?' Without waiting for an answer, she picked them up and let them drop back out of her cupped hand onto the wooden surface. They bumped to a halt, revealing a six and a five. 'Eleven,' she announced, and an ominous hush descended.

'Eleven,' the king repeated drily, still looking down at the dice. 'Unfortunate. The missive states that an uneven number signifies your adultery.' He raised his eyes to Lancelot, his face impassive. 'And your champion's dishonour.'

Lancelot made to speak but was overridden by Agravain. 'I knew it, Your Majesty, I caught them together yesterday evening, with Mordred. I was going to tell you, but the package with the dice arrived before I was able to.'

The king switched his stare to Agravain. 'And yet you had nothing to say before I summoned the queen. How do I know you are not the author of this repulsive rhyme?' He waved a hand at the piece of parchment on the table.

Agravain shook his head vehemently, and Lancelot intervened once more. 'It was luck, Your Majesty, the queen could just as easily have thrown an even score. As for him,' he gestured to Agravain, 'he has never been a true follower of the knights' code. He is using this to win favour with you, at your wife's expense.'

'Very well,' said Arthur, his voice bleak with disappointment. 'The queen will throw again, three times, and we shall see who is telling the truth. I notice, Lancelot, that you have not yet directly denied the accusation.' Lancelot reddened but remained silent, and the king passed the dice to Guinevere. She rolled them, and three times in succession they settled on the numbers six and five.

'They are cursed,' shouted Lancelot, collecting the dice and brandishing them at the king.

Guinevere edged past him to stand in front of Arthur. 'Where these dice come from, and whether they are cursed, I cannot say, but they do not lie,' she said gently. 'It's true, Arthur, Sir Agravain did find us together yesterday, and I can offer no excuse. We spend so little time alone, you and I, and Sir Lancelot has been most attentive, but as your wife the fault is mine. I will accept whatever punishment you deem appropriate.' Lancelot gazed at his feet, and most of the other knights looked on with expressions of profound embarrassment, only Agravain smiling unpleasantly at a job well done.

The king turned to Gawain. 'What do you say, Gawain, as my longest serving knight? Did you know of this, and who the weasel poet is?' Gawain glanced at Lancelot before answering. 'I have no idea who sent the dice to you, Your Majesty, and I am horrified by what they have unveiled. Lancelot's care of the queen, as her champion, is well known and I have always trusted him to abide by the knights' code of honour, in the same way as I have trusted him with my life in battle.' He held up his hands as if he were the one requesting mitigation for the crime. 'I would say merely that he has proven himself a brave warrior and a staunch defender of your kingdom over the years. His lapse in behaviour is an aberration that none of us could have anticipated.' He could not bring himself to admit his earlier misgivings, since that would inevitably raise the question of why he had failed to act on them.

'A worthy speech for your comrade-in-arms,' said Arthur, 'but he has betrayed me, and if the Round Table stands for anything, treachery from within must be seen to be crushed. The same may be said for marriage,' he turned to face Guinevere, 'and the sentence for betrayal is death.' Shock rippled round the room, and Lancelot's head jerked up, but neither of the fated couple spoke and the king continued. 'You will both be burnt at the stake, at noon tomorrow, and until then you will be kept in the dungeons below the castle here.' He stopped, then added, 'Separately, in case you are wondering.'

There was long pause, until Guinevere let out a sob. It seemed to galvanise Lancelot, who drew a dagger from a sheath inside his tunic and stepped back into the empty space behind the table. 'You forget who you are dealing with, Arthur. Yes, I have been found wanting, like many a man before me, but my love for Guinevere is pure of heart, and my readiness to fight for you remains undimmed. I have saved Camelot from invasion and you from death many times, and I defy anybody to kill me in the name of honour.' He flourished the dagger aggressively in front of him as he retreated towards the door of the room. None of the knights attempted to intervene; his reputation in single combat was unparalleled. He put his free hand behind him to push the door open with his knuckles, the dice that he had picked up now clenched in his fist, and stood on the threshold. 'Think on the sentence you have declared, Arthur. I will not stand by to watch it being carried out, not for either of us.' And then he was gone.

*

Three months later – Anjou, central France

After their disembarkation on the shores of Brittany, the English had toiled across France in the summer heat for two months, fighting off skirmishers and seizing hostile country towns in their path as they marched east up the valley of the River Loire. The fields around them had turned to gold and the harvest was beginning to be reaped when they came at last to the city of Benoic, the family stronghold in which Lancelot had sought refuge after his flight from Camelot. This was where he had been born a prince, the son of King Ban, whose premature end from the pox had prompted Lancelot to travel to England and present himself for service at King Arthur's court. Now the great knight's days of royal service were long gone, and he was a fugitive instead, preparing for the battle that must be joined if his honour was to be restored and his life worth living again. He stood on the walkway atop Benoic's defensive ramparts and watched as the English pitched their tents on the far side of the dry water meadow. He guessed that an assault would be launched the following day, once the soldiers had eaten and slept and gathered their strength. Even from a distance he could see the ostlers tending to the knights' horses, magnificent beasts in prime condition notwithstanding the long journey from Camelot, and beyond them were the armourers, whetting sword blades and sharpening lance points. There would be no call for the lances, he reflected, if the English were able to breach the walls and turn the fray into a close-quarters brawl through the streets. Such a waste of his jousting skills as Camelot's tournament favourite over so many years.

In the tented camp Gawain was also looking out across the sun-bleached pasture, assessing the city's fortifications and contemplating, like Lancelot, what form the battle would take. Despite his fall from grace, Lancelot was still a formidable opponent. Several knights from Camelot had thrown their lot in with him, including his cousin Bors, the famous axeman from Brittany whose fighting prowess had generated substantial local support. It would be a bloody encounter, whether inside the walls or on horseback in the meadowland. However, Gawain was confident that justice would prevail – the king and he had ridden too far not to gain the revenge they both deserved. Their grievances were separate, but the redress required was the same – Lancelot must pay in blood for his sins.

For his part, Gawain thought for the hundredth time, it need not have come to this. Although he understood Arthur's distress at the revelation of adultery, he had been dismayed at the death penalty issued to both guilty parties on that ghastly day at the Round Table. He had expected instead that Guinevere would be dismissed to a convent for the rest of her life, to seek redemption for her depravity, and that Lancelot would be banished from Camelot, never to return. That had seemed a fair punishment for his misguided companion who, in Gawain's priggish estimation, had been led astray by the wanton queen. But the king had refused to relent after Lancelot's escape from the castle, and the place of execution had been duly arranged for Guinevere in Camelot's central square, a rough plinth set against a stout pine stake with brushwood piled high around it. Mindful of Lancelot's final words, the king had instructed that the square be guarded against any rescue attempt on his wife, although Gawain had been permitted to abstain from this duty given his long-standing friendship with the errant knight. If only he had been there, perhaps what had followed could have been averted.

On the morning of the burning, as the queen was being led to the plinth, Lancelot had clattered down a narrow alley into the square on a massive charger, accompanied by his brother Hector, Bors and a handful of associates. Kicking the guard at her side to the ground, he had scooped Guinevere up onto the saddle behind him and bellowed his intention to leave without hurting anyone. Caught unawares by his headlong approach, the knights had been slow to react, but as the group turned to ride out, the redoubtable Tristan had moved to block the alley and shouted to the other knights to take similar action on the main streets leading from the square. They had followed Tristan's example and had drawn their swords, ready to carry out the king's death penalty on the adulterous pair by steel rather than fire.

Lancelot had fought alongside Tristan enough to be wary of the Cornwall man's renowned swordcraft and had spurred his horse in a different direction, riding down spectators that had assembled to witness the execution. The street he had aimed for was manned by Gawain's two youngest brothers, Gaheris and Gareth, although whether Lancelot had recognised them in the confusion, Gawain would never know. They had tried valiantly to resist the advancing group, but Lancelot had cut them down where they stood with two brutal slashes of his flailing blade, and he and his men had galloped from Camelot without a backward look.

Once weapons had been bared against Lancelot, the brothers' slaughter had been virtually inevitable, but it was an outrage on his family that Gawain could neither forget nor forgive. On hearing the news, his aversion to the death sentence declared by Arthur had hardened instantly into a personal demand for retribution. In the week after the attack, he had pleaded with the king to organise the pursuit of Lancelot and his followers, and eventually his request had been granted. It had taken a further three weeks to raise the small army considered necessary for the manhunt, by which time scouts had reported that their quarry had reached the south coast and boarded a ship to France. It had come as no surprise that Lancelot had made for his hometown on the Loire, where he would be able to swell the number of troops prepared to defend his cause. The whereabouts of Guinevere was unclear, and Gawain now wondered whether the affair between the wayward queen and her murderous champion had already run its course. He thought again about the blood that would be shed in the next day's battle, the lives of so many men that would be destroyed due to the misdemeanours of an impassioned couple, and an alternative to the pain and waste suddenly came to him, a solution worthy of the Round Table. He berated himself for not thinking of it previously and went to find King Arthur.

A few minutes later, the king and Gawain mounted their horses and rode slowly out through the serried ranks of tents onto the grassland in front of the city gates. From his position on the ramparts, Lancelot was soon able to identify them, and he watched their approach with interest. It was evident they wanted to negotiate and there was nothing to be gained by hiding from them, so he waited until they were within earshot and then shouted down to them. 'Good day, gentlemen, it has been a long trip from Camelot for all of us, and I regret we are not meeting in happier circumstances. But it seems for now that you come to talk, and I promise you no harm.'

King Arthur reined his horse in to a halt and looked up at Lancelot. 'Make no mistake, Lancelot, we do not come in peace. You have sinned against me, and against my trusted friend here,' he gestured to Gawain, 'and you will pay for your transgressions with your life. But before we tear down these puny walls and put you and all your followers to the sword, Gawain has a suggestion. If it spares unwarranted bloodshed amongst both armies, then it has my support. Hear what he has to say.' He nodded to Gawain, who nudged his horse forward several steps, then rested his hands on the pommel of his saddle and craned his neck up to inspect the figure above.

'You killed my brothers Gaheris and Gareth in the square when you rode to the queen's rescue. For that, I must have satisfaction, just as the king must for his broken marriage.

I propose that you and I meet in single combat. There is no reason for fine knights such as Bors and Hector to die, when you are the sole target of our vengeance. Face me, here and now, and once you are gone, that will be the end of the war between our two armies.'

Lancelot studied the two men for a full minute before replying. 'I would consent, but I have a better idea. Stay there while I come out to join you.' He turned his back and disappeared from view down a staircase built into the inner side of the wall. There was a short interval, and then the city gates eased open, and he walked out towards the two riders, clad in upper body armour and sword belt to match Gawain. At ten paces' distance he stopped and looked intently at the king.

'Arthur, I have no wish to boast, but in single combat I will win, and Gawain will die. You know that I am the better warrior. I did not intend to kill his brothers, and I have no desire to kill him, nor to deprive you of his services at the Round Table. My suggestion is that, instead of fighting, he and I gamble for an end to this war. If I win, you still have your leading knight, excluding me of course,' he smiled briefly, 'and if I lose, be assured that the rest of my life will be one of shame and misery here in France. I shall not venture across the channel to England again, where, if you have not heard, I have left Guinevere in the care of her siblings. Either way, our armies may disperse in peace. But Gawain's principles will never allow him alone to agree to this, so you must help him arrive at his decision.' He took a step back and waited calmly for a response.

'Gamble, you say? Meaning what?' the king said.

Lancelot reached into a leather pouch hanging from his belt and produced a pair of dice. 'You will recognise these from the moment at the Round Table that my love for Guinevere was uncovered. Whether they were cursed at that time, I couldn't say, but I have used them often enough since to be persuaded they roll true. If you have any suspicions, it's fair to assume the dice would be weighted against me rather than in my favour. Test them for yourself, if you want.'

Arthur turned to Gawain. 'It is a reasonable proposal, Gawain. With Lancelot's betrayal, I have already lost one of my most valuable knights; I cannot afford to lose another. Nor the wider bloodshed that would come from an all-out battle. I urge you to take up his wager, although I cannot command you on a matter of family honour.'

Gawain held out his hand for the dice, and Lancelot passed them to him. There was an uncomfortable silence as Gawain deliberated, his face twisting with hostility. 'All right,' he growled at last, 'highest score, from a single dice. Sixes and fives will not count, in case the curse remains in place. Let's get this over and done with.' He dismounted and handed one of the ivory cubes to Lancelot. 'My privilege, I believe.' Then he scraped a large patch of grass down to bare earth with his boot, stamped it flat and crouched to throw his dice. Three black dots shone up in the strong afternoon light.

Lancelot joined him, squatting over the playing square. 'The odds are with you, old friend,' he said and rolled the second dice across the dusty ground. It came to rest in the shadow cast by his body, and against the glare of the sun both knights struggled to read the result. Lancelot shifted his weight until the harsh light fell on the two dots showing on the upturned surface. 'You win,' he said solemnly to Gawain. 'I apologise with all my heart for your brothers' deaths, and I accept the disgrace that God has imposed on me.' Then he stood up and bowed to the king. 'Please spare dear Guinevere, Your Majesty. I was more to blame for our romance than she ever was, despite what she said to you at the Round Table that day. She deserves better than me. She deserves to have her husband back.' The king raised an eyebrow but said nothing, and Lancelot turned to walk towards the city gates, as Gawain knelt to retrieve the two dice from the meadow floor.

*

Four months later – Camelot, England

In the growing dusk, Lancelot goaded his horse up the long, low slope to the burial ground on the ridge overlooking Camelot's western approach. It was an old animal, weakened further through malnourishment and barely able to manage the ascent with the knight's weight on its back. He cursed the innkeeper at the coast who had demanded such an outrageous price for it, but speed had been essential and there had been no obvious alternative. At least the horse had survived the ride inland and, now that the journey was nearly over, Lancelot was not inclined to spare it on this final stage. In one sense, he knew, his haste was pointless. Gawain was already dead, and no amount of galloping through the autumn night would resurrect him. But it was the deceased man's birthday, and there was a gift to pledge, an exoneration to convey, which Lancelot felt obliged to do before the clock struck midnight, for no better reason than to salve his own lacerated conscience.

Four short months since that afternoon crouching in the French grass, but a time of dramatic change for King Arthur and all associated with him. The morning after the dice match Gawain had sent a message to the gates of Benoic, stating that he had reversed his decision. Revenge for his brothers' murder could never be achieved at the whim of an ivory cube, and duty must be done; he had issued a fresh challenge to Lancelot for a duel to the death, on the same terms as before, and would present himself in the meadow at noon. Lancelot had come out to meet him and implored him to think again, but Gawain had simply shaken his head and unsheathed his sword to begin the fray. The fight had been pitifully brief, Lancelot's nimble footwork allowing him to evade the first desperate flurry of strokes and then hack down on his opponent's exposed helmet. The helmet had fallen away, sheared in two, and Gawain had staggered back, dropping his weapon and holding his scalp in agony as blood pumped through his fingers. He had begged Lancelot to kill him off, but the disgraced knight had refused, arguing that, after all that had gone before, he must grant a warrior mercy on the battlefield, in line with the chivalric code. He had led Gawain into the king's camp and personally supervised the dressing of the wound before searching out Arthur to explain what had happened. None who had seen the extent of the injury had expected Gawain to live, and he had lain in a twilight world of delirium for several days before rallying sufficiently to be able to rise from his bed.

During that time, dire news from Camelot had reached the king. Gawain's half-brother Mordred had spread a rumour that Arthur was dead and that he would now rule England. To emphasise his control, he had seized Guinevere and planned to make her his queen. With the conflict against Lancelot settled, Arthur had immediately organised his army's withdrawal to the French coast, in order to return to his kingdom and reclaim his throne and wife. Gawain had accompanied him, gathering strength in the course of the journey and fighting at his side in the civil war across England that followed. Despite his recovery, and his indomitable spirit, the exertion had proved too much for his wound, which had reopened and become fatally infected. He had died in Camelot's hospice, sword in hand, valiant to the last.

Lancelot had heard of Gawain's death as he stepped ashore from the channel crossing. Two weeks previously in Benoic, he had received a letter from his comrade knight forgiving him for the slaughter of Gaheris and Gareth and seeking to atone for his part in the rift amongst the fellowship of the Round Table. Gawain had urged Lancelot to join the king in the struggle against Mordred, and Lancelot had answered the call without hesitation, only too late to thank Gawain in person for his change of heart. The least he could do now was visit his friend in his final resting place and confess his own sins. The burial ground loomed into sight, and he eased the exhausted horse down to a walk as he approached the gate of the Round Table's private cemetery. He dismounted, tied the animal to the gatepost and found the freshly dug grave. Then he knelt and put his hands together in prayer.

'Dear friend,' he spoke out loud, 'I accept your offer of forgiveness with the humility of one who has sinned far more. With God as my witness, I take full responsibility for the wound that has led to your death, even though I struck the fatal blow against my will. And besides that, I am ultimately responsible for the mayhem that has been unleashed on England. My love for Guinevere, pure as I thought it, was wrong. It forced Arthur to travel to France, enabling Mordred to usurp him and bringing bloodshed to his kingdom. I failed my queen, my king, my friends and my own honour. Unworthy as I am, I beg your pardon for all of that, and I pledge to do whatever I can to restore Camelot and the Round Table to their former glory.' He bowed his head low to the ground and silent tears streamed from his eyes.

'You are not the only one at fault,' a soft voice came from the darkness beyond him, and he straightened up with a jolt.

'Who's there?' he said, running his hands over his damp cheeks in embarrassment at being caught airing his innermost feelings.

'We have never met, Lancelot,' an old woman stepped into view, long grey hair held in a ponytail, 'but you will know of me from the feud between Gawain's family and Pellinore, who murdered my husband. I am Queen Morgause of Orkney, half-sister to King Arthur, mother to Gawain and, though I shudder to admit it, to Mordred too.'

Lancelot stared at her. He knew her name, naturally, but had never heard of her venturing south to Camelot in all the years he had lived and fought alongside Gawain. 'My Lady,' he rose to his feet and faced her over the grave, 'in other circumstances it would be a privilege to meet you, but I have killed your son,' he gestured sadly at the newly turned soil between them, 'and the fault is mine alone.'

'I heard your prayer,' Morgause cut across him. 'Believe me, there is more to your story than you suspect. Do you remember the first time you saw these?' She raised a hand to show him the two dice he had used to gamble with Gawain. 'You told Arthur they were cursed, didn't you, when they revealed Guinevere's adultery with you that day at the Round Table? Did you never consider who might have sent them to him? Who had most to gain from your death or dishonour?'

Lancelot looked at her in confusion. 'I thought of nothing other than my love for Guinevere,' he said, 'and my refusal to allow either of us to die for it. Surely the only person to gain from that would have been the king?'

'How naïve you men are!' Morgause scoffed at him. 'Did it never occur to you that Guinevere might be using you? For years she and Arthur had been unable to have a child. The gossip from Camelot was that she was barren, a rumour no doubt hatched by you knights in support of their fellow man and spread by others so readily that it reached even my ears in faraway Orkney.' Her voice became steadily more strident. 'But what if Arthur himself had become infertile? What if Guinevere wanted a child so badly, she was prepared to give herself to another man? She would not have been able to disclose her infidelity, so any such child would have been seen as the king's, and hence the heir to Camelot. Ever since Arthur's invasion of Orkney and my husband's murder, I have been trying to position Gawain as the successor to my brother's throne. Do you think I would stand idly by and see him denied his bloodline right by that woman? Or by you, if there was no child, as you wormed your way past my son into Arthur's affections?' She stopped, breathing hard, and Lancelot continued to gape at her.

'I sent the dice and the riddle, you simpleton,' Morgause sighed in exasperation, and then went on more calmly. 'I cursed the dice so that Arthur would learn of your affair with the queen, and in doing so I am at least partly accountable for all the calamities that have followed – your killing of Gaheris and Gareth, this new war with Mordred that is tearing Arthur's kingdom in two and the death of my firstborn, Gawain. I am as guilty as you, and after hearing your words there,' she pointed a toe to the graveside, then thrust an arm forward to display the dice again, 'all I can do is offer you these in apology for my wickedness.'

'But how did you come by them?' said Lancelot, still dazed by this new information after the anguish of his own confession.

'When I heard of Gawain's wound, I came down from Orkney immediately to treat him. I have healing powers, something I learnt from the magician Merlin, but they were not strong enough to help my son.' She smiled mournfully. 'He showed me the dice before he died, explaining how he had got them, and asked me to return them to you with his blessing. I give them to you now, with my own blessing added and all vestiges of my curse removed.' Morgause stretched across the grave to pass the dice to Lancelot. 'Take them, Lancelot, and treasure them in Gawain's name. And where the dice go, may God follow.'

*

And then…

- ✦ Lancelot joins Arthur's forces but is unable to prevent the army's defeat and the king's death at Mordred's hand in the Battle of Camlann. When Mordred himself also dies, chaos descends on England. Still plagued by remorse at his part in the unravelling of the Round Table and the destruction of Arthur's kingdom, Lancelot returns to Benoic in France. Heedful of Morgause's final words to him, he retires to a monastery and devotes the remainder of his life to religious prayer.

- ✦ On his own death many years later, Lancelot leaves his possessions, including the dice, to his brother Hector, now also resident in Benoic. Over the next seven generations, the dice are passed directly from father to son, falling ultimately into the hands of a Frankish statesman, Pepin of Herstal. When Pepin dies in 714, control of his realm is snatched from his nominated heir and grandson Theudoald by Pepin's illegitimate son, Charles Martel, in a civil war lasting three years.

- ✦ Although the dice's story has been largely lost in the mists of time, the legend of their role as a symbol of power dating back to the Roman empire and beyond has persisted. Martel therefore makes a point of seizing the dice when he sends Theudoald into exile, in order to consolidate his position as rightful leader of the Franks.

*

Author's Note

The legend of King Arthur of Camelot and his Knights of the Round Table is just that – there is no substantive evidence of his existence, and the many tales that have been spun around him are thought to originate from the Celtic folklore of Britain and France. In the mid-twelfth century Geoffrey of Monmouth brought the character of Arthur as a great leader undone by the rebel Mordred into European literature with his hugely popular History of the Kings of Britain. Some fifty years later the threads of the knights' quest for the Holy Grail and Lancelot's love for Queen Guinevere were introduced by the French poet Chrétien de Troyes. Early in the thirteenth century the web of storylines was further extended by a group of French romantic prose authors (named the Vulgate Cycle), but it was not until the late fifteenth century that a 'complete' record of the legend was assembled.

Sir Thomas Malory wrote Le Morte d'Arthur *shortly before his death in 1471 and it was printed by William Caxton in 1485. Presented in the form of eight books, Malory's narrative covers: the well-known tale of Arthur's extraction of the sword from the stone to claim his birthright to the English throne under Merlin's magical counsel; the establishment of the Round Table fellowship and code of chivalric honour; the pursuit of the Holy Grail; the love affair between Lancelot and Guinevere and its disastrous consequences; and the death of the king at the hand of the evil Mordred. In particular, Malory's portrayal of Gawain develops the theme that, after the murder of his brothers Gaheris and Gareth, he shifts from being a model of religious piety to a man riven with the desire for vengeance against Lancelot, bringing about not only his own death (despite his belated offer to forgive Lancelot) but also the destruction of the Round Table and Arthur's kingdom. The story is set in the late fifth/early sixth century, and Malory is said to*

118

have identified Camelot and Benoic with the medieval English city of Winchester and the French city of Beaune respectively.

My limited version of events is based loosely on Malory's. I have excluded reference to a host of familiar characters such as Galahad, Percival, Geraint, Bedivere, the Lady of the Lake (Nimue) and the enchantress Morgan le Fay, although I have conflated the latter with her sister Morgause, Queen of Orkney, for simplicity. The suggestion that Lancelot's brother Hector was an ancestor of the historically genuine Frankish king Charles Martel is a fiction. As for the dice, they are my addition to the story, but the events to which they contribute (Morgan le Fay/Morgause's attempt to reveal Guinevere's adultery to Arthur, the two duels between Gawain and Lancelot and Lancelot's visit to Gawain's grave) all feature in different forms in Le Morte d'Arthur.

Note: at the time of Pepin of Herstal's death in 714, the Frankish empire comprised its long-standing homeland territory Austrasia, together with Neustria and Burgundy. On his accession to power, Charles Martel faced an uprising in Neustria, which took several years to quell. Later in his career he extended the empire's reach in campaigns against the Frisians, the Saxons and the Allemanni. Only in 732 did he obtain control over the Duchy of Aquitaine.

Charles Martel

Late August 732 – Metz, north-east France

Charles, Duke of the Franks, waited impatiently as the weary group of visitors was ushered up the steps and through the great oak doorway into the grand hall. He was not normally given to conducting formal audiences at the palace, preferring to be seen out in public amongst his subjects, or better still away on campaign fighting to expand his empire's borders. But he knew from his spies who these people were, and what had prompted their long journey to the Frankish capital, and he intended to milk his advantage to the full. A brief display of pomp and ceremony would help to dispel any suggestion that he was their friend in need, unless of course he chose to be. He had not won his title Martel, or the 'hammer', by making things easy for his opponents.

'Your Highness,' his steward announced in a loud voice, 'these men beg your indulgence. May I present Odo, Duke of Aquitaine, and his companions. The duke has urgent business with you.'

'Does he, indeed?' said Martel, adopting an expression of surprise. 'He has come a long way for it.' He beckoned the group into the centre of the room, while he remained standing at the far end on a dais. The extra height compensated for his squat physique, although in truth it was an unnecessary act of vanity. Few were left in any doubt on meeting him that he was the sovereign leader of the numerous provinces he had absorbed into Frankia by conquest over the previous decade. A muscular build, a tense jawline and pugnacious chin, and a waistbelt equipped with a massive, dented sword and three glinting daggers all contributed to an aura of barely controlled ferocity and a well-deserved reputation for the politics of aggression rather than negotiation. It was a useful veil, concealing a sharp mind and a willingness to deal where it suited him.

'Welcome, Duke Odo,' he said, ignoring the others. 'We meet at last, although not in the manner I had anticipated. I expected to have my sword at your throat on a battlefield outside Toulouse. You have saved me the trouble.' He stopped and waited for the visitor to explain himself.

'I come here in peace, Duke Charles,' replied Odo, 'or should I say in peace between us, although I am looking for a fight elsewhere. You may have heard by now of our battle against the Moors near Bordeaux at the beginning of this month. My army was decimated by their cavalry, and my escort and I were fortunate to escape. We have been riding hard ever since that day, almost three weeks, and we arrived in Metz this afternoon.' He waved vaguely at the men on each side of him and sighed heavily. 'Forgive us, but we are very tired and hungry. I have an important matter to discuss with you, but may I ask that we talk over some food?'

Martel rocked from toe to heel, his hands behind him, as though it was a difficult proposition, and the silence built. At last, he nodded. 'You may. Just you and me,' his eyes remained fixed on Odo, 'the others will be taken to the kitchens.' His gaze switched to the back of the hall, where the steward still hovered, and he raised his voice. 'Gerhard, fetch me a table and two chairs and food for the duke. And get the rest of these men fed downstairs.' He motioned for the escort to make their way to the door and allowed another long silence to descend as the food and furniture were being found. Then he watched as Odo bit into the bread and beef strips that had been brought and drank heavily from a tankard of beer. It struck him that the duke would surely be exhausted – he must be well into his seventies, and to ride all the way from Bordeaux, in flight from his army's shocking defeat, would have tested many a younger man. He knew what Odo's underlying question would be, but he was curious to hear how it would be framed. It was time to set the scene.

'So, Duke Odo, as I said, we meet at last. To be honest, I am amazed it has taken till now. Our armies have fought each other often enough. I defeated your troops in Neustria many years ago, and again in northern Aquitaine last summer. It's no secret that I wish to have Aquitaine for the Frankish empire, so you must have a very unusual reason for appearing on my doorstep.'

'I do, Charles, I most definitely do, but let us go back a step first.' Odo took another gulp of beer and lifted his mug to his host. 'Thank you for receiving me in the palace and for feeding me and my men. I admit we were on our last legs when we arrived here. As for my relationship with you, let us not forget that my generals negotiated a treaty with you after the defeat in Neustria, an agreement that I would not venture into Frankia and that you would leave me to govern Aquitaine unmolested. You broke that treaty last year when your army crossed the border between us at the River Loire and attacked my garrison there. You were nowhere near my capital, Toulouse, so you were no threat to the bulk of Aquitaine, and in any case your forces withdrew over the Loire before the winter came. If anything, you owe me an apology.'

'And yet,' Martel leant forward in his chair, his chin

thrusting towards Odo, 'you are here in front of me, begging for food. An odd way to seek an apology, I would say. You clearly need something more than mere shelter. Come out with it, or leave now.'

Duke Odo had endured sixty years of war and was no stranger to the tactics of bargaining. He let Martel's belligerence pass and said mildly, 'I concede I have a problem, Charles, but unlike the years gone by, this time you and I share that problem, and we should address it together.'

'The Moors?' Martel blew out his cheeks in derision. 'They have looted Bordeaux and humiliated your army. I fail to see why that should be my problem.'

'Think back over the last twenty years,' said Odo. 'First, they cross the sea from Africa and establish themselves within months as masters of the Iberian Peninsula, foisting their Islamic religion on every city they come to. Then, twelve years ago, they cross the Pyrenees and build a fortress in Narbonne, securing their supply lines by sea, which allows them to send raiding parties northwards into Aquitaine and Burgundy. You'll remember they besieged Toulouse, and it was only thanks to me that they were beaten off. Since last year they are on the march again, into the Rhone Valley and now across my lands to Bordeaux. I don't know where they've gone since we fought them there, but it is rumoured that they plan to invade Neustria, their first target being Tours, where they will ransack the Abbey of St Martin and steal its famous treasures.' He swallowed some more beer and licked his lips, conscious that he was at the crucial point in his mission to Metz. 'I urge you to bring an army to the Loire and help me resist their advance before they reach Tours. I can rally troops to meet us there, and between us we can send the Moors back to Narbonne with a bloody nose. If we persist, we may even drive them over the Pyrenees. I acknowledge we have had our differences in the past, but I ask you now to put these aside in the light of this new menace.'

Martel stared at the duke across the table, his face impassive. Then, suddenly, he burst out laughing. 'A good effort, Odo, I give you that. But have you not heard the adage: my enemy's enemy is my friend? I would be better off having the Moors clear out what remains of your resistance to them so that I can then occupy Aquitaine and chase them away to Narbonne myself. Why would I help you, when I have been fighting you for over ten years?'

'So, they take Tours? And then what, Charles?' It was Odo's turn to lean forward, and he began to jab an index finger at Martel. 'What is to stop them advancing deeper into Frankia, towards Paris and Metz, and putting all the churches and abbeys in their path to the torch? These are not short-term attacks on Aquitaine or Frankia, or on you or me as individual rulers; the Moors will not just retire south with their booty when the winter comes; this is an invasion, part of a strategy to impose themselves and their Islamic faith throughout our lands, as they have done across Persia and North Africa over the last hundred years. It is an assault on Christianity itself, and I need you to join me in halting them before they destroy the very fabric of our society.' He sat back in his chair, visibly fatigued by the emotion of his plea. 'Bring your troops to the Loire and help me staunch this creeping death to our civilisation. I appeal to you in the name of God, not Aquitaine.'

'Again, well spoken,' said Martel, 'and you could be right. But at the moment the Moors are not my enemy – they have not set foot in Frankia and, whatever you may say, my sources tell me their actions ever since crossing the Pyrenees have been restricted to opportunistic raids rather than any real pattern of invasion. I see no danger from them, or from their religion.

You have come a long way, Duke, and I will grant you and your men a bed for the night here in the palace and safe passage to Aquitaine in the morning. But my answer to your request is simple. No.'

Odo rose abruptly from the table, his brow creased with disappointment. 'Sleep on it, Charles. Who knows, the Holy Spirit may come to you in the small hours. Once again, I thank you for your hospitality. I will find your steward myself.' Then he walked stiffly down the long room to the door and disappeared without another word.

Martel watched the duke's retreating back with niggling respect. It would have been a brave decision for the old man to make the long journey from Bordeaux, risking imprisonment or execution on arrival, and plead his case from such a position of weakness. And despite Martel's dismissive comments, he was aware that the threat posed by the Moors was more serious than an occasional raiding party. His spies in Aquitaine had reported a large movement of troops towards the border with Frankia in recent weeks, and any theft of the treasures from St Martin's Abbey in Tours would be a grievous loss, both to his empire and to the Christian Church. Take advantage of his foe's vulnerability, or join his cause to protect their mutual religious interest in blocking the spread of Islam? He would follow the duke's advice and dwell on it overnight.

Martel was an early riser, and he paced up and down the grand hall irritably the next day while Duke Odo and his men were shaken from their beds and brought to him. 'You seem in no hurry to leave,' he said, as they filed into the room.

Odo ignored the gruff tone. 'Good morning, Duke Charles,' he answered politely. 'I am honoured to be granted a second meeting with you. May I take it that you have reconsidered your opinion since we spoke yesterday?'

'I have given it further thought, yes. But not thanks to

a visitation from the Holy Spirit, I can assure you.' Martel reached into a purse between two of the daggers on his waistbelt and withdrew his hand curled into a fist. 'I hear your plea as a fellow Christian and yet, as your enemy, I am conflicted. In my experience, contrary to Christ's Sermon on the Mount, the meek do not inherit the earth, and certainly not Aquitaine.' A grim smile flickered across his lips. 'So your request falls on stony ground, to use another well-worn saying from the Bible. However,' he paused for dramatic effect, 'I recognise that the Moors may in time push north into Frankia, and for that reason there may be justification in lending my support to you. One could argue it both ways, and in the circumstances my conclusion will rest in the hands of fate rather than in the name of God.' He raised his upturned fist to Odo and opened the palm to reveal its contents. 'We will wager with these dice, and if you win, I shall bring my army to the Loire and fight the infidel, as you have asked. If you lose, I will also come to battle, but only on the condition that you cede the rule of Aquitaine to me as overlord once the Moors are defeated. Those are my terms – take them or leave them.'

Duke Odo appeared to hesitate, although he had expected some form of condition like this to be levied. For all Martel's posturing, he was a committed Christian and would not wish to be seen encouraging the violation of the abbey at Tours, one of the richest and most prestigious holy shrines in Western Europe. As for the surrender of outright control within Aquitaine, that could be contested at a later date, just as Martel had broken their previous treaty. 'Agreed,' he said, and they moved to the table he had eaten from the previous evening to begin the rolling of the dice.

*

9 October 732 – Tours, central France

'Six days, Charles! Six days skirmishing and we have achieved nothing. How much longer do you intend to sit on this hill and watch the Moors laughing at us?'

'Until I am ready, Odo. You accepted that the decision would be mine when I agreed to bring my army here, and if it means waiting for another week, then that is what we will do. Let the Moors mock us all day long, until the moment we slaughter them.'

'But we have the advantage,' Odo riposted. 'We can swoop down on them when they are not in battle order and put them to flight in minutes. The longer we stay here, the more our troops will lose heart. They will be tempted to desert and make their way home before the winter sets in. We are already outnumbered, as it is.'

'And that, my dear duke, is exactly the point.' Martel moved from the shadows of his campaign marquee to its entrance and drew the front screen to one side. 'You, of all people, should understand my plan. Look down there.' He nodded to the plain stretching out below them in the evening light, partly obscured by a scattered fringe of trees on the upper slopes of the hill the Frankish army occupied. 'For every two of our men, the Moors have three. We have no cavalry other than the few you have been able to call up, whereas they have several thousand, and you know only too well what damage they can do to foot soldiers.' He had not intended to remind Odo of the defeat at Bordeaux, now that they were allies, but he was increasingly exasperated by the duke's lack of military fieldcraft. No wonder he had suffered such a mauling.

'You said yourself that we have the advantage,' he continued, 'and you are right. We hold the high ground, so why abandon it? It takes the sting out of any charge by their cavalry and, better still, the weight of their attack will be broken by the trees. We will fight on our terms, not theirs, and the difference in numbers will be irrelevant. Trust me and be patient.'

'Patience is not a word I would associate with you,' replied Odo, with a hint of sarcasm.

'There is a time for everything, which is why I have grown my empire in the last fifteen years at my neighbours' expense. Think how long I waited to gain control of Aquitaine!' Martel grinned at the memory of the dice game in which he had won the duke's allegiance. 'You told me in Metz to sleep on my thoughts. You should do the same. We can talk again tomorrow if nothing has changed. Until then, get some rest. Your horsemen will be vital when the fighting starts, and I need you fit to lead them into battle.' He stood back to allow Odo to leave the marquee and pulled the screen into place behind him.

He looked moodily round the tent's interior and then untied his sword belt and flung it onto the camp bed set up along the rear wall. Although he was loath to admit it, Duke Odo was right in a couple of respects. Martel was not a patient man and the enforced roost on the hilltop was testing his natural preference for action, even though he was certain his strategy in this case was the correct one. Furthermore, he knew from long experience that delay in joining battle sowed boredom and fear amongst soldiers. He had pushed them hard in the two-week march from Metz to defend Tours before the enemy reached its gates, and they had been primed for combat on arrival. But over the last six days their appetite for fighting would have gradually diminished, and soon they would begin to steal away during the night to the safety of their homeland. Then his army, already undersized, would be unable to withstand the Moors' attack, despite the benefit of the high ground. How much longer could he wait for his opposing general to make the first move, before having to take the battle to him?

He sat down on the bed in the gathering darkness and shifted to extract the sword belt from under him. As he did so, his eye fell on the purse looped onto the belt, and an idea occurred to him. The fates had brought him here, with Odo as his subordinate, so maybe the answer to his quandary lay with the dice once more. He fished them out of the purse and held them for a moment in his hand, recalling the rumour he had first heard at his father's court in Herstal, that they were not only a centuries-old token of governorship but a tool for decision-making as well. *According to Odo*, he thought wryly, *God will show the way, but some extra direction from the fates will do no harm.* He let the dice fall onto the coverlet and bent down in the gloom to read them. Five and two. An omen for the seventh day. The Moors would attack tomorrow, and Martel's troops would be ready for them.

*

10 October 732 – Tours, central France

Martel was up well before daybreak, stirring his officers and issuing instructions for the coming battle. He had no doubt the Moors would launch their assault on the hill that day – it was simply a question of when. His final stop was at Duke Odo's tent, as the first glimmer of light was beginning to show, and he shouted through the canvas for the older man to wake up. There was a pause while Odo struggled in the darkness to find his clothing, and then he emerged into the cold autumn air, blinking at Martel's lantern.

'Get your men prepared, Odo, and tell those with horses to have them saddled up immediately. The Moors are coming!'

'How can you be sure?' the duke mumbled, still half asleep.

'Oh, they're coming. Trust me, as I said yesterday. We will form a shield wall on the lip of the hill, just above the trees. I will command the line from the centre, and I will send skirmishers forward into the trees to disrupt the enemy's first charge. I want you on my left flank. If the shield wall holds, there will be a moment when we can launch our own attack, and that will be your job. You and your cavalry can swing round the side of the hill and fall on their camp. Don't move until I send you the signal. And then ride like the Horsemen of the Apocalypse!' Martel clapped Odo on the back and turned away. 'Get some food first,' he shouted as he disappeared into the grey pre-dawn murk, 'it's going to be a long day.'

Down on the plain, the leader of the Moorish army, Abd al-Rahman al-Ghafiqi, was also awake. An accomplished general, with a substantial force of well-trained troops, he had been wrestling with the same issues as Martel since arriving outside Tours. It was a fact, borne out by the victory at Bordeaux, that in open terrain infantry were no match for cavalry, and he had three thousand mounted warriors at his disposal. But an uphill attack would sap their pace, and the trees would dilute the impetus of their charge. Far better to tempt the Christians onto the flat ground where their shield wall would weaken as they advanced and Abd al-Rahman could deploy his infantry and his cavalry in unison. After six days' stalemate, this remained the right strategy, but the soldiers were getting restless, and provisioning was becoming a problem for the static army. He knew he had superiority in numbers, and the lure of the fabled treasures within Tours' city walls was too much for him. He would attack today and be inside the Abbey of St Martin by sunset.

Unlike Martel, it took the Moorish general several hours to prepare his troops for action. There was an interval while a minor squall passed through, and his officers requested that they wait for the slippery grass incline to dry out in the following breeze. Then there was the call to prayer, followed by the midday meal, and the combat formation fragmented as the food wagons moved amongst the men. It was not until early afternoon that Abd al-Rahman was able to give the order to charge, and his first contingent of cavalry accelerated towards the base of the hill. By the time they reached the incline they were at full gallop, and they swept up to the trees, confident that whatever opposition lay beyond, they would crash through it and put the splintered enemy regiments to the sword. Their general had neglected to do his homework.

Following Duke Odo's visit to Metz, Martel had sent out a call to arms across northern Frankia, and within a fortnight he had assembled an army of nearly twenty thousand troops. After ten days' march, they had entered Orleans, where Odo had rallied another four thousand men from Aquitaine, a third of them mounted. The combined force had continued towards Tours on small country lanes, eschewing the main Roman roads to avoid detection by Moorish scouts. This had gained them the advantage of their hilltop position, blocking Abd al-Rahman's approach to the city and allowing him no chance to assess their strength. They were outnumbered, but by a factor of three to two, instead of the two to one that the Moorish general had assumed. Thanks to Martel's armourers in Metz and Orleans they were also far better equipped than Odo's troops in Bordeaux had been.

Reduced to little more than a trot on the hillside, and with their manoeuvrability impeded by the woodland, the Moorish cavalry presented easy targets for the waiting Frankish skirmishers. The riders were unable to use their usual tactic of slashing down at speed on the foot soldiers, who dodged amongst the trees and turned their weapons on the horses to devastating effect, jabbing at their underbellies with spears and severing their hindquarter tendons with blades. The untidy mob that succeeded in cresting the hill were met by a solid wall of infantry, standing ten ranks deep behind a shallow trench and banging their shields in intimidation. Horses reared up at the barrier before them and men tumbled to the ground, only to be trampled by a beast frantic to escape or hacked to death by a soldier permitted momentarily to step out from the wall. Hundreds of Moors were killed in that first charge, while the Franks lost almost no one.

Abd al-Rahman could hear the noise and guessed from the loose horses running wild from the trees that the attack had faltered, but he was unable to assess the reason for the failure or the extent of the destruction. Still convinced that he was facing an outmatched foe under poor leadership from Duke Odo, he ordered a second unit of cavalry forward, to be followed by a squadron of infantry. The cavalry met the same fate as their colleagues, and by the time the foot soldiers had struggled up the hill the woodland was littered with yet more injured horses, writhing in pain and kicking out at anyone approaching them. Their riders lay all around, cut to pieces by the skirmishers once they had been unseated. Further on, the bodies of horses and men had begun to pile up in front of the shield wall, making a concerted infantry assault on the Franks virtually impossible. Nonetheless, in acts of extraordinary bravery, groups of Moors smashed repeatedly into the wall, penetrating it briefly by weight of numbers but quickly repelled when Martel brought additional troops up from the rear.

The fighting continued all afternoon, the Moorish general throwing wave after wave of cavalry and infantry into the fray, with rising frustration and always with the same result. The Franks suffered losses, but nothing on the scale of the thousands inflicted on their enemy, and despite their fatigue amongst the carnage, they stood firm. The light was beginning to fade when Martel finally saw his opportunity to strike back.

Odo's troops had been largely spared from the front line, and the Frankish commander now sent the duke the signal to launch his horsemen into battle. Fresh and eager to avenge their humiliation at Bordeaux, they thundered down the left shoulder of the hill onto Abd al-Rahman's position in the open plain. The element of surprise proved crucial, and they raced through the camp, slaying all before them, including the general himself, before wheeling away to evade the rush of Moors returning from the hillside to defend their leader. As darkness fell, calm finally descended on the battlefield, and the only noises to be heard in the chill of the starlit night were of wounded men and animals crying out in agony. By morning, even those were silent.

Soon after dawn, Martel and Odo led a detachment of horsemen down through the trees to gauge the enemy's remaining strength, in preparation for another day's fighting. From a distance there appeared to be no sign of activity on the plain, and they edged forward warily for a closer inspection. It soon became clear that the Moors had struck camp in the middle of the night, leaving their tents behind them, and by mid-morning scouts were able to report that the battered remnants of the enemy army were in rapid flight south. The infidels' inexorable advance northwards, all the way from the tip of the Iberian Peninsula, had been halted. The forces of Islam had been turned and the treasures of St Martin's Abbey in Tours protected by the Franks, and as Duke Odo of Aquitaine had foretold, it would prove a pivotal moment for the future of Christianity across Western Europe, even though it had cost him his Duchy. Charles Martel was hailed as the saviour of the faith, although he felt it expedient not to celebrate the part played in his success by a pair of dice.

*

And then...

+ The dice pass to Charlemagne, Charles Martel's grandson, who gives them to Pope Leo III as an act of contrition on being made Holy Roman Emperor in 800. They are retained by the Vatican until, many incumbents later, Pope John XII gifts them to Otto the Great in 962 when crowning him Holy Roman Emperor, in recognition of Otto's successful resistance to the heathen Vikings and Maygars.

+ In 974 Otto's son, Otto II, loses the dice in battle against Harald 'Bluetooth', King of Denmark, and they duly pass to Harald's grandson Cnut, King of England between 1016 and 1035. They become part of the English monarchy's regalia of office and are inherited by William the Conqueror when he is crowned king in Westminster Abbey on Christmas Day, 1066.

+ Before his death in 1087, William bequeaths the English throne, and therefore the dice, to his son, William Rufus, who dies suddenly while hunting in the New Forest thirteen years later. Rufus's younger brother, Henry, moves swiftly to seize the throne before any other claimant can thwart him, ensuring, like those in centuries past, that he holds the dice to support his bid for power.

*

Author's Note
    The Battle of Tours is often credited with being the turning

point in the medieval fight against Islam's advance into south-west Europe. After Mohammed's death in 632, the religion he had founded was spread rapidly by his followers through military conquest, initially across much of the Middle East and Northern Africa. In 711 the Moors (a combination of Arab and Berber troops) invaded the Iberian Peninsula via Gibraltar, occupying Toledo and making incursions over the Pyrenees into Gaul. By 720 they had established a local base in the old Visigoth city of Narbonne, and the following year they besieged Toulouse, the capital of Aquitaine. They were repulsed by Duke Odo but over the next decade they continued to raid northwards, culminating in an attack on Bordeaux in mid-732, where they inflicted a heavy defeat on Odo's army. The duke was obliged to seek the help of the Franks, his erstwhile enemy, and their leader Charles Martel agreed to assist on the condition that Odo ceded control of Aquitaine to him.

Details of the battle are limited. The site was probably somewhere north of Poitiers on the approach to Tours, and Frankish forces are thought to have numbered twenty to twenty-five thousand, with the Moors fielding thirty to forty thousand. Six days of skirmishing preceded the principal encounter. As described, the Franks occupied an area of high ground screened by trees, greatly reducing the potency of Abd al-Rahman's repeated cavalry charges when they were finally launched, and Odo's troops were able to counter-attack the enemy camp, killing the general in the process. The Moors abandoned their position overnight, having suffered heavy losses, and ultimately retreated to the far side of the Pyrenees.

The battle was undoubtedly an important victory for the Europeans but is considered unlikely by many historians to have been the single defining factor in stemming the tide of Islam's advance. It is unclear to what extent the Moors' march through Aquitaine towards Frankia was part of a full-scale invasion strategy rather than simply another raid, for which the treasures at the Abbey of St Martin in Tours would have been a compelling attraction. Abd al-Rahman's successor brought a fresh army to Narbonne in 735, and Charles Martel and his son Pepin the Short fought numerous engagements in Aquitaine and Burgundy over the following three decades before the Moors were expelled from Gaul for the final time. Aside from the defence of Christianity in Western Europe, these events allowed Martel and Pepin (and later Pepin's son Charlemagne) to consolidate and expand the Frankish empire, creating the structure for a 150-year dynasty across the region. There is no reason to believe that Martel resorted to dice to support his decision-making.

Norman/English Monarchy

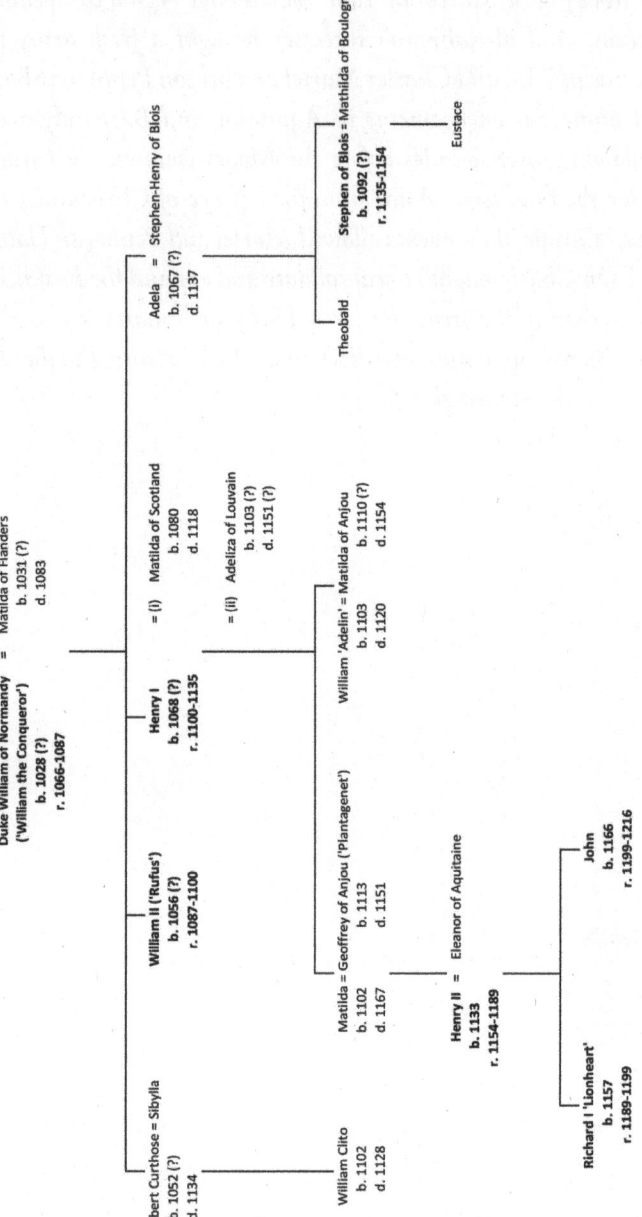

Note

For simplicity, only individuals directly relevant to the White Ship story are included

Kings of England in bold typeface

The White Ship

25 November 1120 – Barfleur, Normandy, France

After seven days on the road, Berold was in a very bad mood. He was cold, dirty and extremely hungry. His feet hurt and he had not slept in a proper bed since leaving his hometown of Rouen. His grievance had festered and swollen with every step of the way and, putting aside the matter of the money itself, his mind kept returning to the attitude of his debtors. If they thought they could avoid paying the butcher's bill just because they were rich and powerful, they were wrong, and in an hour or so Berold would tell them to their faces. He looked up from the muddy track towards his destination on the northern horizon. Barfleur's church spire was now clearly visible, and he guessed that the harbour would be close beyond. He would be there before sundown after all.

The first part of the journey, as far as Caen, had been relatively simple. As soon as he had discovered that the king and his entourage had left the ancient castle in Rouen, seat of the Dukes of Normandy for over two centuries, he had begun to plan his pursuit. The word was that the nobility were travelling to the coastal port of Barfleur, in order to sail to England for the winter months. By mid-November his butcher's shop was beginning to enter its usual seasonal lull compared to the busy summer trading period, and his wife and son could manage it easily enough in his absence. The publican in the city's central marketplace had mentioned a while ago that he would be taking a cart to Caen to buy cider – the local crop around Rouen had suffered a severe blight that spring – and Berold had hoped that he might catch up with the royal party there. He had begged a ride and had spent an uncomfortable three days sitting amongst the empty barrels in the back of the wagon as it jostled westwards across Normandy. At least it had saved his boot leather and had provided him with shelter from the elements at night.

On arrival in Caen he had gone immediately to the king's residence, the massive hilltop stronghold built by Duke William of Normandy in the previous century. It was not difficult to find and, after attempting to tidy himself up at an inn nearby, he had presented himself to the guards at the gatehouse. Their indifference as Berold explained his purpose had turned to scornful laughter when they finally revealed that the king and his friends had moved on that morning. The royal company was indeed heading to Barfleur, they had assured him, and they would be happy to show him the way by kicking him down the road. He had run from them as fast as his sizeable belly permitted, their shouts of derision ringing in his ears.

For the average adult in reasonable health, the walk from Caen to Barfleur would normally take three days, but Berold was not cut out for such an expedition. His business in Rouen had flourished in the last four years, as the kings of France and England had taken up their positions around Normandy's capital to dispute control of the region. The fortunes of the opposing armies had ebbed and flowed, but their soldiers had always needed to be fed, regardless of the short-term shifts in ascendancy. Berold had become the principal supplier of meat to both forces, and he had grown fat on the profits. The recent months since the last major battle, at Brémule outside the city, had been particularly fruitful, King Henry of England's warriors celebrating their victory in style and then bringing their families and servants across the channel to join them as they administered the peace. They had eaten the finest cuts of beef and lamb and had paid little attention to the price. Berold's standard of living had changed accordingly and now he was in no fit state to hike long distances. At the end of the third day on foot, exhausted by the unaccustomed exercise and the fitful sleep of two nights in the open air, he had collapsed in an orchard next to the village of Carentan, with a full day's journey still ahead and a mounting concern that the king's ship would have sailed by the time he reached Barfleur.

Setting off at sunrise the following morning, he had followed the road as it veered north and had walked continuously all day. His thighs chafed from the harsh rub of his breeches, and he could feel the blisters on the soles of his feet getting ever bigger. His last meal had been a mouthful of bread and cheese at first light, bought from a hawker on leaving Carentan, but since then he had dared not stop, even for a moment's rest or food, in case he missed his quarry. Now he could smell the sea, and his mood lifted at the view of Barfleur's church. He would get his money before dark and spend some of it on a well-earned supper at the harbour's public house. He walked on, his pace increasing as the anticipation of success overcame his weariness, and soon found himself passing workshops and stalls on the town's periphery.

Although he could not know it, Berold's timing was opportune. Another hour on the road would have made his mission considerably trickier, and another night would have seen his debtors slip through his fingers altogether. The royal group had arrived two days before him, but their expectation of a speedy passage across the water to England had been frustrated by a brisk northerly wind. They had been obliged to wait until it swung round to the south, which it had finally done late that morning. During the delay, dozens of other nobles and their retinue had also descended on Barfleur, eager to participate in King Henry's victorious departure from Normandy and to take advantage of any sovereign favour being dispensed in the process. By mid-afternoon the town was crammed with people, and negotiations as to who should travel with the king were reaching fever pitch. Once all the courtiers, barons, churchmen, knights, squires, wives, children, bodyguards and servants were accounted for alongside Henry and his inner circle, the number trying to board easily exceeded the capacity of the royal vessel, and no one wanted the indignity of being demoted to a secondary transport.

The appearance of a ship's captain called Thomas FitzStephen in the harbour master's office, outside which the debate raged, provided a welcome solution to the issue. Once he had shouldered his way through the crowd and been granted an audience with the king, he announced that he was the owner of a large and recently refitted craft at anchor offshore called the *Blanche-Nef*, which he would be honoured to put at the monarch's disposal. It would accommodate many more passengers than the vessel the king planned to use and would make the crossing under sail to Southampton more swiftly thanks to its modern construction. If the wind dropped, its fifty oarsmen would prove a first-rate substitute for powering him and his companions to their destination. The harbour master supported FitzStephen's proposal; he knew both the captain and the *Blanche-Nef* well, and the king would be in good hands.

With a following wind the voyage between Barfleur and Southampton normally took around twelve hours, and it was a journey Henry had made many times. He was keen to embark and to leave the chaos of the crowds in the town behind him. His own ship was ready to depart, and he saw no reason to disturb that arrangement, particularly given that they would be sailing through the night, when a reduction in the trip's duration of an hour or two was meaningless. But FitzStephen's offer could be applied in a different way. The *Blanche-Nef* could take Henry's teenage son, William Adelin, the flock of young attaching to him and a swathe of the older nobility. The king would leave port shortly before dark and FitzStephen could follow later, making up some of the time if his ship was as fast as he claimed. FitzStephen and the harbour master were both delighted, the former because he could bask in the glory of being permitted responsibility for Prince William, the king's favourite child and precious heir, the latter because at one stroke it resolved the argument still boiling outside his door.

By the time Berold entered Barfleur two hours later, the crush of people seeking passage to England had split into two factions. Those selected to travel on the king's ship were now gathered round him on the waterfront, chatting and laughing as they waited for their belongings to be taken aboard the vessel. Beyond them, grooms led whinnying horses across the gangway; servants bustled between them dragging heavy wooden baggage chests; kitchen staff bearing platters of food beat a steady path to the quay from the hotel where the king's party had been lodging; and local traders circled the throng advertising their wares at the top of their voices. Amid this noisy hive of activity, the royal purser Geoffrey de Clinton stood alone, watching the loading operation with a beady eye and occasionally bellowing a command to anyone foolish enough to impede progress.

The other group, those due to travel on the *Blanche-Nef*, were now nowhere near the king. In the hotel in the town square where he had been staying with his father, William Adelin was holding his own court for the first time and relishing it. After making his decision in the harbour master's office, the king had introduced the prince to Thomas FitzStephen and had explained that the captain would bring the boy, his young attendants and the remaining nobles to England in a second vessel. It would sail later in the evening, once FitzStephen had summoned his crew. William Adelin had bridled at the suggestion that he was being relegated to the second ship until it dawned on him that he would have the evening on shore with his friends, without his stern, authoritarian father there to keep him in check. As soon as the king was distracted, he and his contemporaries had headed for the hotel where they had settled down, drinks in hand, to enjoy themselves before embarkation. They were quickly joined by the older nobles instructed to travel with FitzStephen.

Not surprisingly, William Adelin was the centre of attention, a slim seventeen-year-old who had fought with distinction in his first battle, Brémule, and had been formally assigned the dukedom of Normandy by his father as a consequence. As such he was heir not only to the rich lands around Rouen and Caen but also to the kingdom of England that his grandfather, William of Normandy, had won from the Anglo-Saxons some fifty years previously. He was everyone's friend, and the young nobility, also savouring the rare moment of freedom from their parents and tutors, swirled round him like moths to a flame.

Passing the church on the corner of the square, Berold came to the main avenue sloping down towards the harbour. He could hear boisterous voices from within the hotel behind him, and he could see the large crowd at the quayside. He paused briefly, wondering where best to look first for his money, and then picked out the figure of de Clinton standing by the gangway, King Henry a handful of paces further along the wharf. He recognised both of them from his frequent visits to the castle in Rouen over the last few years, and while he had no intention of disturbing the king himself, de Clinton might be able to direct him to the man he sought if he could get the purser's attention long enough to make his case. He advanced down the slope and waited until a reluctant horse had been persuaded to leave the security of the cobbled quay for the royal ship bobbing gently on the water. There were no other obvious distractions, and he addressed de Clinton with a bow.

'Sire, forgive this interruption, but you may remember me from Rouen. I am the butcher there, and I have had the honour of supplying the castle kitchens with meat for many years. My name is Berold.'

De Clinton inspected him with displeasure. The butcher was never the tidiest of men, and after his long journey he had fallen well below even his modest standards, his fleece coat rumpled and spattered with dried mud, his chin bristling with stubble. He was saved by his notable girth, which had been the subject of great amusement amongst the court at Rouen.

'Berold? Yes, the fat butcher. How could I forget you? Why on earth are you bothering me here?'

Berold longed to retort with a critical comment about de Clinton's appearance. This was exactly the type of attitude he associated with the people who had failed to pay him, the casual abuse, the dismissive intolerance, the refusal to accept the part that tradesmen like Berold played in the nobility's comfort and good health. But that was not going to change in a hurry, and in the meantime, he had no wish to be locked up in the local stocks for impertinence or, more likely, thrown into the harbour's cold seawater. He had never learnt to swim and would probably sink like a stone.

'Sire, I beg your indulgence,' he answered. 'There is a minor problem, which you might be able to help me with. I am owed a substantial sum for the beef and lamb I have provided for the king's table in Rouen over the summer. And for all the poultry too. I delivered my statement of account to the castle a month ago and had expected to be paid before the king left to come here. I need to find whoever handles these things and receive payment before the ship sails.' He gestured at the gangway, then reached within his coat for an order book, which he proffered to the purser. 'I have the list of supplies set out in here and the price of every item.'

'You've come all this way for a food bill?' De Clinton glared at him, baffled that anyone could be troubled by such a triviality. 'Why couldn't you wait till next year, when the king returns to Rouen?'

'My business, Sire. Without payment I will struggle to continue my business through the winter.' Berold's voice became more plaintive. 'My family depends on it. I've always been paid in the past, and I'm sure it's just a mistake. But it's a lot of money and I must speak to someone about it.'

'Well, there's no point talking to me. The man you want is the king's chamberlain, Maudit. He will be travelling with the prince, not the king. Go on up to the hotel, and keep out of my way. If I catch you down here again, I'll make certain you don't get paid at all.' He turned his back on Berold to emphasise that the conversation was closed and began to berate a lady's maid as she staggered onto the ship with a heap of thick woollen cloaks in her arms. The butcher looked at the hotel standing above the harbour, where William Adelin's followers had swelled to such a number they were now spilling out of the front door, and he understood for the first time what de Clinton had meant. The figures he could see must belong to a second group sailing in a separate vessel, and he would find the chamberlain amongst them. Although he did not know Maudit by sight, he had heard of him and was pleased to learn that he was the person to speak to. He walked slowly back up the slope, leg muscles aching with fatigue, and plunged into the crowd at the hotel.

Of the first four people he asked, three refused even to acknowledge Berold, and one claimed to have no idea who or what the chamberlain was. They were all so young, hardly more than children, but dressed in the finest cloth that money could buy and conducting themselves with the airs and graces of fully grown adults. They included a smattering of girls, daughters to the older generation down on the quay, no doubt, and the boys were clamouring for their attention. The pack was at its loudest and most dense around the fire at the hearth of the hotel's main reception room, where the prince stood warming himself. Here, at least, several older men were in attendance, one of whom the butcher presumed must be Maudit. He worked his way through the press and succeeded in attracting the attention of the one furthest from the prince. 'My apologies, Sire, but I am looking for the king's chamberlain. Do you know if he's here?'

'What do you want?' shouted the man brusquely through the din around them. Berold launched into the explanation he had given Geoffrey de Clinton, but the man simply put his hands to his ears and then pointed to the door of a side room. They threaded their way there and Berold shut the door behind them. As he began to talk again, the older man cut across him. 'You have a message from the king? What does he say?'

'No, Sire, I am here to see his chamberlain about payment for a butcher's bill in Rouen.'

'A butcher's bill? Today? This is not the time to be discussing tradesmen's bills.'

Berold could feel his hackles rising at the flat rejection but realised a more obsequious route was called for, much though it irritated him. 'Sire, permit me to explain. My name is Berold, and I have had the great privilege of serving the king's household in Rouen over the last four years. Payment for this summer's supply of meat has yet to be made, which naturally I take to be nothing more than an oversight, and I am told that I should speak to King Henry's chamberlain about it.' He decided not to mention that he had chased the king's entourage across Normandy for an entire week after a debt that should have been settled a month ago. 'If you could help me find him, I would be most grateful.'

'I am Robert Maudit, chamberlain to His Majesty. As I said before, I have more important things to be doing this afternoon than worrying about paying bills.'

'I understand that, of course, Sire, and I am honoured to meet you.' Berold bowed, as he had done to Geoffrey de Clinton, and produced his order book. 'I have the account here, if you would be kind enough to look through it. It is clearly set out, with the total at the bottom. It will take very little time.'

Maudit breathed a loud sigh of annoyance and took the order book. As he began to flick through the pages, a horn sounded from outside the hotel, and the noise in the reception room next to them died at once. 'The king's messenger,' the chamberlain said to Berold. 'Leave the account with me, and I may look at it later.' He tossed the book onto a table between them and added, 'If I have time,' before crossing to the door and rejoining the group crowding round William Adelin.

Berold's interpretation of Maudit's final words was, 'if I can be bothered', and he stood in the side room considering what else he could do to obtain payment that day. He was loath to part with the order book, his sole record of the sum owed, but he feared that to remove it and attempt to re-present it to Maudit later in the evening would only invite trouble. With reluctance he left it lying on the table and followed the chamberlain into the next room. As he did so, the crowd parted to allow a tall, weather-beaten man to approach the prince at the hearth.

'Your Highness, I bring news from the king.'

'Hello again, FitzStephen,' replied William Adelin, 'I heard the horn blaring, but I am surprised to see you. Have you been relegated from ship's captain to messenger?' He smirked at his petty joke, and a sycophantic ripple of laughter washed round the listeners. Thomas FitzStephen ignored it. He would not let himself be provoked by a seventeen-year-old, especially not one on whom his future wealth depended. All he had to do was deliver the prince safely to Southampton and the *Blanche-Nef* would be hired out to the nobility of England and Normandy for years to come. He smiled respectfully at the prince.

'I am delighted to be able to tell you that the *Blanche-Nef* will be ready to board in two hours' time, Your Highness. The king's ship will be leaving port in the next few minutes and once it has gone, there will be space for my vessel in the harbour. Then I just need an hour or so to prepare the decks for you, your attendants and the other nobles that were unable to accompany His Majesty.' He glanced quickly at Robert Maudit, whom he had met with King Henry earlier in the day, and received a tiny nod of approval. The prince might like to think he was in charge of events in his father's absence, but FitzStephen knew that the chamberlain had been instructed to travel with the second ship as an informal guardian for the precious cargo and therefore required an element of discreet consultation. 'As I was about to come up here from the quay the king saw me and asked me to deliver a message to you. And he told me to bring his herald, since this is official business.' He held up a small velvet pouch that had gone unnoticed by the prince and his friends until that moment, although Maudit had spied it in the captain's fist and guessed what it presaged.

William Adelin took the pouch from FitzStephen and examined it warily. The party with his companions had barely begun and he had no wish for it to be interrupted by officialdom, whatever that entailed. He untied the ribbons at the pouch's neck and emptied the contents onto the mantelpiece behind him. Two ivory dice rattled out onto the painted wooden surface, grey with age and distinctly un-regal. And yet, something told him these were no ordinary toys.

It was Robert Maudit's turn to catch FitzStephen's eye. He nodded again and stepped forward. 'Your Highness, you won't have seen these dice before, but they are part of the insignia of the English throne. Your father, your uncle and their father before them have all owned the dice. When the king opted this afternoon to sail on a separate ship from you, he told me he would give you an item to demonstrate your command in his absence. Once you are reunited with him in England, you will have to return the dice to him. But for now, you are our sovereign lord, and we are your subjects. Captain FitzStephen, do you have anything to add from King Henry?'

'Only one word, Your Highness.' FitzStephen gazed round the room and said solemnly, 'Godspeed.'

There was a long silence as William Adelin contemplated the dice. Then he turned, grinning, from the mantelpiece and reached out to shake the royal chamberlain by the hand, shouting as he did so across the heads of his audience, 'Well, let's drink to that!' A huge cheer erupted, and glasses were raised all round. The party could continue, for as long as he chose.

Berold looked on in dismay. Getting Maudit's attention for a second time amid the mass of revellers was going to become increasingly difficult. He resigned himself to the knowledge that it might be a long evening and decided he too needed a drink.

*

Six hours later – Barfleur, Normandy, France

The *Blanche-Nef* was underway at last. Berold watched as the final mooring line was unlooped from the quayside bulkhead and flung over the ship's rail. Crew members at the bow and stern used long staves to push off from the wharf and after a few seconds the oarsmen were able to take their first strokes. The ship glided towards the harbour entrance, and for a brief moment the butcher was able to enjoy the quiet starlit night as it illuminated the water. Then the noise began again, the uproar of drunken voices from the horde of young on the vessel's foredeck.

Berold's concern about the likely course of events at the hotel had proved correct, more so than even he had feared. The prince and his friends had set about enjoying their liberation from their parents with gusto. When Thomas FitzStephen had reappeared midway through the evening to confirm that his ship was ready for boarding, William Adelin had pressed a wine glass into his hand and insisted that the captain drink with him. Looking on, Robert Maudit had remarked politely that the king was expecting the *Blanche-Nef* to follow his own ship out to sea fairly quickly, and the prince had hooted with laughter. 'Stop fussing, Maudit, we have a superior ship. FitzStephen promised this afternoon we would make far better time across the channel than my father. There's no rush to set off. Calm down and have some more wine. Why don't we get some food too? And FitzStephen, have the hotelier send some barrels of beer down to your crew. That will keep them happy while they're waiting for us.'

After another two hours, the prince had finally been induced to leave the hotel for the quay. The raucous crowd around him had surged down the gentle slope and onto the *Blanche-Nef*, where they had been met by the crew, also now in high spirits thanks to the copious amount of alcohol they had been given. There had been an awkward incident as the prince was approaching the gangway, when his path was blocked by three priests seeking to bless the royal voyage with holy water. William Adelin had shoved them out of his way, and a couple of his more inebriated attendants had offered them slurred advice about what they could do with themselves. Neither Maudit nor FitzStephen had been on hand to intervene, but Berold had seen one older man detach himself from the boarding group, claiming that he was feeling unwell and would travel to England the following day instead. Whoever the nobleman was, he seemed to be suffering from neither illness nor intoxication, and the butcher presumed it was instead a healthy dose of superstition that had prompted the change of plan.

As for Berold himself, it looked as though he was going to be leaving Normandy for the first time in his life. Twice during the evening he had tried to renew his conversation with the king's chamberlain, and each time Maudit had brushed him off. As the prince left the hotel, the butcher had retrieved his order book from the table in the side room and brandished it in the chamberlain's face – something he would never have done without several glasses of wine to fortify him – but once more he had been ignored. He had followed the crowd down to the harbour, where his rebellious nature had taken the upper hand. He would not watch his debtor disappear onto the ship, never to be seen again. He would board and talk to Maudit in the cold light of day, even if that meant pursuing him onto the shores of England.

A burst of whistles and cheers went up from the bow of the *Blanche-Nef*, and Berold walked forward to find out the cause. In the dark he was able to move around at will amongst the nobles, despite his humble trade and scruffy attire, and he joined the group of young clustered in a circle close to the ship's dinghy, which was held in place on the deck by sturdy oak wedges. Wriggling to the front of the spectators, he found William Adelin and four others sitting on the floor playing a game of dice. Coins were scattered on the deck's planking, and the butcher recognised the dice from the hotel. He was a keen gambler himself, and he stood observing the game for a few minutes, as money changed hands and the crowd at his back shouted encouragement to the players. He was conscious of a sharp breeze now that the ship was out of the harbour and gaining speed under the clear night sky. The oarsmen had been boasting when he boarded that they could catch the king's ship and he imagined that, spurred on by their beer supply and a possible tip from the prince, they were rowing flat out to prove their case. He took a swig from the beer mug that a crew member had thrust into his hand at the gangway, and suddenly he was pitched forward, the mug spinning across the deck towards the prince.

Bodies were falling all around him as the *Blanche-Nef* came to an abrupt halt. The young nobles' wine-fuelled shouts of excitement switched instantly to yells of consternation, accompanied from the side of the ship by a hideous scraping, rending sound. Water began to splash over the rails and, as Berold picked himself up from the pool gathering on the floor where the prince had been sitting, the trickle swiftly became a flood. Waves poured in and the whole vessel listed heavily towards the source of the grinding noise, followed by a mighty crash as the central mast snapped at its base and smacked down onto the deck, flattening a score of oarsmen and shearing into several pieces as it landed. All along the ship, the heaving mass of passengers and crew slid in unison to the lower rail, and in doing so the angle of the deck steepened further. Cries of fear rose into the night as people struggled to clamber up the welter of flailing bodies beneath them, or to cling on to anything fixed to the deck, and then a huge wrench ran through the *Blanche-Nef*'s hull. It yawed upwards and, as if in slow motion, the craft rolled over onto the reef it had struck. Every single one of the three hundred on board was tipped into the sea, many crushed on the rocks under the ship's splintering timbers, others swept free into the open water.

Uninjured, but terrified at his inability to swim, Berold thrashed his arms around him in a frantic effort to avoid being dragged down by the weight of his soaking fleece coat. He managed to hold his head above the surface enough to see a wooden spar drifting past, a large cross-piece from the shattered mast. After four attempts he eventually heaved himself up onto it. Waves continued to break over him, but with his upper body out of the breath-sapping cold of the sea itself, he was able to take in the scale of the disaster from the light of the stars.

The *Blanche-Nef* was ruined, hoisted keel-up onto the reef she had hit outside the harbour, and now being pummelled into fragments by the surf. On the rise and fall of the swell, Berold caught glimpses of bodies, some face down and motionless, some still striving desperately to stay afloat and shouting for help. One of the voices belonged to a girl, her high-pitched screams slicing through the darkness. After a minute or two, a rhythmic slapping noise behind him caused him to look round and there, incredibly, he could just make out the oars of a small boat moving in her direction. It did not occur to him to hail it, his humble position amongst the nobility still an instinctive impediment, and he watched as the rowers leant down to haul the girl aboard. Only then did he realise what he was witnessing. William Adelin had been standing in the middle of the ship's dinghy, pleading with the girl not to give up before the boat reached her, and was now crying out, 'Thank God', over and over again as he hugged her.

The butcher's survey of the horrific scene was broken by a sudden lurch, as a swimmer sought to climb on to the far end of the spar. Berold was dislodged but he grabbed hold of the timber beam with one hand as he slid into the sea and levered himself up into his previous position. The other man was now all but submerged again, and the butcher crawled along the spar to pull him up by his collar. After a lengthy battle with the greedy waves, they were able to sit back to back on the mast piece, exhausted by their efforts and quivering with shock.

When the butcher was sufficiently recovered to look around him again, the starlit spectacle had altered once more. The dinghy was about fifty paces away, capsized, with a dozen or more figures floundering nearby. One by one, they slipped under the surface and after five minutes he could see no survivors from the wreck besides himself and his companion on the spar, who was still retching from the salt water he had swallowed. The waves lapped up against their improvised raft, and the cold from Berold's wet clothes in the bitter winter breeze was intense. He had no idea where the tide's current would take him, but he guessed from the rocks they had hit that he must be close to the coastline, and that if he could stay alive long enough, he might be washed up onto the beach or rescued by a fishing boat. Two things were clear to him: he was not going back into the sea, and Robert Maudit was almost certainly unavailable to settle his debt.

Still, Berold mused as he sat shivering on the shattered mast, it hadn't been a completely wasted voyage, assuming he could reach dry land. When the first impact of the shipwreck had propelled him across the deck, he had found himself lying amongst the gaming coins and dice being used by William

Adelin and his friends. With mayhem all around he had taken the opportunity to scoop them into his coat pocket, and he could still feel them there, next to his sodden order book. Compared to his butcher's bill the money was a drop in the ocean, an unfortunate expression in the circumstances but better than nothing at all.

*

28 November 1120 – Wilton Abbey, Salisbury, England

Theobald of Blois, King Henry's nephew, braced himself and stepped into the abbey. He had been the one to break the news of the shipwreck, and of William Adelin's disappearance, to the king the previous evening, and it had been an excruciating moment for both of them. Henry had been awaiting word of his son's arrival at Southampton for the best part of two days before any of his courtiers had felt sure enough of the rumours coming into port to pass them on to him. After his own ship's successful channel crossing, the king had ridden to Salisbury, expecting to be joined by the prince in an hour or two. As day turned to night, his impatience had turned to concern and then, the following morning, to mounting anxiety. Being the closest relative present, Theobald had been given the dreadful task of speaking to him, and the king's anguish had been terrible to see. He had howled in despair at the loss of his one legitimate son, heir not simply to the throne of England and dukedom of Normandy, but also to the king's work of two decades in securing their borders through conquest, marriage and diplomacy. Twelve hours later, he remained inconsolable, lashing out at anyone attempting to commiserate and now said to be beseeching God within the abbey to deliver his son from the deep. Theobald's only hope was that the fresh news he now bore would come as a relief to the agony of conjecture regarding the fate of all those on the *Blanche-Nef*.

'Your Majesty,' he said tentatively, shutting the door behind him and moving up the aisle towards the figure kneeling at the abbey's altar. The king looked round, his face furrowed in torment, but did not reply. 'Your Majesty, I have a man with me who survived the shipwreck and is able to describe some of what happened. Would you like to meet him, or shall I write up his report for you to...?' He stopped in confusion as the king leapt to his feet.

'What news of William? Has he been found?'

Theobald gulped. 'No, Your Majesty, there is still no sign of the prince, but the man...'

'Where is he?' Henry barged past him and ran to the door, flinging it open. Outside, on the paving stones leading from the abbey garden, Berold stood waiting in the bright sun, accompanied by two guards. He had been told of the king's distress and did not believe that what he had to say would improve matters.

'Who are you?' the king spat the words out. 'What do you know of the shipwreck?'

'My name is Berold, and I was there, Your Majesty. I am a butcher from Rouen, and I was there seeking payment for supplies to your household over the summer...'

'I don't care why you were there. Tell me what happened on the *Blanche-Nef* and where my son is.'

For once, Berold's defiance in response to such high-handedness did not come to the fore. As a father himself, he understood the king's grief for his son, and he continued as if he had not been interrupted. 'I spoke to your chamberlain at the hotel in Barfleur and then followed him on board. By chance I was standing near the prince when the ship struck the rocks, and we were all pitched into the sea.' He went on to explain how he had clambered onto the broken mast piece and watched as those in the water around him had vanished, one after another, beneath the surface. Even his companion on the spar, Geoffrey de l'Aigle, Berold recalled him saying, had eventually succumbed to exhaustion and been washed away by a wave. The butcher had clung on till daylight when he was spotted by a fisherman and taken into harbour, almost comatose from the cold. It seemed he was the sole survivor of the entire ship's company, and he could put it down only to his thick sheep-wool fleece and the good fortune of finding the piece of timber. Once he had revived and told his story to the harbour master, he had been bundled onto a boat and brought immediately to England to repeat his eyewitness account to what remained of the royal court there. They had wasted no time in presenting him to the king in person.

'But my son, damn you.' The king took Berold by the shoulders and shook him in frustration. 'What of him?'

'I saw him in the ship's dinghy, rescuing a girl from the water. I assume that his guards had managed to launch the boat and were rowing him to safety but that he heard the girl's shouts for help and told them to go back and get her. The next thing I knew, the dinghy had capsized, and everyone nearby was drowning.' The king let out a heaving wail of pain, and Berold looked to Theobald for assistance. The courtier took up the story.

'It is likely, Your Majesty, that the dinghy was swamped by others trying to climb aboard after the prince had rescued the girl. So far, no one except the butcher has been picked up alive, and very few bodies have been found along the shore. After all this time, I think we have to assume that the prince drowned. It is little consolation to you, but it appears he died very bravely.'

A gust of wind blew through the garden and leaves eddied around the group at the abbey door. The only sound came from the king as he sobbed wretchedly, and Theobald had no idea what else to say. He began to usher Berold away, but the butcher elbowed him aside and stepped square in front of the king again. 'Your Majesty, there is one other thing. Also little consolation, I fear, but perhaps something to cherish, nonetheless.' He felt in the pocket of his breeches and withdrew two dice. 'I was in the room at the hotel when the ship's captain delivered these to the prince, and I was watching your son playing a game with them on the ship when it struck the rocks. I had heard the captain say the dice were important, and I was able to grab them as we all slid down the deck into the water.' The butcher omitted the fact that he had also snatched up a fistful of coins. 'I know they are something to do with being King of England, but more significantly, they were being used by the prince in his final moments. I give them to you, not as your subject here in England but as one father to another.' He held the dice out and waited for the king to take them, uncertain whether he had overstepped the mark.

King Henry's face contorted and then relaxed into an expression of aching sadness. 'You are a good man, Berold,' he said, reaching for the dice. 'They are the only thing from Normandy that I will have to remember William by. Go home to Rouen with my blessing, and make sure Theobald here sorts out your payment claim before you leave.' Then he turned away, his cheeks wet with silent tears, and walked back into the dark interior of the abbey, closing the door gently behind him.

*

And then...

+ King Henry never truly recovers from the loss of William Adelin, the presence of the dice haunting him for the rest of his life. After his death they remain part of the English royal regalia, falling in due course into the hands of his great-grandson Richard the Lionheart.

♦ In 1190 Richard takes the dice with him on the Third Crusade to the Holy Land, where he learns to play a new game called Hazard. On his return to England, he introduces Hazard to his court and its popularity soon spreads throughout the country.

♦ The dice continue to be transferred down the line of English monarchs, passing after another seventy years to Richard's great-nephew Edward I. In 1292 Edward gifts them to John Balliol, to mark the latter's appointment as King of Scotland in a selection process where Edward, as theoretically independent arbitrator, has asserted his authority to become that country's overlord.

*

Author's Note

The details of the Blanche-Nef *shipwreck (or the* White Ship, *using its English name) are known to us principally from the works of William of Malmesbury and Orderic Vitalis, both monks writing in the two decades after the event. Although I have fictionalised the story by recounting it from the perspective of Berold, the bare facts of the tragedy are as I have described them. Departing from Barfleur (near Cherbourg) after a successful campaign fighting the King of France for control of Normandy, King Henry chose to stick to his prearranged travel plans, leaving his son and many of the royal court to follow him on the newly refitted* Blanche-Nef. *Captain FitzStephen's crew were supplied with alcohol and by the time the ship left harbour in the dark, both they and the passengers had been drinking for several hours.*

Priests seeking to sprinkle holy water on the vessel were ridiculed, and a few nobles (including Stephen of Blois, Henry's successor as King of England) disembarked, whether for reasons of superstition, concern regarding the raucous behaviour onboard or ill-health as Stephen claimed, is uncertain. Under a starlit sky, directed by a drunken helmsman, the ship struck a rock called the Quilleboeuf just one mile into the voyage and quickly capsized.

Some 300 people perished that night, including William Adelin, around 155 nobles, 90 servants and the entire 50-strong crew. The butcher from Rouen was the sole survivor, thanks probably to his thick fleece coat and his good fortune in being able to clamber onto a wooden spar and stay afloat until his rescue the following morning. To what extent he embellished his account of the minutes immediately after the ship's ruin is unclear, but his report did include the prince's attempt to save a girl (possibly his half-sister Matilda of Perche, one of King Henry's many illegitimate offspring), the swamping of the dinghy and the appearance for a time on the spar of the knight Geoffrey de l'Aigle. There is no record of Berold sailing to England to meet the king, nor obtaining payment for his butcher's bill, but he is said to have lived for a further twenty years. William Adelin's body was never found, and King Henry is fabled never to have smiled again.

Besides the huge loss of life, the shipwreck was a political disaster for Henry. In addition to his heir, at a stroke it removed a swathe of the aristocratic ruling class, the warrior knights and the administrators on whom his realm relied. Had William Adelin lived, he could have boasted a bloodline co-mingling the ruling families of Normandy, England and Scotland, a wife from Normandy's southern neighbour and long-term rival Anjou and victory over France (at that time a region around Paris much smaller than the France of today), promising succession to power over a vast and stable empire. In his absence, Henry's only other legitimate child was a daughter Matilda, whom the barons of

England were reluctant to accept as their queen. On Henry's death in 1135, his nephew Stephen of Blois swiftly arranged to have himself crowned king, prompting a vicious fifteen-year civil war against Matilda known as the Anarchy. Peace was finally achieved by Stephen's agreement to allow Matilda's son Henry ('the Second') to succeed him on the English throne.

As for the 'And then' section, there is nothing to suggest that Richard the Lionheart took dice to the Holy Land, but the two-dice game of Hazard (a precursor to the American game Craps) is thought to have been introduced to Europe by knights returning from the Crusades of the eleventh to twelfth centuries. Nor is there any indication of dice being used as a token of goodwill in the appointment of John Balliol as King of Scotland under the protection of Edward I of England.

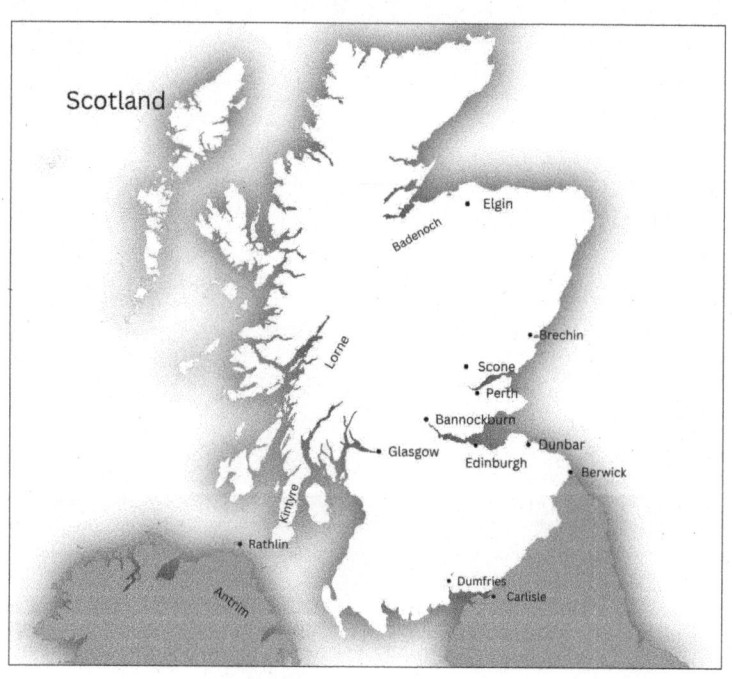

Robert the Bruce

10 July 1296 – Brechin, Angus, Scotland

'Say the words, man. Tell me what I've come to hear. I'm in no mood to let this nonsense continue.' The English king's voice was as cold and merciless as the great sword laid out on the table before him.

The figure standing on the far side of the table cleared his throat and leant forward to lay his hand on the sword's blade, his head bowed. 'I, John Balliol, King of Scotland these past three and a half years, hereby abdicate my throne, and in doing so I offer my fealty to you, Edward, King of England.' He looked up at Edward. 'I recognise that I was wrong to have put my troops into the field against your army at Dunbar and to have led you this far north before submitting to you. However,' he withdrew his hand and straightened his back in a belated act of defiance, 'the atrocities committed on your orders at Berwick were unacceptable and I yield now only because I have no wish for them to be repeated elsewhere in my kingdom.'

'No, Balliol, you are wrong on both counts, as well you know.' King Edward lifted the sword and pointed it aggressively at him across the table. 'You have not ruled Scotland for over a year now. A handful of your associates took that responsibility away from you last summer and immediately set about forming an alliance with France against me. In February your nephew, Comyn, attacked my castle at Carlisle, and in April you made a public renunciation of your allegiance to me, the allegiance that brought you to the throne in the first place. The sacking of Berwick was entirely justified given these acts of rebellion, and you are submitting now not out of choice but because you have lost what little remaining support you had from your nobles.' The bleak menace of the king's recitation grew with every sentence. 'You have nowhere else to hide. Since your coronation I have been Lord Superior over the realm of Scotland, and you are no longer fit to act as its king in my name.' He looked round the hall. 'If anyone here seeks to dispute that, now is your moment to do so.' He turned slowly in a full circle, sweeping the blade in front of him at chest height as his gaze raked across the audience. Nobody spoke.

Edward resumed his position facing Balliol and sheathed the sword at his belt. He maintained his grim expression, although in truth he was pleased with events so far that day. His royal counterpart's abdication had been inevitable once the English army had occupied Scone, the age-old seat of the Scottish monarchy outside Perth. Edward had wanted it to be delivered at Scone in the presence of the Scottish nobles, the real powerbrokers for the country, in order to assert his conquest and maximise their humiliation at a single stroke. But Balliol had been a difficult quarry to hunt down in the chase north from Dunbar, and when Edward's general, John de Warenne, had cornered him at Brechin's castle with a score or more knights in train, the English king had decided to force the abdication there and then. He had ridden through the night from Scone to Brechin and had sent a message ahead instructing de Warenne to have the Scots assembled for his arrival. He was familiar with many of the faces from his visit to Scotland four years previously, when he had presided over the selection of Balliol as king. Most of them would also have witnessed Balliol paying homage to Edward as his overlord shortly after the coronation, so their part in the recent uprising against England was as much an act of treason as Balliol's own breach of fealty. Lessons must be learnt, and the brutality of Berwick had been as important as the formality of this abdication rite.

With all eyes on him, the English king allowed the silence to build as he stared at Balliol. At last, he growled, 'Your submission is accepted.' Then he looked about him again and picked out the owner of the castle in whose dining hall they were gathered. 'Maule, I have been in the saddle for twelve hours. I need food and ale. Get it organised.' He was deliberately abrupt, another tool in forcing his superiority on the Scots, and he ignored the ensuing request by Sir Thomas Maule to his squire to bring the best provisions available from the kitchens. Sir Thomas had been the first to welcome Edward at the castle gate that morning and had been treated with similar contempt then too. Being caught playing host to the fugitive Scottish king had put him in a uniquely exposed position, and he had soon realised that anything short of complete subservience to his English visitor would provoke a swift and violent end.

'While I am waiting,' King Edward pulled a chair out from under the table and sat, offering Balliol no invitation to join him, 'let us be clear on the conditions of your abdication. First, you will be sent south, to be held prisoner in the Tower of London for the rest of your life, and you may consider yourself fortunate that you are keeping your head. Second, my army will garrison all the principal castles across Scotland. Third, every nobleman in the land will swear allegiance to me, on this day next month, and they will do so under the walls of Berwick as a reminder of what happens when an oath to me is breached.' He broke off and glared at the men standing round the wood-panelled walls of the hall beyond Balliol, daring them to defy him. 'That means that all of you here will meet me at Berwick, and I charge you to ensure that my edict also reaches your compatriots. Fourth, all the royal records, the crown jewels and other regalia of office will be removed from Scone and taken to London, in recognition of the fact that I am now your direct king.'

Edward paused again, his eyes swivelling back to his captive across the table. 'And fifth, John Balliol, you will return the dice that I gave you when you were appointed to the throne. They were a token of my patronage, and since you have forfeited that, they are no longer yours to hold.'

Balliol's face, normally the flesh-pink hue of a middle-aged man who had eaten and drunk to excess for decades, was drained of colour, and he swayed on his feet as if about to faint. Then he blinked several times and composed himself. Even he conceded that his brief reign had been a disaster. Ever since the coronation Edward had found ways to undermine him, treating Scotland as a vassal state and raiding its coffers to prop up his own treasury. The final straw had been the demand for military assistance in England's war against France. Having viewed their king's pusillanimity with increasing irritation for three years, the Scottish nobles had been unable to tolerate this assault on their personal wealth. A self-styled 'Council' of twelve ringleaders had effectively snatched the reins of power from Balliol and formed a pact with the French monarch, King Philip, during the course of the previous winter. Naturally, this had enraged the English king and his invasion of Scotland had followed on within just a few weeks. After the loss of Berwick in March, a stand at Dunbar the following month might have saved Balliol, but he had been too faint-hearted to lead his troops into battle. Cowering behind the lines, he had watched as the Scots were soundly defeated. In the three months since then he had been on the run, shedding followers at every step, a laughing stock throughout his kingdom and a danger to those diehards, such as Maule, still prepared to offer him shelter.

Realistically, imprisonment had always been the likely outcome of his agreement to abdicate, but he had hoped that his Norman ancestry and his connections at the English court might have limited his detention to that of house arrest at one of his many properties in England or France. A life sentence at the infamous Tower of London was terrible to contemplate, but perhaps not so terrible, once he had reflected on it, as losing his head to a spike on its battlements. The more urgent concern was the requirement to produce the dice. He knew all too well that they had been a prized possession of the English monarchy for centuries and that Edward's decision to give them to him on his accession to the Scottish throne would not have been taken lightly. To confess that they were now lost was to dice with death – literally, it occurred to him – but there was nothing else to be done.

'Your Majesty, I regret to say that I cannot return the dice, much as I would like to. They have been mislaid.' He waited for the explosion of temper that he had anticipated and was not disappointed.

'You imbecile,' bellowed Edward, slamming both fists onto the table's surface and rearing up out of his chair. He rammed the table to one side and took two steps towards Balliol, in a forcible demonstration of his nickname 'Longshanks'. The tallest person there, the English king towered over Balliol and his posture bristled with rage. 'You lost the confidence of your people; you lost your country in battle; you surrendered your throne. Are you telling me now that you have even managed to lose the symbol of my support for your original appointment? Can't you keep anything safe?'

Balliol quailed at the tirade. 'They were taken from me last summer, Your Majesty, when my nobles took matters of state into their own hands. I'm not sure where they ended up. It is possible that Bishop William Fraser, who was one of the Council, kept them in his capacity as a former Guardian of Scotland before my coronation, but he went to France last winter to negotiate the alliance and is still there.'

'So the dice are now with my enemy, the King of France?' Edward snarled, his temper rising still further.

'I cannot say. It may be that he passed them to another member of the Council before he left.' Balliol risked looking away from the English king to address the others in the room. 'Does anyone here know the whereabouts of the dice? Wishart,' he gestured to a stout figure wearing a crucifix, 'you were a guardian yourself, in years gone by. Do you have any idea?'

The man began to reply, but King Edward cut across him, still staring at Balliol. 'This is not a debating chamber. The return of the dice is a condition of peace. If you are unable to deliver it immediately, there will be consequences.' With nothing more to say, Balliol hung his head in contrition and the king switched his gaze to the clergyman. 'I remember you, Wishart, from the selection process that led this fool to the throne. What do you have to say?'

Robert Wishart, Bishop of Glasgow, stepped forward and bowed low. 'Your Majesty, I was indeed a guardian in the period leading up to the coronation four years ago. You and I met then, and I am honoured to be in your presence again now. But on the subject of the dice, I cannot help. I know Bishop Fraser, of course, but only through church dealings, and I haven't heard from him since his departure for France last year.' A wily veteran of court diplomacy, Wishart did not mention that he had been a member of the Council alongside Fraser, that his role in Scottish government had extended far beyond the church for over a decade and that he knew exactly where the dice were. 'We could send a messenger to Paris to see if the dice can be retrieved—'

'I have no interest in speculation or delay,' Edward interrupted him once again. Turning back to his prisoner, he drew his sword with a dramatic flourish and pressed the tip against Balliol's chest. 'You have failed your country in every way. You have squandered the protection of the English crown and been negligent in the care of its property. I should kill you now, but instead I will take something far more precious to your people than your pathetic life.' He jabbed the sword and Balliol staggered backwards. 'I will take something that represents the history of Scotland in the same way that the dice have traced the history of England. I will take the coronation stone from Scone on which you and countless kings before you were enthroned. And understand this: even if the dice are found, the stone will not be restored to you. Ever.' He gave the sword a final prod for good effect and then lowered it. 'Now get out, all of you. And Maule, bring that food before I burn your castle down.'

Balliol and the Scottish nobles filed out of the hall in silence. Wishart was the last to leave, one hand deep in a pocket, fingers curled round the two ancient dice.

*

10 February 1306 – Dumfries, Scotland

Dark banks of cloud hung over the small town, delivering a persistent drizzle and a constant trickle of water down the street gutters into the River Nith, already dangerously full from a long winter of snow and rain. Two men hurried across the stone bridge straddling the river and climbed the slope to the Greyfriars church looming above them. It was noon, but the light was so poor it could have been early evening. They ducked under the church porch, unclasped their sodden cloaks and pushed open the massive oak door to the interior. The wall lamps were unlit and the thick glass windows on each side of the nave provided little natural illumination. But despite the dimness it was plain to the three nobles awaiting their arrival by the altar that the newcomers were armed with swords and dirks, as they themselves were. The two men advanced up the church's central aisle and the younger of them – tall, heavy-set and wearing a thick reddish-brown beard – was the first to break the tomb-like hush of the building. His voice was brittle with antagonism.

'I have come a long way, Bruce, so I hope you have something worthwhile to tell me.'

Robert Bruce, dark, lean and a head shorter than his visitor, stepped down from the altar plinth. 'We are in a church, Comyn. Let us try to be civil, or is that too much to ask of a man from the north?' Without waiting for a response to his barb, he continued. 'Allow me to introduce my colleagues. This is Roger Kirkpatrick, a neighbouring landowner to me here in Galloway, and then John Lindsay, from Fife. Who do you have with you?'

John Comyn, Lord of Badenoch, nodded sourly to Bruce's attendants and twitched a thumb at his companion. 'My cousin, Sir Robert Comyn. He has travelled with me all the way from Elgin, almost a week on the road, so let's not waste any more time. You called this meeting. What do you want?'

'You know very well what I want, Comyn. But since that is a matter between you and me alone, I suggest we get our friends to wait outside.' Bruce motioned for Kirkpatrick and Lindsay to leave the church, and after several seconds' hesitation, John Comyn jerked his head at his relative to follow suit. The door thudded shut behind them and the men remaining at the altar eyed each other warily.

'We had an agreement,' Bruce stated in a calm tone. 'Having Scotland remain a fiefdom of England and King Edward is intolerable to both of us. Your uncle John Balliol should never have allowed that to happen, and ten years on it is high time we won back our independence. Your bloodline to Balliol prohibits you from being a candidate for the throne, and despite our differences in the past you agreed in November that you would support me when I launch my own bid to be king. In return, I would transfer my lands here in Galloway to you.'

'Correct,' said Comyn, 'so what has changed?'

'What has changed,' Bruce's voice took on a harder edge, 'is that someone has been whispering to King Edward. I was in London before Christmas and received a warning that he was about to arrest me for treason. I rode north immediately and wondered all the way to the border who his informant might be. A few enquiries told me what I already suspected. That whisper could only have come from you.'

'Rubbish.' Comyn glanced up at the south-facing window, and then to its counterpart across the aisle, as though searching for deliverance from a preposterous challenge. 'That is an accusation as vile as your weather here in the south-west. You said it yourself, we both wish to be rid of Edward. Why would I consort with him, to the detriment of our country?'

'Because you still crave the throne for yourself. Admit it, Comyn, you want it so badly you are prepared to trade with King Edward, just as your uncle Balliol did in his pitch for the crown fifteen years ago. Scotland would be no more independent under you than it was under him.'

'How dare you?' Comyn snapped at Bruce. 'I have been fighting the English ever since the Battle of Dunbar. I was imprisoned in the Tower of London for a while alongside Balliol; I fought alongside William Wallace for seven years; and, unlike you, I had no hand in his betrayal last summer. How dare you argue I am beholden to Edward?'

'I had no part in Wallace's capture and execution,' Bruce replied, his voice rising. 'We can trade charges all afternoon, but I know where the treachery lies. So answer me this. One simple question. You promised me your backing in my claim to the throne. Does that still stand?'

'The Bruces were considered second best when Balliol was chosen as king. Through him the Comyns have a closer connection to the Scottish royal line than your family, and we command a stronger following amongst the nobles than the Bruces ever will. I have had time to think more clearly since November, and I do not regard you as a credible leader for our country.'

'So you are going against your word and taking the English king's money? And that makes you a more credible choice? What was it worth, Comyn? How much does the throne of Scotland cost?'

'Damn you, Bruce,' Comyn thundered. 'I've always loathed you, and I would rather support the claim of a pox-ridden beggar than have you crowned King of Scotland.' His fingers bunched into fists, and he shifted his weight onto his front foot as if to punch his rival in the face.

'You filthy traitor,' Bruce shouted, stepping back and drawing his sword in warning. Oblivious to the threat, Comyn swung an arm at him and Bruce reacted instinctively, raising the sword and hacking down at his adversary's shoulder. Twisting sideways on bone, the blade cut deep into Comyn's neck, and he sank to his knees, clutching helplessly at the wound. Blood sprayed across the flagstones below the church's altar, and Robert Bruce threw his weapon down, aghast at the unintended assault. Even in the semi-darkness he could see that the injury was probably fatal, and his fury evaporated as the consequences of his actions rushed in on him. The killing of a powerful fellow noble was bad enough, but in a sacred place to which he was known to have purposely invited the victim? Whatever the provocation, it would smack of premeditated murder to all but his most faithful friends, and an abomination in the eyes of God.

His mind recoiling at the enormity of the crime, he watched vacantly as Comyn slumped forward onto the ground. But after a few moments the sight of his enemy lying prostrate in a widening pool of his own blood brought the way forward into sharp focus. The deed was done, unintentional though it was, his decision to seize the throne had already been taken, and the one serious contender was gone. There was nothing to be gained by wavering now on his chosen path. He would have himself crowned, but first he required absolution from the church for the killing, and he knew a man he could rely on for that. Robert Wishart had sponsored Bruce's grandfather in his failed attempt versus John Balliol to become king and remained an ardent champion of the Bruce family. More to the point, Wishart still held the bishopric of Glasgow after all these years, a burgh less than two days' ride away. There was no time to lose, and Bruce reached down to retrieve his sword before striding out of the church into the incessant drizzle beyond.

Six weeks later, Wishart stood to one side as his accomplice, William de Lamberton, Bishop of St Andrews, gently settled the makeshift crown on Robert Bruce's head. With the Scottish regalia still in the hands of King Edward of England, the two bishops had commissioned a replacement gold circlet from a local craftsman in time for the hastily arranged ceremony at Scone. It was rudimentary but sufficient to mark the occasion in the absence of the royal jewels and the great coronation stone.

'Rise, Your Majesty,' said de Lamberton, and Bruce climbed from his knees to the applause of the onlookers. There were only some fifty gathered, given the limited time available to rally them since Bruce had declared himself king, but it was enough to celebrate the event and confirm the bulk of the senior nobles' support for him across Scotland. Needless to say, there was no sign of any Comyns from the north in Scone's throne room, nor of their powerful kinsmen, the MacDougalls of Lorne in the west.

As the clapping and cheering abated, Wishart moved forward to address the new monarch, right hand outstretched to be shaken, the other hidden from view. 'Congratulations, Your Majesty. It feels odd to be witnessing this ancient ritual without you being seated on the great stone. However, if anyone can restore the stone to us, it will be you. It is good to see the throne back in the hands of someone who genuinely believes in the independence of our fine country.'

'Thank you, Wishart,' replied Bruce, breaking the handshake. 'Your role in bringing me here has been critical, not merely in terms of organisation, but also in your remission of my sins last month. As you will remember, I swore on the lives of my children that John Comyn's death was an accident, and when I sought our Lord's forgiveness at your cathedral, I meant every word I said.'

'I believed you,' Wishart nodded, 'and when I said I would do everything in my power to assist you, I also meant it. Which means the time has come to give you another item, along with the crown, to salute your accession to the throne. I daresay you have heard of the dice that Edward of England gave to Balliol on his coronation, and the fact that Balliol thought them lost when he abdicated.'

It was Bruce's turn to nod in affirmation. 'I've heard the story, yes. What of it?'

Wishart brought his left hand from behind him and held it, open, in front of the king. The two dice nestled in the crease of his palm, cracked and chipped from centuries of use, unlikely emblems of royalty compared to the more usual gold, silver and precious stones. 'They were never lost. I hid them, away from Scone and unbeknown to Balliol, when the Council of nobles took control of the country before he abdicated, and I have been safeguarding them for the last ten years, waiting for the person who can win back Scotland from the English. You are that man. Take them, and treasure them, as much as you do your crown.'

Robert Bruce picked the dice out of Wishart's hand. 'I certainly will,' he replied solemnly as he began to inspect them. They were as old and worn as his crudely fashioned crown was new and burnished, and yet curiously beautiful in the fragile antiquity of their appearance. 'Today is simply the beginning,' he said, still staring at the little ivory cubes, 'there is much work to be done if we are to assert ourselves against King Edward and the Comyn clan, and no doubt many bumps in the road to full independence. These will be my guiding light and will accompany me wherever I go. Thank you again.' He tucked the dice into a pocket and his face broke into a broad smile as he looked up at the bishop. 'Now, there's no point being king if I can't have a drink to rejoice in it. Come on, Wishart, stop being so serious and find me some of your best wine.'

*

1 January 1307 – Isle of Rathlin, Northern Ireland

James Douglas climbed nimbly over the rocks to the mouth of the cave, his stocky frame silhouetted against the iron-grey sky above. He flung the armful of driftwood he was carrying down beside a bundle of smaller sticks that he had collected earlier and brushed wet sand from his tunic. Then he knelt by the two wood piles and rearranged them into a single stack, placing the thinnest twigs at the bottom and spreading the bigger stems in a series of latticed layers above. Once he was happy with the structure, he sat back on his heels and extracted a tinderbox from an inside breast pocket. He removed a fire steel, a flint and a fold of charcloth and set them down carefully on a flat rock next to him, his body shielding the flimsy scrap of material from the crisp breeze blowing in off the sea. From another pocket he took out an assortment of wind-dried feathers and leaves that he had found caught in the split trunk of a tree on the cliffs above the cave. Leaning forward again he poked them into the base of the miniature bonfire and then began to strike the steel across the sharp edge of the flint, waiting for a spark to fall onto the charcloth. As he worked, he was conscious of being observed from within the cave, but he ignored the scrutiny and continued his efforts to generate a flame. Creating fire outdoors was a painstaking process, especially in midwinter on a rain-lashed coastline, and he could not afford to waste his diminishing supply of resources. He had no way of knowing how much longer they would be required to camp on this miserable pimple of an island.

At length, the centre of the charcloth ignited. Holding a corner, he flicked the burning fabric in amongst the feather and leaf tinder and watched as the fire curled its way into the twigs and on up to the larger sticks above. Once it was firmly established, he adjusted the angle of his body to allow the breeze to fan the flames and then crouched on his haunches to warm his hands in the smoke billowing upwards, enjoying its soft heat and pungent saline aroma. He estimated it would take ten or fifteen minutes before he could begin cooking, and there was no rush to prepare the food. Snared rabbit was quick to skin for roasting, and he had long since stopped bothering to wash the oats before boiling up the daily pot of porridge. After ten days living in the cave, royal privilege was a distant memory.

As he gazed into the flames, the young man's thoughts turned to the nine-month journey that had brought him to this wretched state. Immediately on learning of the coronation, he had ridden to Scone to enlist in the fledgling army assembling under the new king's banner. The need for that army had soon become apparent, as the news of King Edward's forces marching towards the border rolled northwards ahead of them. After the desecration of Berwick ten years earlier, the Scots were under no illusions as to Edward's intentions. By seizing the throne Bruce had triggered another invasion, and no amount of diplomacy would appease the old English king. The sovereignty of Scotland would once again be settled on the battlefield. It was just a matter of where and how.

King Robert, as Douglas now struggled to refer to him, had shown remarkable leadership in rallying the nobles to his cause, not least in the face of the gossip surrounding John Comyn's death. In years gone by Bruce's support for the country's independence had been questioned by many, and his dislike of Comyn had been widely recognised. The allegation of acting for personal gain had been difficult to dispel and the double crime of sacrilegious murder impossible to ignore. But the backing of the influential churchmen Wishart and de Lamberton had been helpful and the confiscation of his estates by King Edward had been enough to win round those continuing to doubt his commitment. The ranks of the army had swelled rapidly, notable exceptions being the Comyns from Badenoch and their MacDougall of Lorne kinsmen.

And then the reality of war had set in. Douglas's memory of the early summer was one of continuous fight and flight, a succession of minor engagements seeking and failing to halt the English advance on Scone. The last of these losses had been the rout at Methven, outside Perth, two days before the June solstice, when a squadron of English cavalry had surprised the Scots in their camp and scattered them to the four winds. The king had fled into the Perthshire hills with a handful of aides, only to be met by a group of Comyn sympathisers in an ambush from which he and Douglas were lucky to escape unscathed. The two men had continued their retreat westwards, living off the land as they picked their way through hostile MacDougall territory to the Argyll coast. By October they had found refuge with a Douglas cousin on the Mull of Kintyre, but in early December seeping rumours of their location had obliged them to move on again. A long-standing friend of the Bruce family, Hugh Bissett of Antrim, had organised a boat to ferry them the short distance across the open sea to the Irish coast, where he had welcomed them to his castle on Rathlin Island.

Their arrival on the tiny islet had been greeted with the news that Bruce was now officially outlawed, that his wife, sisters and daughter had all been captured and imprisoned in England and that his brother Neil and numerous close associates had been hanged on King Edward's orders. Bruce's mood, already dark with defeat, had declined still further as he contemplated the ruin he had brought to his family and supporters, and Bissett's announcement a week later that a MacDougall patrol was coming to the island had been the final straw. The two fugitives had been dispatched with little more than a bag of oats, some snares and a cooking pot to hide in a cave on the shoreline until the patrol departed. Here the king's depression had taken full hold. Devoid of all energy and inspiration, he had lapsed into brooding melancholy, barely speaking and relying wholly on his twenty-year-old attendant to make the best of their pitiful situation. His sole distraction seemed to be a pair of dice, and he would toy with them for hours on his own, though to what purpose Douglas could not imagine. More than a week on, the young man had still not devised a way to raise his king's spirits, and he was beginning to despair of the future for them both.

A strip of dry lichen blazed briefly as the flames spread into the upper logs of the bonfire, catching Douglas's eye and breaking his train of thought. He was in danger of descending into Bruce's pit of despondency, he realised, when he should be celebrating a rare dry day, not to mention the dawn of the new year. Perhaps 1307 would bring a reversal of fortune after the disasters of 1306. Anyway, it was time to skin the rabbit he had trapped the previous evening, and he stood to retrieve it from the cave's entrance where it hung, lifeless, from a jagged spur of the rock wall below the ceiling. He untied the wire knotted around its back legs, and in doing so his attention was drawn along the wall to a spider scuttling across a fissure in the rock, spinning a fine, silken filament out behind it. A hand's breadth beyond the crevice it stopped, evidently intent on fixing the gossamer to another snag in order to create the first loop of a web across the wall. Suddenly it slipped, and dangled from its starting point, before scrabbling up the delicate thread and resuming its journey. Douglas watched, mesmerised by the effort and agility, as it spun and slipped and climbed five more times, never once indicating frustration or fatigue.

'What are you looking at?' a sullen voice called out from the cave's recess, and Douglas turned towards the noise. 'A spider, Your Majesty,' he answered, 'come and see. It's building its web. It's really struggling but it never gives up.' He heard Bruce lurch to his feet with a sigh and clamber over the rock-scattered floor to join him. The spider ignored them, setting off yet again across the fissure to fix the strand. 'Look, it's on its seventh attempt.'

The two men watched in silence as the arachnid marched along the rock wall, its eight spindly legs carrying it over the rough surface at impressive speed. This time, its destination was different, a blunt spike slightly above its previous target. Apparently satisfied, it began the return trip, and they both found themselves holding their breath. The first loop remained in place and the web's tissue now extended in the opposite direction, until at last a second strand was safely harnessed across the section of wall. They exhaled in unison, and a smile lit up the king's features for the first time in weeks.

'Six failures, you say?'

'Yes,' replied Douglas, also grinning at the strange little episode they had witnessed. 'Incredible. Nature's lesson in stubborn determination to us humans. And on the first day of the new year, too.'

'Today is New Year's Day?' The king sounded bewildered. 'I had lost track of time.'

'Good riddance to 1306. December is behind us, and soon the days will be getting longer and the weather warmer. The MacDougall patrol must surely leave Bissett's castle soon, and then we can plot our return to Argyll.' Douglas injected all the enthusiasm he could muster into his words, in the hope that Bruce's change of mood might be sustained.

'Six failures,' the king repeated, 'the same as us last summer on the battlefields against Edward's army. But faith and perseverance brought our wee friend here success at the seventh time of asking.' He walked out of the cave mouth and stared over the sea below them. Then he spoke again, his voice husky with excitement. 'You said it is a lesson to humans. But it's more personal than that, Jamie. It's a sign, to you and me. Think about it. We lost six times, but if we have faith and keep trying, we *will* beat the English the next time we confront them. The seventh attempt, in the new century's seventh year.

And if you don't believe me, look at this.' He led Douglas back to where he had been sitting in the shadows of the cave and gestured to a smooth rock embedded in the sand. The two dice lay at rest there and Douglas peered down to read their faces: six and one, making seven. Robert Bruce snatched them up into a fist and shook it vigorously at his companion. 'It's the sign I've been waiting for. Scotland's tide is about to turn. Trust me, Jamie, just trust me.'

*

And then...

+ Robert Bruce returns to the Scottish mainland in early 1307 to launch a skirmishing campaign against the occupying English army and his rivals amongst the local nobility (principally the Comyn and MacDougall clans). His strategy is immediately successful and gathers pace steadily over the next few years so that by 1314 he controls the whole country, prompting another invasion by the English. Their army is soundly defeated at the Battle of Bannockburn, near Stirling.

+ Despite the victory, Scotland remains formally subservient to the English crown, and in 1320 Bruce gifts the dice to one of his leading nobles, Sir Andrew Leslie, for his part in submitting the *Declaration of Arbroath* to Pope John XXII in Rome. The *Declaration* asserts Scotland's status as an independent nation, which the Pope duly acknowledges.

+ On Sir Andrew Leslie's death, the dice pass to his son Sir Norman, also an advisor to the Scottish monarchy. After Robert Bruce's successor, King David II, has entered into a fresh war with England and been held captive for several years, Leslie finally negotiates his release in 1357, on terms that include giving the dice to the English king, Edward III.

+ Over the next 150 years the dice pass down the line of English kings once more, falling ultimately into the hands of Henry VIII.

*

Author's Note

The genesis of the long-running conflict between England and Scotland in the late thirteenth/early fourteenth century, or the First War of Scottish Independence as it came to be known, was the death of Scotland's king Alexander III in 1286. When his sole heir, a young granddaughter, died four years later, there were a number of claimants to the vacant throne, so the royal guardians invited the English king Edward I to adjudicate in the selection process for a successor. John Balliol was chosen in 1292, ahead of Robert Bruce's grandfather, the other principal candidate, and Edward took the opportunity to appoint himself Lord Superior, effectively subordinating the Scottish crown to English rule. Over the next three years Edward steadily increased the assertion of his authority, eventually inducing a 'Council' of Scottish nobles to confiscate the reins of government from Balliol, who then renounced his allegiance to the English king. Edward's reaction was swift – in March 1296 he invaded Scotland, sacking the town of Berwick with extreme brutality as he crossed the border and winning an easy victory the following month at the Battle of Dunbar. From there the base storyline of Balliol's abdication, the removal of the ancient coronation stone from Scone and the role of Bishop Robert Wishart in the country's political affairs is historically accurate.

Likewise, the emergence ten years later of John Comyn and Robert Bruce as contenders for the restoration of the Scottish monarchy, Comyn's murder, Bruce's absolution from Wishart and his hasty coronation are all true. It was well known that Comyn and Bruce disliked each other intensely, but precisely why Bruce called the meeting in the Dumfries church and whether the murder was premeditated, is unclear. His family had tended to align themselves with the English king in years gone by, and he may have played an early part in the manhunt for William Wallace, Scotland's brief patriotic saviour until his capture and execution in 1305. But shortly after this Bruce appears to have had a change of heart. His attempt to wrest command of Scotland back from Edward on becoming king was initially disastrous, and in killing Comyn he had made dangerous enemies of the Comyns of Buchan and John MacDougall of Lorne, powerful kinsmen of the dead man. However, as set out in the 'And then' section, he recovered from the defeats of 1306 to win full control of the country over the next few years, culminating in 1314's victory at Bannockburn. Formal recognition of Scotland's independence was provided first by the Pope in 1324, in response to the Declaration of Arbroath, *and then by Edward I's son, Edward II, at the* Treaty of Edinburgh–Northampton *in 1328.*

The presence of the numerous supporting characters in this chapter is generally correct, the imposters being the dice and the spider. Where Bruce spent the winter of 1306/07 is uncertain, the islands of Rathlin, Arran and the Hebrides all having been touted as possibilities. The familiar story of the spider is almost definitely fictitious and was first told in relation to James Douglas. A further five centuries passed before it was attributed to Bruce, by Sir Walter Scott in his Tales of a Grandfather *written in 1828. Nonetheless, with or without inspiration from a spider, that winter was indeed the turning point in Bruce's fortunes. He died at the age of fifty-four in 1329, a national hero, and it was only after his death that he was entitled Robert 'the' Bruce, referring to the old Norman family name of 'de Brus'. Scone's coronation stone (known as the Stone of Destiny) was finally repatriated to Scotland in 1996, after precisely seven hundred years in London's Westminster Abbey.*

King Henry VIII

From the King to Lord Chancellor & Cardinal Thomas Wolsey
1 January 1527 – Greenwich Palace

Cardinal Thomas,

With the dawn of the new year, I have come to a decision. Though it pains me to address the matter, it must be done. My Queen Katherine has fought a valiant battle in her bid to provide me with a son and heir but, now in her forty-second year, she is surely beyond child-bearing age. I dare not entrust England's throne to our daughter Mary – the barons chose civil war over a queen in defiance of my namesake King Henry's legacy four centuries since. Yet any son from another must be legitimate, therefore must I have a new (and fecund) wife. Before which, I will divorce Katherine and send her back to her countryfolk of Aragon. When I come to Hampton Court next week, we shall discuss this further. Until then,

H. Rex

*

From the King to Anne Boleyn*
25 May 1527 – Greenwich Palace

My Dearest,

In turning over in my mind the contents of your last letters, I have put myself into great agony, not knowing how to interpret them, whether to my disadvantage, as you show in some places, or to my advantage, as I understand them in some others, beseeching you earnestly to let me know expressly your whole mind as to the love between us two.

It is absolutely necessary for me to obtain this answer, having been for above a whole year stricken with the dart of love, and not yet sure whether I shall fail of finding a place in your heart and affection, which last point has prevented me for some time past from calling you my mistress; because, if you love me with an ordinary love, that name is not suitable for you, because it denotes a singular love, which is far from common. But if you please to do the office of a true loyal mistress and friend, and to give up yourself body and heart to me, who will be, and have been, your most loyal servant (if your rigour does not forbid me) I promise you that not only the name shall be given you, but also that I will take you for my only mistress, casting off all others besides you out of my thoughts and affections, and serve you only. I beseech you to give an entire answer to this my rude letter, that I may know on what and how far I may depend. And if it does not please you to answer me in writing, appoint some place where I may have it by word of mouth, and I will go thither with all my heart. No more, for fear of tiring you.

Written by the hand of him who would willingly remain yours, H.R.

*

From the King to Queen Katherine
17 June 1527 – Windsor Castle

Katherine,

I need not tell you that our marriage has suffered in recent years, my court and state affairs taking me away from Greenwich Palace while you have devoted yourself increasingly to God's great work. In this I honour you, but I cannot continue to inhabit a spiritual structure that is no longer pertinent to the future of England. With sadness in my heart, I must therefore have a divorce, from which to protect the patrimony of my throne. Shortly, I shall seek papal approval from Rome to this end. Understand that this in no way denies the love and respect in which I have held you, My Queen, over these last eighteen years, nor the rigours you have undergone in bearing and losing five children, being left only with young Mary. I return to Greenwich on midsummer's day, whereon we shall speak more of this.

H. Rex

*

From the King to Anne Boleyn*
10 July 1527 – Greenwich Palace

My mistress and friend: my heart and I surrender ourselves into your hands, beseeching you to hold us commended to your favour, and that by absence your affection to us may not be lessened: for it were a great pity to increase our pain, of which absence produces enough and more than I could ever have thought could be felt, reminding us of a point in astronomy which is this: the longer the days are, the more distant is the sun, and nevertheless the hotter; so it is with our love, for by absence we are kept a distance from one another, and yet it retains its fervour, at least on my side; I hope the like on yours, assuring you that on my part the pain of absence is already too great for me; and when I think of the increase of that which I am forced to suffer, it would be almost intolerable, but for the firm hope I have of your unchangeable affection for me: and to remind you of this sometimes, and seeing that I cannot be personally present with you, I now send you the nearest thing I can to that, namely, my picture set in a bracelet, with the whole of the device, which you already know, wishing myself in their place, if it should please you.

This is from the hand of your loyal servant and friend, H.R.

*

From Anne Boleyn to the King
26 August 1527 – Hever Castle, Kent

My Lord,

I can scarce believe the treasures you are bestowing on me. Even as I write I wear the bracelet you sent last month, while further gifts have since arrived by the day. The ruby pendant hangs neat below my throat, and the diamond love-knot brooch is pinned to my breast. But closest to my heart is the knowledge of our secret. Why then is my betrothed so far from me? When may we shout our love to the heavens and beyond? When shall we marry? Come soon, and soothe my yearning soul.

Your humble servant and ardent love, A.B.

*

From the King to Pope Clement VII
19 September 1527 – Greenwich Palace

Your Holiness,

Our secretary, William Knight, who presents this letter in humble observance of your heavenly excellence, is able to furnish you with additional documents supporting our royal petition. But, in short, we write seeking your good offices in the annulment of our marriage to Queen Katherine, late of Aragon and soon to return to that place. Many years ere now she was wed to our brother Prince Arthur, who died of the sweating sickness soon thereafter. Seven years on, Katherine, as Dowager Princess, contrived to enter into a second marriage with her brother-in-law, ourself the King of England. It has come to our attention that, under canon law, such a union is prohibited, in which consequence the marriage cannot be considered valid. Annulment is therefore both legally requisite and morally appropriate. We know we may rely on Your Eminence's signature to the deed and await your response with all gratitude.

This written by the hand of a loyal supplicant within the firmament of God's great Church,

Henry Rex

*

From Queen Katherine to Pope Clement VII
2 October 1527 – Greenwich Palace

Your Holiness,

You will by now, I warrant, have received an application from my husband, King Henry of England, requesting the termination of our marriage. He argues that it was never valid, which I dispute on terms that cause me some embarrassment yet must out. He states, I understand, that because I was prior married to his brother Arthur, who died after only five months, a subsequent union with Henry as Arthur's widow was a breach of Church law and so never took formal effect – hence, he claims, it should now be annulled. Yet in truth I write to advise that, given our young age and poor grasp of nature's ways (I was not yet sixteen and he younger still), the marriage was not consummated on the few occasions I lay with Arthur before his illness struck. It follows that my marriage to Henry was my first, and its validity, therefore, not in doubt. I trust you will find in my favour and sustain the union into which the king and I entered in good faith so many years ago.

I describe this delicate matter in semblance of confession, Holy Father, not to be spread abroad to laymen's ears. Only my nephew, Archduke of Austria and Emperor Elect Charles V, may know of it, in the event that Henry seeks his support in bringing the argument to you. I am told Charles is currently to be found in Rome, and I ask you to send him my good wishes as loving aunt and proud princess of Aragon.

In God's grace, your humble servant, Katherine, Queen of England

*

From the King to Lord Chancellor & Cardinal Thomas Wolsey
13 January 1528 – Greenwich Palace

Cardinal Thomas,

My envoy Knight is returned today from Rome, with no success in his quest for my divorce. In its war against France, he reports, Emperor Elect Charles V's army has sacked Rome and holds Pope Clement prisoner. Knight was barred from presenting my case in person, and worse, it is rumoured that the emperor, Queen Katherine's nephew, refuses to condone the proposal to annul. His Holiness dare not incur the emperor's displeasure in taking a different path.

This *cannot* stand. The Bible states (Leviticus 20, verse 21): 'If a man shall take his brother's wife, it is an unclean thing: he hath uncovered his brother's nakedness; they shall be childless.' My marriage is invalid, and the Lord's punishment has been to withhold the creation therein of a male heir. You are a cardinal to Rome, Thomas; it therefore falls to you to find a solution. Petition the Pope once again, and be sure you do not fail. I mean to marry Anne Boleyn; we are betrothed, and I will not be frustrated in my desire.

H.R.

*

From the King to Lord Chancellor & Cardinal Thomas Wolsey
21 July 1528 – Greenwich Palace
Cardinal Thomas,

Five months have passed since your petition to Pope

Clement. When'er we speak of it, you tell me the business
is in course, yet I see no result. Tell me now, straight out,
what you have achieved, and when I may be rid of Queen
Katherine. My patience is stretched thin. I must know.
H.R.

*

From Lord Chancellor & Cardinal Thomas Wolsey to the King
22 July 1528 – Hampton Court

Your Majesty,

In reply to your missive of yesterday, you will recall
my news last month that His Holiness has instructed
my fellow cardinal, Campeggio, to come to England
and hold a papal court to settle the question of the
annulment. He has yet to leave Rome, but I am assured
that his departure is imminent. Once we learn of his
arrival on our shores, preparations for the court hearing
will commence directly. You have my undertaking that
all haste is being made to expedite the process.

Your obedient minister and servant in all things,
Thomas Wolsey

*

From the King to Anne Boleyn*
3 August 1528 – Greenwich Palace

Mine own sweetheart, this shall be to advertise you of
the great loneliness that I find here since your departing;
for I ensure you methinketh the time longer since your
departing now last, than I was wont to do a whole

fortnight: I think your kindness and my fervencies of love causeth it; for otherwise I would not have thought it possible that for so little a while it should have grieved me. But now that I am coming towards you, methinketh my pains be half removed... Wishing myself (especially an evening) in my sweetheart's arms, whose pretty dukkys I trust shortly to kiss.

Written by the hand of him that was, is, and shall be yours by his own will, H.R.

*

From Anne Boleyn to the King
8 September 1528 – Hever Castle, Kent

My Love,

What tidings from Rome? Forgive me, but I long to be married, and the months slip away unnoticed by all but me and you, my precious paramour. Is the cardinal on his way? Surely by now? When might we see an end to this trial? Would that the strength of my ardour were matched by the urgency of His Eminence. Pray tell me the answer in writing, at once, if I cannot have it (and more) from your lips themselves.

Your betrothed, A.B.

*

From the King to Anne Boleyn*
16 September 1528 – Windsor Castle

Darling One,

The reasonable request of your last letter, with the

pleasure also that I take to know them true, causeth me to send you these news. The legate which we most desire arrived at Paris on Sunday or Monday last past, so that I trust by the next Monday to hear of his arrival at Calais; and then I trust within a while after to enjoy that which I have so long longed for, to God's pleasure and our both comforts.

No more to you at this present, mine own darling, for lack of time, but that I would you were in mine arms, or I in yours, for I think it long since I kissed you.

Written after the killing of a hart, at eleven of the clock, minding, with God's grace, tomorrow, mightily timely, to kill another, by the hand which, I trust, shortly shall be yours.

Henry R.

*

From the King to Lord Chancellor & Cardinal Thomas Wolsey
17 December 1528 – Greenwich Palace

Cardinal Thomas,

Once again, we seem mired in a bog of obstruction. Cardinal Campeggio has been in England since mid-October and still I hear nothing of any court hearing. How so? A full year is lost since my secretary Knight's retreat from Rome. The queen's case that her marriage to my brother was never consummated is now common knowledge, and I hear it said that she shares many letters with her nephew, the emperor elect Charles V. He is no friend, such that he will begin to poison Pope Clement's mind against me if the petition for divorce continues to run. As Lord Chancellor you surely have the power to make Campeggio proceed immediately. Let it be done, without further notice, else I will hold you personally responsible.

H.R.

*

From Lord Chancellor & Cardinal Thomas Wolsey to the King
18 December 1528 – Hampton Court

Your Majesty,

You rightly question the cardinal's actions, or lack thereof, as do I on your behalf. But I fear we must tread carefully. Only the Pope Clement can grant the annulment you seek, and since Campeggio's hearing represents the papal court over which Pope Clement presides, even the Lord Chancellor of England is at his pleasure. We cannot force the issue, much though I would wish to do it for you. Regarding the emperor elect, a treaty between his empire, France and the papal territories is considered close, and favourable to Your Majesty's interests beyond these shores. I will continue to press on both subjects, of course, and remain,

Your obedient minister and servant, Thomas Wolsey

*

From Lord Chancellor & Cardinal Thomas Wolsey to the King
24 May 1529

Good news at last, Your Majesty. Pray excuse this scribbled note, but I am come just now from Cardinal

Campeggio, who advises that the court hearing will begin one week hence. Other news too, perhaps explaining the age-long delay in reaching this moment. Since Pope Clement's predecessor Pope Julius granted formal approval to your union with the queen at the time you were wed, any agreement now to an annulment would require the original approval to be struck out. My sources in Rome tell me that Pope Clement has been reluctant to address this. That the hearing will now proceed suggests he has overcome his concerns. In haste, as I travel back to Hampton Court.

Your humble servant, as ever, Thomas Wolsey

*

From the King to Sir Thomas More
26 October 1529 – Greenwich Palace

Sir Thomas,

I am pleased to confirm your appointment as Lord Chancellor in place of Cardinal Wolsey. As you heard last week, Wolsey's negotiations with France's king and emperor elect Charles V have come to nothing, and the parties' Treaty of Cambrai has disadvantaged our country severely. My dissatisfaction at the outcome is exceeded only by Wolsey's further failure to obtain the Pope's annulment to my marriage with Queen Katherine during the summer. Cardinal Campeggio's court hearing delivered no firm conclusion on the matter, whose pursuit remains of the utmost import to me. This shall be your primary duty going forward. Come down the river to Greenwich tomorrow and we shall decide how best for you to proceed. I will have

Rome change its mind, and a new queen, whatever steps need taken to achieve it.

Henry Rex

*

From Anne Boleyn to the King*
9 December 1529 – Hever Castle, Kent

My Lord,

Did I not tell you that whenever you disputed with the queen she was sure to have the upper hand? I see that some fine morning you will succumb to her reasoning and that you will cast me off. I have been waiting long and might in the meanwhile have contracted some advantageous marriage, out of which I might have had issue, which is the greatest consolation in this world. But, alas! Farewell to my time and youth spent to no purpose at all.

Anne B.

*

From Queen Katherine to Holy Roman Emperor Charles V
20 March 1530 – Greenwich Palace

My Dear Charles,

News has just reached me of your coronation as Holy Roman Emperor in Bologna last month, at the hand of His Holiness Pope Clement. I write in congratulation, since while I know this crown has been awaiting you for many years now, I believe it has required success across the battlefields of Europe and the treaty table of Cambrai to finally secure it. A worthy result for a great prince of Aragon!

You will doubtless be aware of my husband King Henry's continuing frustration in his quest for the annulment to our marriage. Since Wolsey's failure last year, the cardinal has been ousted from the office of Lord Chancellor and replaced by Sir Thomas More, a man whose wisdom and piety I much admire. Whether he can withstand the king's determination to thwart Pope Clement on the petition, only our God in Heaven can be sure. Meanwhile, Henry's extravagance – always a concern for the ministers of his Exchequer – grows ever bigger on the costs of war, royal building works and personal baubles for his favourites. He is reduced to gambling large sums, usually for the worse. Pray forgive this venting of my spleen, for I speak out of turn as I remain his wife and queen, and also,

Your loving aunt, Katherine Regina

*

From Sir Thomas More to Mister Miles Partridge
6 November 1530 – Chelsea, London

Sir,

I am informed that you are lately become His Majesty's chief companion in the pursuit of hunting and gaming, such that you organise his entertainments and draw from the Exchequer the monies necessary to pay for them. As his principal minister, I must caution you in such activities. There are many demands on the coffers of state, and gambling debts rank low amongst them. Encourage your master towards the hunting field, in which he excels already, rather than the other, for which the dice and cards indicate his talents are ill-fitted. Trusting that I may depend on your discretion in this, I thank you,

Sir Thomas More, Lord Chancellor

*

From Mister Miles Partridge to Sir Thomas More
11 November 1530 – Gray's Inn, London

Dear Sir Thomas,

I write to acknowledge your letter of last Thursday, which awaited my return from Windsor's deer forest. I understand your concerns and you have my word that I shall assist wherever possible, subject always to His Majesty's pleasure.

Your obedient servant, Miles Partridge

*

From the King to Mister Miles Partridge
30 March 1531 – Greenwich Palace

Partridge,

You seem strangely disinclined for the gaming table these past weeks. Where is your appetite, so strong in months gone by? I have just the proposal to tease it out. The four bells of Jesus Chapel in St Paul's Churchyard have lately come into the Crown's possession. There being plenty other bells ringing close by – those of the cathedral and St Mary Bow in Cheapside to name but two – the din is enough to have my four silenced. We will have a wager on them, a game of dice whereby I might win one hundred pounds, or else you take the bells for breaking up, and the belfry's stonework too. A tidy profit for you on their sale, I don't doubt. What do you say? Attend me here at Greenwich and let the dice do their business. I await your arrival.

Henry Rex

*

From Mister Miles Partridge to the King
17 April 1531 – Gray's Inn, London

Your Majesty,

Since my good fortune in our wager, I have made arrangements for the bells and tower of Jesus Chapel to be brought down. However, I lack the formal authority sought by the churchyard warden. May I humbly request your seal to prove my claim? If your mind is changed, then you have only to say it. The dice were uncommonly kind to me that day, and Your Majesty's charity is scarce deserved.

Your most loyal and unworthy subject, Miles Partridge

*

From Sir Thomas More to Queen Katherine
8 May 1531 – Chelsea, London
My Lady,

I trust this finds you well and comfortable in your rooms at Greenwich. How much longer those lodgings can remain yours, I regret I cannot say. The king continues to pursue the annulment with great vigour and is ever more brazen in showing off your rival. I am joined by others, both here and in Rome, in resisting the course he follows, yet I worry that it is soon to take a sharp new turn, the worse both for the country and for you. He speaks openly now of challenging the word of His Holiness Pope Clement, of installing the Lady Boleyn in his palace and removing you to a nunnery. He has confiscated Church properties, selling them to raise money, and his proclivity for gaming exceeds all that has gone before. Only last month he wagered the bells of Jesus Chapel at St Paul's Churchyard for one hundred pounds and lost them to a roll of the dice. The bells are being broken up for sale as I write. I hesitate to bring such tidings but believe you should prepare yourself for a new life beyond the world of throne and court. With my commiseration for the contents of this missive, I remain,

Your most humble servant, Thomas More, Lord Chancellor

*

From Queen Katherine to Holy Roman Emperor Charles V
5 November 1531 – Hatfield Palace

My Dearest Nephew,

Much has changed for me in recent months, some of it perchance known to you already, some likely not. The king, having taken his mistress Boleyn to Greenwich, would have me consigned to a nunnery, which I resisted, hence now quartered here in Hatfield at Cardinal Morton's favour, and soon to move on, I fear. My tribulations are so wearisome, my life so disturbed by the plans daily invented to further the king's wicked intention, that it is enough to shorten ten lives, much more mine. Beyond my own position, he outwits others too, threatening all manner of tyranny on the Church and taking its property for his own. In April he wagered away a precious set of chapel bells in a single dice game; would you believe such a thing? I can only stand steadfast in my conviction that I remain his wife and queen till death do us part. For your share, I ask simply that you continue your support for my suit in Rome, with my heartfelt thanks and love,

Katherine Regina

*

From Sir Thomas More to Queen Katherine
16 May 1532 – Chelsea, London

My Lady,

Some news which I would want you to hear from my pen before that of another. I have today stepped down from my role as Lord Chancellor on the grounds of ill-health. That, at least, is my reason given to His Majesty. For your eyes only, however, I can report my true purpose. The king will not be diverted from his determination to reject Rome's papal authority and to establish instead a Church of England whereof he shall be the Supreme Head. In doing so he will achieve his original goal, the annulment of your marriage and the liberty to marry Mistress Boleyn. I cannot countenance any of it, and thus I take my leave of office. In doing so, my allegiance to you, My Queen, burns bright as always,

Your loyal servant, Thomas More

*

From Sir Thomas More to Queen Katherine
14 February 1533 – Chelsea, London

My Lady,

It is with a dark heart that I write to share the news at court this week. The king is married and, more than that, or perhaps the cause of it, Mistress Boleyn (I cannot call her queen to you) is with child. His Majesty will have Archbishop Cranmer of Canterbury declare your marriage annulled and that of your successor validated. Would that I might find a means to halt this, but my standing is much diminished. You have my word, however, that I will do nothing to support it.

Your servant, as ever, Thomas More

*

From the King to Sir Thomas More
3 June 1533 – Palace of Whitehall

Sir Thomas,

You should know I am mightily vexed at your absence from my queen's coronation two days past. Archbishop Cranmer's declarations last month were clear to all who heard them: my previous union is rubbed out and my marriage to Anne confirmed. It was right and proper that she be crowned queen consort and that my subjects salute her. In keeping your distance, and your silence, there in Chelsea, you have snubbed her and, in doing so, affronted your king. I would have

expected better from a sometime advisor and friend.
   Henry Rex

*

From Sir Thomas More to Queen Katherine
10 April 1534 – Chelsea, London

My Lady,
   Further dire news on your situation, I regret to report, and also now mine. You know, of course, of the child born to Mistress Boleyn and the king last September – Princess Elizabeth. In consequence of this and his eagerness to formalise the split from Rome, the king seeks to push two bills through Parliament. The first will be an Act of Supremacy, creating the imposter Church of England and his position at its head, thereby legalising his marriage to Boleyn. The second is to be an Act of Succession, declaring your daughter Mary illegitimate (and so unable to ascend the throne) and entitling Boleyn's issue (Elizabeth, in the absence of a brother) to rule after him.
   I have made clear to the king my refusal to support the Acts, and I fear I shall be arrested and hanged because of it. No matter – you remain the queen and Princess Mary the rightful successor – and I shall take those truths to the grave if God so desires. As a small token of my estimation for you in such difficult circumstances, I enclose this ancient pair of dice. You will remember me telling, three years past, of the king losing the Jesus bells in a wager. These are the dice used, but more so, they are part of the monarchy's regalia of office. I took them from His Majesty's desk at Greenwich, shortly after the bells'

loss, so agitated was I at the sacrilege and considering that the king had forfeited the licence to hold them. Now, in my looming straits, it is time that they pass to you, ready for the day that Mary might yet follow you as queen.

Your constant servant, Thomas More

*

From Queen Katherine to Sir Thomas More
23 May 1534 – Kimbolton Castle, Cambridgeshire

Dear Sir Thomas,

I am come to Kimbolton only this week, your letter of early April being held from me until my arrival here. I am heartily tired of this shuttling between houses, my fifth since being removed from Greenwich, and pray I may be permitted to rest here. But my concerns are nothing in compare to yours, now that I have learnt of your arrest. It is as you foresaw, and I am deeply grateful for the stance you took on my behalf these several years. Be assured that I continue to regard myself wife and queen, and that the dice you sent are thus in good hands. Trusting you are in fine spirits, and knowing that God is with you in your adversity,

Katherine Regina

*

From Queen Katherine to Holy Roman Emperor Charles V
31 December 1535 – Kimbolton Castle, Cambridgeshire

My Dear Nephew,

Events here have moved apace since the last letters

between us noting the birth of Mistress Boleyn's daughter Elizabeth. I have chosen not to trouble you with my woes, and you will know most of it already. King Henry's split from Rome is done, the new Church of England established, and with it the position of Boleyn as his queen and Elizabeth as his successor. My friend and counsellor Sir Thomas More (having the king's ear from being Lord Chancellor in years gone by) defended my cause to the last, but he was executed for treason in July on refusing to recognise the new order, and now I am alone. Worse, I am dying, and as the year closes, I have little time left, I think, to arrange my affairs. Hence I send you these dice, emblems of this land's royal house, that would rightfully come to my daughter Mary on the king's demise. I ask you to hold them on her behalf, as future Queen of England and dutiful subject of Rome's divine office. May she ascend the throne one day, with your patronage and God's grace.

With my love, as I go in peace to our Lord, Katherine Regina

*

From Gerolamo Cardano to Holy Roman Emperor Charles V
15 December 1552 – Pavia, Duchy of Milan, Italy

Your Most Excellent and Imperial Majesty,
My long journey to treat the Bishop of St Andrews in Scotland, following my visit to you in Brussels last summer, is now complete, and I have returned to my hometown to find your gracious letter proposing my appointment as physician to the Imperial Court. I am greatly flattered by your expression of confidence in

my skills and pleased to learn that my treatment of your gout has been successful. It is a curious and very painful affliction, and I pray you suffer no reoccurrence. As to your request, I fear I must decline and trust you will understand my reasoning. I have much work to do at my position as Professor of Medicine here in Pavia's university and also at my private studies in the fields of mathematics and the sciences. You will recall our speculation about the arithmetic behind dicing and cards when we met, and I welcomed your wise observations thereon. I believe there is more substance to the world of Chance than we mortals grasp and will continue my search for enlightenment on this and the many other mysteries of the universe around us. I know I will have your support and have the honour to remain, at all times,

Your Majesty's most humble and obedient servant, Gerolamo Cardano

*

From Holy Roman Emperor Charles V to Gerolamo Cardano
25 July 1554 – Coudenberg Palace, Brussels

My Dear Cardano,

Since our meeting two years ago, and your letter thereafter, I have dwelt on the subjects of your studies and their importance in our quest for knowledge beneath God's celestial vault. During that time, I have also been giving much thought to my own position as emperor of such a broad dominion, and I have arrived at two conclusions. Like the Roman empire before it, mine is too large and diverse to be governed single-handed from here in Brussels, and I am minded to split it between my heirs. I have taken my first step today, in abdicating my responsibility as Duke of Milan in favour of my son Philip. In addressing the future of the Duchy, my contemplations come again to your work there, and this pair of dice enclosed. They belonged to the late King Henry of England and came to me from his spurned consort Katherine, my aunt, in her hope that I might pass them to her daughter Mary, now queen of that country. Such is the confusion of the Tudor monarchy, I no longer believe myself obliged to pursue her wishes. Instead, I give them to you, as an accolade of your ascent to the pinnacle of science over the last decade and as a tool in your continuing endeavours. In praise of our Lord and yet applauding your efforts to better understand the fates, if not master them.

Charles, Emperor

*

And then…

+ Gerolamo Cardano expands his studies of the sciences, mathematics, astrology, astronomy and philosophy, gaining fame throughout Europe while continuing in his role as Professor of Medicine at the universities of Pavia and then Bologna. In 1564 his analysis of risk culminates in the writing of *Liber de Ludo Aleae*, a systematic computation of probability based partly on his long experience gaming at cards and dice.
+ Prior to his death in 1576 he gifts the dice to the University of Padua, from where he had gained his first doctorate (in medicine) at the beginning of his illustrious career.

+ Over the next 170 years the university keeps the dice in its library display cabinet, in celebration of its acclaimed alumnus.

*

Author's Note

The story of Henry VIII's divorce from Katherine of Aragon and marriage to Anne Boleyn in the pursuit of a male heir is well known; perhaps less familiar is the lengthy period over which this was played out and how his quest gradually mutated into the more dramatic objective for which he tends also to be remembered – the country's religious schism with Rome and the creation of an independent Church of England with Henry as its Supreme Head in place of the Pope. Katherine had borne the king six children over seventeen years, only Princess Mary surviving beyond infancy, before he began to look for a new wife. The machinations with the Vatican to obtain an annulment to the marriage, which Henry convinced himself had been contrary to canon law and was therefore cursed not to generate a healthy son (per Leviticus 20:21), ran on for several years before his frustration led him to abandon the authority of the Catholic Church. It was not until late in that process that Anne permitted him to sleep with her, swiftly resulting in a pregnancy (the future Queen Elizabeth), a secret marriage and finally, in mid-1533, Anne's coronation. Katherine refused consistently to acknowledge the annulment, continuing to assert her position as rightful wife and queen through to her death of cancer in January 1536.

The roles in these events played by Thomas Wolsey, Thomas More, Cardinal Campeggio, Pope Clement VII, Queen Katherine's nephew Emperor Charles V and Archbishop of Canterbury Thomas Cranmer are all based on fact. The letters themselves are of course fictitious, with the exception of those from Henry to Anne Boleyn of 1527–1528, and hers to him of December 1529 (each marked with an asterisk). Henry's love letters are part of a collection of seventeen to Anne found in the Vatican, presumed to have been stolen from her during the annulment negotiations. As for the wager between the king and Miles Partridge for the bells of Jesus Chapel at St Paul's Churchyard, this story is considered to be true, although I have brought the likely timing of it forward by several years. Henry was an enthusiastic gambler, in numerous formats including dice, and in describing the episode I have merged the increasing need for money generated by his extravagance with his growing exasperation at the English clergy and his readiness to confiscate its property. In reality, the latter behaviour only began in earnest in 1536, leading ultimately to the dissolution of the monasteries throughout the country.

The final exchange of letters between Gerolamo Cardano and Emperor Charles is fabricated, although the backdrop is largely accurate. Already established as an eminent physician and scientist, Cardano travelled to Scotland to treat the Bishop of St Andrews (for asthma) in 1552 and declined a position around the same time as personal doctor to Charles. Cardano was one of the most influential scholars of the Renaissance, across a broad spectrum of subjects, and a key figure in the foundation of probability theory. An inveterate gambler himself, he was the first person to explore a definition of 'the odds', almost a century before the French mathematicians Blaise Pascal and Pierre de Fermat. His 1564 Book on Games of Chance (Liber de Ludo Aleae) was not published until 1663. Emperor Charles's abdication from the Duchy of Milan in 1554 was the opening step in the split of his empire between his son Philip and his brother Ferdinand, and he retired to a monastery in 1557, crippled by gout, where he died the following year. Cosmopolitan, cultured and pragmatic in the advance of new ideas, despite a strict theological upbringing, it might not have been out of character for him to have corresponded with Cardano and encouraged him in his studies.

Giacomo Casanova

19 April 1746 – Venice

The young man had not intended to look back after stepping across the threshold but, as the heavy metal doors clanged shut behind him, he could not resist one final glance over his shoulder. The mighty walls of the Arsenale cast a long shadow in the early-morning sun, and the cool shelter of their ochre-red brickwork seemed suddenly reassuring compared to the harsh light bathing the wharf ahead. The huge, winged lion sculpted in white stone above the gateway gazed down impassively, while its companion statues guarding each side of the entrance refused to meet his eye. Were they mocking his decision? Surely nobody but an impetuous fool would abandon a promising military career in the illustrious Republic of Venice? *Too late*, he thought, resuming his path towards the wharf; there was more to life than sitting in a barracks waiting to be sent to die in some worthless scrap on the frontiers of the once great empire. What had the tutor from his teenage years, Abbé Gozzi, drummed into him? Carpe diem. Giacomo Casanova had never been one to agonise over his actions, and if ever there was a moment to 'seize the day', this was it. He strode on into the light, one hand clasped protectively round the wad of bank notes in his breeches' pocket, regretting nothing.

Casanova's visit to the Arsenale, the republic's ancient naval dockyard and temporary headquarters to its army, had been set in motion a fortnight previously on the island of Corfu, several days' voyage southwards down the Adriatic Sea. After his expulsion from the Church as a nineteen-year-old apprentice – his conduct with the local girls considered ill-suited to his training at the seminary of San Cyprian and his subsequent post as scribe to a cardinal – he had bought a commission in a regiment allocated to the defence of Corfu, one of the republic's dwindling number of territorial holdings around the Mediterranean. Eighteen months of tedium in the heat and dust of the island's garrison parade ground had convinced him that he was not cut out for army life, and with some trouble he had finally obtained permission from his commanding officer to resign. He had sailed to Venice to sell his commission, and the formalities had been completed quickly that morning in a drab cubicle deep in the maze of buildings within the Arsenale. He had surrendered his ceremonial sword and epaulettes, and in return the regimental clerk had handed him his money. Rather to his surprise, he had even made a profit on the cost of the commission, just as well given that he had gambled away most of his monthly wages in Corfu on card games with his fellow officers. There had been nothing else to do there, no enemies to fight, culture to enjoy, women to woo. But now he was home, a free man with the spring sun on his back, cash in his pocket and the world at his feet. He needed a plan for his future, and the best way to concoct that was over a cup of coffee in St Mark's Square.

His route to the centrepiece of the city state took him through the winding side streets so familiar from his youth.

As he walked, he passed the church of San Zaccaria, the towering gothic masterpiece of Gambello, architect of the Arsenale's equally splendid gates, he now recalled, and turned into the Calle San Provolo. On the bridge over a small waterway behind the Doge's Palace, he stopped to watch a gondola glide by and, leaning his elbows on the stone parapet, he continued to look down onto the water long after the craft's wake had settled. Memories of his childhood came flooding in: the early years in his grandmother's house behind the San Samuele theatre where his mother had been an actress; the cramped apartment between the theatre and the wide curve of the Grand Canal where he had lost his virginity to one or other of the Savorgnan sisters (for the life of him he could not remember which); the shuttling to and from nearby Padua while studying for his university degree there; his introduction around that time to the thrill of gambling by friends at the Ridotto casino; the later kindness of his benefactor Malpiero, so suddenly withdrawn when he was discovered frolicking with the man's sweetheart. Venice had been a riot in those carefree days before the boredom of the army, and there was no reason why it should not be so again.

His twenty-one-year-old reflection stared up at him from the still surface of the tiny canal, a profusion of jet-black curls framing a swarthy complexion, a wide sensuous mouth and a strong beak of a nose. Not classic good looks, he would readily acknowledge, but effective enough along with gallant behaviour, an easy charm and an infectious enthusiasm for life's pleasures to bring him what he wanted. What that might be going forward would emerge from the coffee awaiting him beyond the palace.

Ten minutes later he was sitting at a table outside Caffè Florian on the southern flank of the square, enjoying the view of the Basilica's magnificent façade: the four bronze horses looted from Constantinople's Hippodrome pawing the ledge over the central arched doorway and the five massive domes adorning the roofline above. It was a sight he would never tire of, but his cup of coffee had been delivered, and he must apply himself to the mundane matter of employment. He dragged his eyes down to the crowd bustling past and began to mull over his options. All manner of human endeavour was laid out in front of him: noblemen, clerks, beggars, musicians, lawyers, sailors, craftsmen, artists, swindlers, farmers, shopkeepers, wordsmiths, financiers, clerics, soldiers... he had tried the last two, so they were off the list, but what else might he turn his hand to that would assure him money and enjoyment in equal measure?

The scratch of a novice's violin sounded from a room facing onto the square, triggering a memory of his tuition on the instrument from Abbé Gozzi, and he wondered briefly whether a job as a musician was a possibility. But the pay would be thin and the routine of daily performances dreary. His law degree from Padua could bring him office work, probably as dull as soldiering, and the side interests he had developed at the university in philosophy, science, mathematics and medicine, though appealing in principle, would require years' more education and expense than he could bear. No, something more immediate and livelier was called for. He gazed out into the throng seeking inspiration, and suddenly it came to him, the fleeting echo of a scene that had first flickered into his consciousness that morning standing on the bridge of the Calle San Provolo. He would be a professional gambler, starting at the Ridotto and then moving between the other great casino salons of Paris, Madrid, Vienna and Prague. He would mingle with the aristocracy of Europe, divesting them of their abundant gold and spending it on their beautiful women as he went. He had the brain to beat the odds, the stake in his pocket to launch the plan and the nerve to pull it off. He took a sip of coffee and smiled contentedly.

The more he dwelt on the idea, the better it felt. His sure-fire success would secure him a place in history beside famous Italian mathematicians like Archimedes, Fibonacci, even the extraordinary da Vinci. At the Ridotto he would be mixing with the cream of Venice, senators, business leaders and local men of culture such as the celebrated artists Tiepolo and Guardi, who were known to frequent the casino. In the world of brilliant minds at the betting tables, he would be the Descartes of his generation, the Cardano of gaming theory. And so another image from his student days reared up, Cardano's dice in the display case of Padua's university library.

Casanova sat bolt upright in his chair, deaf to the noisy horde spread across the paved expanse of St Mark's Square. He must have a talisman for his project, to invite the good fortune every gambler needs alongside skill and cool-headedness. He had learnt about Cardano in his mathematical studies at Padua. His tutor had shown him the dice that Cardano had donated to the university and told him the story attaching to them, that they were thought to be over a thousand years old, relics of the English monarchy and then key tools in Cardano's understanding of risk. Casanova's interest had been piqued initially by the simple fact that he shared an almost identical forename, Girolamo, with Cardano. After that, they had caught his eye every time he visited the library, and he had often inspected them through the glass window of the display cabinet. They had not been much to look at, the ivory dirty grey and cracked with age, but they had an allure he could not dispel, and it had remained with him in his later years as trainee cleric, scribe and infantryman. He could picture the dice again now in the cabinet, to the left of the tablets commemorating the work of Copernicus and Galileo at the university, and to the right of the sketches by Fallopio, Padua's most eminent anatomist and physician. He had always considered them wasted as memorial trophies. If their role in Cardano's experiments was to be believed, they should still be in the hands of a master gambler. Giacomo Girolamo Casanova was that man, and he would steal them from the university that very night.

He drained his cup of coffee and stood up to leave. As he did so, two immaculately coiffed ladies detached themselves from the crowd on the square and approached Caffè Florian, evidently set on finding seats in the sunlight. He called out to attract their attention and gestured to the three chairs at his table. 'Ladies, feel free to sit here. It would be my rare pleasure to have you join me.' With company such as this, he reckoned, his new career could wait an hour or two. If the Almighty was smiling on him, which often seemed to be the case, his acquaintance with the women might even lead him to fresh overnight lodgings, whereupon his visit to Padua could be deferred to another evening. 'Allow me to buy you a drink. A cup of Florian's excellent coffee, perhaps, or some Chinese black tea? Or an orgeat? It's too early for anything stronger, for me at least, but if you would rather have a glass of brandy, then please, be my guests.' What a day to be alive, with romance across the table and a fortune over the horizon.

*

26 July 1755 – Venice

Casanova was fast asleep when they came to arrest him, the din of their heavy boots as they stamped their way up the staircase a distant clap of thunder in his dreams. Even the insistent knocking on the door and the raucous shouts for him to give himself up made little impression. His mind was fogged by the wine he had drunk the previous night, and in his semi-conscious stupor he rolled onto his stomach and stretched an arm out to embrace the warm body lying supine next to him. It was therefore something of a shock when he found himself being shaken awake, none too gently, by the chief of the State Inquisitors' militia, a coarse fellow whose clutches he had successfully evaded during numerous escapades over the last eighteen months.

'Arise, Lothario,' the man said in a sarcastic growl, snatching the single sheet off the bed to reveal the naked bodies of both Casanova and the girl alongside him. The ten soldiers that had crowded into the room behind their captain stared openly at her embarrassment, prompting Casanova to leap to his feet and collect a coat from a nearby chair. He flung it over her and then turned his attention to the intruders.

'Steady, Merrettini, there's no call for discourtesy from you or your men. Whatever business you have with me, leave this fine lady out of it.'

'She's no lady, from what I've heard of the hussies you mix with,' Merrettini leered. 'I might buy some time with her myself once I've finished with you. Cover yourself up, you filthy whoreson, and get your shoes on. You'll need them on the walk to the Piombi, unless you want us to drag you.'

Casanova was wide awake now, piecing together his predicament as he donned his shirt and breeches in the emerging glow of dawn. He remembered locking the door when he brought the girl Marlena, an actress he had been pursuing for a week or so and certainly no prostitute, up to his bedroom in the middle of the night. His patron Senator Bragadin, one of his staunchest supporters and owner of the apartment he had been inhabiting for the two years since his return from Paris, must have supplied Merrettini with the key under duress. There was no fault in that; Bragadin would have tried to block the arrest, but even pillars of the community could not afford to defy the Inquisitors for too long. And seizure by the militia had been on the cards for a while now, as Bragadin had been the first to warn Casanova. But incarceration in the Piombi was a surprise. Casanova knew of it, the prison across the Bridge of Sighs at the back of the Doge's Palace, a five-storey warren of trial and torture rooms, topped by seven cells under the roof reputed to house offenders of high status. He supposed that, if he had to be arrested, he should take pride in his distinguished accommodation, although he doubted that he would be there for long. A few days in relatively comfortable custody as a rap on the knuckles, and then he could revert to his life of leisure and pleasure, his reputation potentially enhanced rather than diminished by the experience. It would be as well, however, to know what the charge was.

'The trouble with you, Merrettini, is that you have no manners. The *signorina* is a star of Venetian theatre, with a level of refinement you will never enjoy.' Casanova stooped to retrieve his silk stockings and silver-buckled shoes from under the chair. 'As for the rude awakening you have given us both, you have failed to mention why you are here. I will be delighted to come with you to the palace but not until I understand what trumped-up charges are being levied against me.'

'You'll hear soon enough,' muttered Merrettini, somewhat deflated by the calm with which Casanova was treating his capture as he dressed. 'Cardsharping, blasphemy, debauchery, take your pick, although personally I'd go for the way you cheat people with your claims of occult powers. I've never heard such rubbish. Anyway, no more chatter. Out you go,' and he pushed his prisoner towards the door. Casanova blew a kiss to the girl as he went, wondering for the first time whether the charge might be more serious than he had anticipated.

Two months later, his fears were confirmed. Long regarded as a thorn in the side of religious and social rectitude, the Inquisitors had chosen to make an example of him in their efforts to maintain order. His ceaseless and often indiscreet love affairs, his feast-to-famine gambling enterprises and his interests in astrology and Freemasonry had upset too many husbands, fathers, senators and churchmen to be allowed to continue. He was an affront to common decency and as such he was sentenced to five years' imprisonment in the Piombi cell he had already been occupying with another so-called enemy of the state. Merrettini spat in his face as he was led back through the corridors from the palace courtroom to the gaol, and Casanova's humiliation was complete when he discovered he would now be kept in solitary confinement, his company shrunk to just a handful of books, a mattress full of fleas and the pair of dice that had been in his breeches' pocket when he was arrested.

For a mind such as his, overspilling with curiosity for the worlds of art, science and philosophy, besides the thrust and parry of general discourse with both men and women, time passed very slowly. However, once the initial despair over the length and conditions of his punishment had subsided, his natural ebullience revived, assisted by his friend Bragadin's successful petition to have him provided with improved bedding, two changes of clothes and a steady supply of journals. He was even granted an armchair in which to sit and read by the dim light of the barred window high on his cell wall. By the summer of the following year, he had also begun to devise a means of escape.

It had taken a single moment of extreme good fortune. During his regular afternoon exercise trudging round the prison courtyard, he was usually supervised by a guard, but one day he had been left unattended very briefly, as the man staggered off, stricken by diarrhoea, to relieve himself. Continuing on his circuit, Casanova had suddenly spotted an old iron bar in the weeds abutting the yard's wall. A rough fist-sized piece of rock lay next to it, probably a remnant of the repairs carried out to the wall's buttresses that spring. He had looked about him to ensure he was still unobserved and then stuffed both items hurriedly down his shirt front. Once restored to his cell, he had hidden them in the horsehair padding of his armchair, careful not to attempt a breakout until he was confident their disappearance had gone unnoticed.

Over the next two months, he worked first at fashioning the iron bar into a spike, using the rock to sharpen it. It was a slow process, operating only at night and requiring a minimum of noise. Eventually the spike was ready to be used in earnest and, on a moonlit evening after his food tray had been collected, he stood on his bed and levered one of the wooden panels down from the ceiling above. Pulling himself up into the loft space, he was able to explore the underside of the roof, searching by touch for a joint that he might be able to gouge his way through. The prison was famous for its impenetrable lead-plated roofing, and it was rumoured that no one had ever managed to escape through it. After some lengthy probing, he found what he wanted and elected to return to his chamber. He estimated he would need several hours to bore through the lead and descend to the canal below, and it was too late to start now. In any case, the following day was the last of October, All Hallows' Eve, a fitting date to slip away into the darkness across the Venice skyline. It would be a great story for the girls in Paris, his intended goal since he would obviously have to abandon his hometown to avoid recapture.

Dropping soundlessly down onto his bed, he began to lift the ceiling panel into position. As he did so, he heard a gentle tapping on the partition wall next to him. He froze. The noise stopped and in its place he heard a muffled whisper, too low for him to make out the words. No guard would behave in such a way, and he knew a prisoner had recently arrived in the adjacent cell. He decided to risk his night's exertions and tapped back more loudly for a few seconds before resting to listen once again. This time the whisper was clearly audible.

'Signor Casanova, I heard you above me in the loft. If you are escaping, take me with you.'

'Who are you, and why are you here?' Casanova whispered in response. It was common practice for the Inquisitors to plant spies in the Piombi, in a bid to flush out the names of inmates' associates, and he had not yet had the opportunity to learn the identity of his neighbour.

'My name is Balbi. I'm a priest and they've locked me up for fathering three beautiful children. You might remember me from the San Cyprian seminary.'

Casanova cast his mind back to his clerical training, some thirteen years previously. He had had at least five careers since then, with the multitude of new faces that entailed, and the details of San Cyprian were hazy. Nonetheless, he could vaguely recall a boy named Balbi, and it was highly unlikely that a spy would use such an obscure cover.

'I do remember you, Balbi. Yes, I'm planning to escape through the roof, but not tonight. Anyhow, why should I bother taking you with me? It will be less noisy on my own, and less trouble for me to hide if I have to.'

'I've been in prison here before, so I know the building well and I can help you. Making it onto the roof is the easy part.'

It was a fair point, Casanova conceded. 'All right, once we've eaten tomorrow evening, I'll undo one of your ceiling panels from above and you can climb up to join me.' He went on to outline the rest of his plan and then they agreed to maintain silence until the getaway was launched.

The following day seemed interminable, but at last the gaoler came to retrieve the meal tray. After listening intently to ensure the man had withdrawn to his post at the far end of the corridor, Casanova removed his spike from the cushioning of the armchair and got to work. Minutes later he had hoisted Balbi into the loft space and the two men began to take turns digging their way through the lead plate above their heads. It was well after midnight before they had created a hole wide enough to wriggle through, and Casanova passed a bundle of belongings up to the priest before joining him on the sloping external roof. Mist swirled about them, making the lead surface slippery but shrouding them from view in the event of anyone looking up from the back quarters of the palace prison. Unfortunately, the cloud presented a different obstacle.

'I'm sorry, Balbi.' Casanova's muted voice was taut with frustration. 'I assumed we could jump into the canal from here, but without being able to see exactly where we would land, it's too dangerous. We need to find another way down.'

'Don't worry, I know this place inside out.' Balbi smiled in the dark. 'As I said yesterday, I've been in prison here several times. Once for each child, in fact. There's a dormer window into a disused attic on the far side of that chimney breast.' He pointed across the roof. 'If we can open the window, we can drop into the room and then use the back staircase to escape. The only difficulty is the height of the dormer. We might break a leg getting down.'

'Not a problem.' It was Casanova's turn to grin, as he gestured to the bundle he had brought from his cell. 'My bedsheets,' he explained, 'with the spike and some fresh clothes wrapped up inside. We can unlatch the window with the spike, tie the sheets to the frame and shin down. Then we can change out of these prison clothes and walk out. If we're lucky no one will see us, and even if they do, we can claim we are visiting, and they may not recognise us.' Balbi grunted his approval, and they moved cautiously over the treacherous roof. Ten minutes later they were in the attic room, peering out of its doorway to confirm that the route to the staircase was clear.

'Wait,' Balbi hissed suddenly, reaching across his companion to pull the door shut. 'This is not the time. If we're caught, no one will believe we are visitors in the middle of the night. But if we leave in daylight, shortly before the breakfast food trays are delivered, we'll stand a better chance of getting out unchecked.'

The thought of a delay at this stage went against all of Casanova's impetuous instincts, but he saw the sense in the priest's suggestion. It would be five hours or so until dawn, and he wondered how best to pass the time. He dared not sleep and although, as always, he had his dice in his pocket, there was no light by which to play with them. He would catch up on some much-missed conversation instead, even if it was with a disgraced cleric who had become a father to more than just his flock. He sat down on the floor, his back to the wall, and spoke softly.

'Wise counsel. I have a question, though. How did you know it was me in the cell next to you?'

'Oh, they gave me your name the day I arrived.' Balbi slumped against the wall next to him. 'They said I was a vile licentious sinner and that I'd be in good company living next to you. It seems they did not appreciate your skill as an escapee. How did you come up with your plan?'

Casanova felt the dice beneath his clothing, hard against his thigh. 'I once broke into the University of Padua to steal something precious to me. I always knew that if I could break into a building, I could find a way to break out of one. It merely took a while to organise.' He chuckled quietly and added, 'Well met, Father Balbi. By midday tomorrow, we'll be doing what we do best again with our women. For now, we have a long wait, so tell me what you've been up to ever since those days at the seminary.'

Their hushed conversation ran on throughout the night, Balbi talking at length about the conflicting joys of his double life as priest and parent. In response Casanova described his own erratic path to the Piombi cell since leaving the army, his brief and hopelessly disastrous spell at the Ridotto as a professional gambler, his time as a violinist at the San Samuele theatre, his reinvention as a Venetian nobleman under the patronage of Senator Bragadin, his flight from the republic after a false charge of rape, the Grand Tour leading him to Paris and his eventual return to Venice two years past. He glossed over the rakish reputation he had acquired from his amorous exploits and dismissed the allegations of trickery and occultism that had sprung from his constant struggle to finance his lifestyle. There were plenty other things to discuss, not least the two men's shared interest in Greek mythology and the arts. The hours flowed by unnoticed, until the first grey of dawn began to show in the dormer window above them. They rose, flexed their stiff legs, eased the attic door open and crept along the corridor to the staircase.

By the time the sun had risen in full, they had left the building and were paddling fast towards the Grand Canal in a stolen gondola. They had faced only one challenge in their escape, from a sleep-addled guard who was fooled into thinking they were guests of the Doge. Incredibly, they had been able to persuade him that, after attending an official dinner at the palace the previous evening, they had wandered drunkenly through its maze of rooms before falling asleep on the prison's side of the Bridge of Sighs. The man had escorted them to the Piombi's front door himself, and they were still laughing at their good fortune as they merged with the morning traffic on the city's great arterial waterway. Finding them there would be like hunting for a needle in a haystack.

*

30 October 1787 – Prague

'It is truly an honour to meet you,' said Casanova, bowing politely to the composer seated at the table overlooking the Charles bridge. The café was brimming with people seeking shelter from the rain squall sweeping down the River Vltava, but this was the only man he was interested in speaking to, the talk of the town after the opera's opening performance the previous night.

'Thank you, *signor*,' replied Mozart, using the older man's formal title in an unusual show of respect. 'You have quite a reputation yourself. Da Ponte here has told me all about you.' He pointed to the bench on the far side of the table. 'Please, sit down, both of you, and let me know what you thought of my *Don Giovanni*.'

Lorenzo da Ponte nodded to his employer and followed Casanova onto the bench. There was a pause as they settled themselves, and then Casanova began. 'It was magnificent, Mozart. There is no other word for it. I enjoyed the *Marriage of Figaro* last year, but this is in a different league. Naturally, I was familiar with the old Spanish legend of Don Juan, but what you have done with it is remarkable. The music is exquisite, and the overture in particular—'

'You are too kind,' Mozart broke in. 'You should save some of the credit for your friend here. Without da Ponte as my librettist, the story might not have come out so well. As for the overture, would you believe me if I told you I wrote it just two days ago? The whole thing has been an awful rush.' He shook his head at the memory of it. 'But I am indebted to the members of the National Theatre here in Prague. They were much more enthusiastic about *Figaro* than my Vienna audiences, and in January they commissioned me to write a follow-up. The premiere was supposed to be two weeks ago, in front of the Archduchess Maria Theresa, but the score wasn't finished, and they were patient enough to postpone. They seemed to like it, so it was worth the wait.'

'It was magnificent,' repeated Casanova, 'the audience were in raptures. I doubt they will see the like of it ever again. For my part, I am indebted to da Ponte for the opportunity to meet you. We have known each other for over a decade, but it was only by chance that I bumped into him yesterday in the main square after attending mass. He got me into the theatre for the performance, and I bullied him into arranging an introduction to you this morning.'

'Well, I'm delighted he did. I recognised your name from Vienna, but he tells me you have been living here in Bohemia for a while. What occupies you nowadays, after such a varied career?'

Casanova's expression darkened, and he brushed a hand through his lank grey locks before leaning forward across the table. 'My circumstances are not what they were, Mozart. I have had all kinds of jobs over the last forty years, and I have travelled the length and breadth of Europe, mixing with some of the greatest men and women of our age, but now I am reduced to the role of librarian for a local nobleman, Count von Waldstein. I ought not complain, he pays me a reasonable sum each month, and we share certain interests, such as Freemasonry. But the work is tedious and the company, besides that of the count, is dismal. To be honest, I'm bored and depressed, and I can't find a way out of it.'

Mozart and da Ponte exchanged glances. This was not the Casanova the librettist remembered from their previous encounters, nor the character he had described to Mozart earlier that morning. To be sure, the Venetian had aged more than his three score years, his skin pockmarked with the effects of disease and his sunken cheeks accentuating the hook of his nose. More than his bodily features, it was his bearing that had changed so much. He appeared to have lost that zest for life that had spawned such a succession of adventures. Da Ponte wondered if a gentle reminder might jolt him out of his gloom.

'Come now, Giacomo. You and I have been kindred spirits in the pursuit of both employment and pleasure. Think of all your achievements – the creation of the state lottery in France, your translation of the *Iliad* from the ancient Greek, your meetings with the likes of Empress Catherine of Russia and Benjamin Franklin of America, your essays on philosophy that even Voltaire struggled to gainsay. What about all your excitements over the years at the gambling tables and the ladies you have wooed and won? I gather you've upset a few people in the process, but there's many a royal court that would welcome a man of your education and experience.'

'Too late,' Casanova answered morosely. 'I've used up all my favours. I am yesterday's man in the corridors of power, and I'm too old and decrepit for any beautiful woman to notice. I can't afford to leave von Waldstein, and I've even lost my appetite for gambling. I've wasted far more than I've ever won, and I've finally realised it's no way to run one's life.'

'Impossible!' said Mozart heartily. 'I gamble and I seem to lose all the time, but nothing will stop me believing the next hand at cards or throw of the dice will be the win of the century. Anyway, if gambling's not the answer, why don't you write a record of your exploits? From da Ponte's description of you before we met, you've crammed more into a single lifetime than most of us would manage in ten. You may have lost a fortune or two, but it would be a much bigger waste for you to take your story to the grave.'

Casanova leant back in his chair and stared at Mozart. Da Ponte began to speak but Casanova cut him off with a curt downward stab of his index finger. Half a minute ticked by on the heavy brass clock mounted on the café wall above them. Then the Venetian smiled, a vestige of the radiating cheerfulness da Ponte remembered from their escapades together over the years but a smile nonetheless.

'With last night's *Don Giovanni*, Mozart, you have established yourself as one of the world's finest composers, and for that alone you deserve a gift. But you are also a gambler, like me, and a Freemason too, I understand. Most of all, you have just given me fresh purpose in my old age. I will return to von Waldstein's library, accepting my lot, and I will write my memoirs. For all this, I wish you to have my most favourite possession.' He dug into his waistcoat pocket and extracted two small grey dice, which he pushed across the table. 'These belonged to a famous mathematician of the sixteenth century, Cardano. Before that it is said they graced the palms of royalty for a millennium or more, their true origin lost in the well of history. They may not have brought me huge wealth, but in owning them I have enjoyed great fortune instead. May they bring you the same, and at the very least another opera with my friend to rival your last. It is time I left you and Lorenzo here in peace, but I say again, it has been my honour to meet you.' He stood, reached over to shake hands solemnly with both men and walked out of the café as they looked on in silence.

*

And then…

+ The dice are sold as part of Mozart's effects on his death in Vienna in 1791. They come up for sale again in 1838 and are purchased by a young Irish cavalry officer serving in Austria, Captain Louis Nolan. A modest gambler and lover of opera, he buys them for their association with Mozart but is otherwise unaware of their long history.

+ In 1839 Nolan transfers to the British Army. Over the next fifteen years the dice are his constant companion as he serves in India and then as a cavalry tactician around Europe. At the outset of the Crimean War in 1854 he is a staff officer in the expeditionary force commanded by Lord Raglan. As always, the dice travel with him to the new theatre of operations.

*

Author's Note

The word 'Casanova' has come to mean someone noted for their amorous adventures or, more negatively, a seducer and philanderer, yet the man himself deserves to be remembered for a career of extraordinary variety besides his love affairs. A native of Venice, Giacomo Girolamo Casanova entered the nearby University of Padua in 1737 at the age of twelve, graduating five years later with a law degree and a grounding in science, maths, medicine, philosophy and music. During that time he shuttled to and from his home city while also training to be an abbé, or church cleric, and was introduced to the twin lures of girls and gaming tables. This broad array of interests led to a succession of enterprises over the next fifty years, some more fruitful than others but all underpinned by the pursuit of the opposite sex, the switchback of gambling and an interest in the arts. Casanova was, at different times, a soldier, violinist, salesman, spy, silk manufacturing factory owner, social commentator and essayist, translator of ancient Greek poetry, mathematician, diplomat, author and, finally, librarian. His more successful activities included creating a state lottery for the King of France, selling government bonds in Amsterdam to fund France's involvement in the Seven Years War, acting as secretary to the Venetian ambassador in Vienna and writing the Histoire de ma Vie, a mine of information for future generations on European social life in the mid/late eighteenth century. In the course of it all he travelled throughout Europe, covering an estimated forty thousand miles and mixing with a remarkable range of royalty and celebrities of the age as he went. He survived a duel over an actress in Warsaw, in which he self-medicated a wounded hand to avoid the amputation proposed by doctors, came close to suicide through depression in the late 1780s and finally died in 1798 at Castle Dux, the home of Count von Waldstein outside Prague. The Histoire suggests that he had affairs with over 120 women during his lifetime, although it is acknowledged that some embellishment may have crept into both the number and the frank details of his liaisons.

Casanova's attempt to set himself up as a professional gambler after leaving the army at the age of twenty-one was a disaster. He then acquired a patron, which allowed him to live the life of a gentleman in Venice for three years until a reputation for decadence forced him to flee the city. He embarked on a Grand Tour, finding his way to Paris where he lived for two years until obliged to move on again thanks to his libertine lifestyle. On return to Venice he resumed his previous habits and was eventually arrested by the Inquisitors. My account of his imprisonment and subsequent escape from the Piombi cells is based on his own description of it in his memoirs, albeit simplified.

The details around the writing and launch of the opera Don Giovanni, Mozart's second collaboration with the librettist Lorenzo *da Ponte, are generally accurate. It is known that Casanova met da Ponte in Prague in October 1787 and, being long-standing friends, it is therefore highly possible (but not certain) that da Ponte introduced him to the composer. Mozart was a keen gambler, as a (usually ineffective) means to finance his participation in the aristocratic circles that would generate commissions for him. The idea that he persuaded Casanova to write his memoirs, or that he received a gift of dice from the Venetian, is my invention, although the two men did have a common interest in Freemasonry. Mozart went on to write a third opera with da Ponte, Cosi Fan Tutti, which premiered early in 1790, before his untimely death the following year at the age of only thirty-five.*

The Charge of the Light Brigade

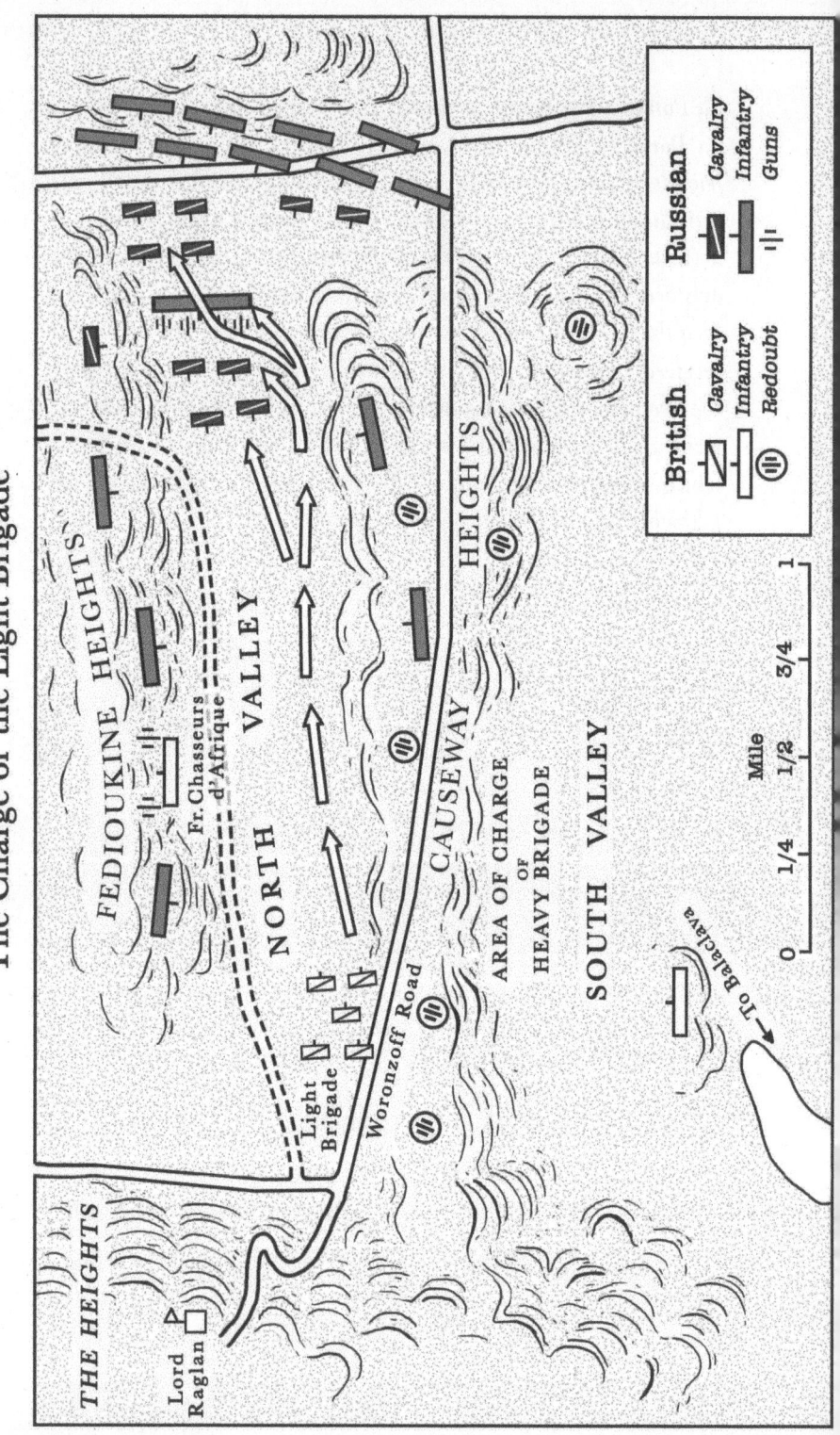

The Charge of the
Light Brigade

25 October 1854 – Balaclava, Crimea

Captain Louis Nolan watched in disbelief. Outnumbered five to one, the Heavy Brigade had charged the Russian cavalry and broken their formation. It was an extraordinary feat by General Scarlett's mounted troops, and the enemy were now retreating in disarray, slowed down by the cumbersome field guns they pulled behind them. It was the perfect moment for Nolan's colleagues in the Light Brigade to be launched into action, to perform precisely the role they were trained for. Unimpeded by the bulky armour worn by the Heavy Brigade, and equipped instead with lances and sabres designed to cut down an army in flight, they should be galloping in pursuit. In a matter of minutes, the Russian cavalry could be destroyed and their cannons captured. The town of Balaclava would be safe from attack and the siege of Sevastopol, the principal objective in this miserable war, could recommence with the renewed vigour of a glorious victory. And yet the Light Brigade sat, immobile, on their horses, as the Russians escaped. It was a monstrous dereliction of duty by the senior officers, and he could only shake his head in disgust at the lost opportunity.

'It should not have come as any surprise,' Nolan muttered to himself. Unlike the Heavy Brigade's well-regarded General Scarlett, the Light Brigade was led by the stupidest man in the British Army, Lord Cardigan. The fact that both brigades were under the control of the Earl of Lucan, overall commander of the Cavalry Division, was equally laughable, given his failure to exercise effective leadership ever since the army had landed in the Crimea. Lord Lucan was known to be a tough, disciplined soldier, but he was unduly harsh on his men and, in Nolan's opinion, utterly devoid of common sense. Two weeks previously there had been a similar chance for the cavalry to attack a significant Russian skirmishing force, in ideal riding country, and Lucan had inexplicably refused to order the charge. Nolan had told him to his face what a mistake he was making; the troops had cursed him openly; and his immediate subordinate Cardigan had continued to rage at him for days afterwards. As a result, Lucan was on speaking terms with neither Nolan nor Cardigan and, worse still, his relationship with the army's commander-in-chief, Field Marshal Lord Raglan, whom Lucan held ultimately responsible for the muddle, had collapsed.

Nolan turned his horse away from the view of the stationary Light Brigade to survey the knot of staff officers surrounding Raglan some thirty yards upwind of him. They were gathered on a hill looking out over two valleys extending parallel to the east. The southernmost of the two, the scene of the Heavy Brigade's successful engagement a few minutes ago above the port of Balaclava, was separated from its northern neighbour by a ridge, which the British had named the Causeway Heights. Over the previous fortnight Raglan's artillery had established a series of gun emplacements on the road running along the heights, most of which the Russians had seized at dawn that morning. Pursuit by the Light Brigade would have allowed the

British to reclaim those redoubts – another failure by Lucan, and by association Lord Raglan. Nolan could see the field marshal chatting to the quartermaster general, Richard Airey, and wondered what the next blunder would be.

It was impossible to dislike Raglan, an urbane and amiable gentleman in his mid-sixties who had lost an arm at Waterloo and had spent the following four decades as a desk soldier operating in the shadow of his mentor the Duke of Wellington. On Wellington's death he had found himself at the head of the army, with no experience of leadership in the heat of war. His skill was in defusing controversy, although even he had been unable to work with Lucan, and he was entirely unsuited to the command of a battlefield, where intuition, tactical awareness and clarity of purpose were essential. He was weary and out of his depth, and the army was suffering terribly as a consequence of it. The six weeks since disembarkation in the Crimea had been a masterclass in vacillation and poor decision-making. Communication with Britain's French and Turkish allies in the joint war against the Russians had been sporadic at best, generating a strategy for besieging Sevastopol that was both geographically and militarily inept. In addition, due to lack of reconnaissance, water supplies had been virtually non-existent in the early days, and no serious efforts had been made to fend off the resulting cholera and dysentery that were ravaging the troops. As one of Raglan's aides-de-camp, Nolan had suggested solutions to all these issues, but his ideas had fallen on deaf ears.

The problem, he knew, was that he was considered ill-equipped for staff officer duties beyond the narrow realm of mounted brigades. A superb horseman, he had spent all his fifteen-year career in the British Army studying and teaching the application of cavalry in battle. He had been brought into the fold for this alone and ignored on wider military affairs. Despite his specialist knowledge, he was still a humble captain, and his intelligence, confidence and vivacity were lost on the old men conducting the war. They saw him instead as boisterous and outspoken, and now they would not even listen to his advice within the cavalry division, preferring him to keep his distance until summoned. He longed to be involved in the fighting itself, rather than stuck on a hilltop supervising it, although he grudgingly admitted that Raglan's position gave him an excellent vantage point from which to direct his troops. If only he would do so with more urgency...

Nolan's thoughts were interrupted by a flurry of movement amongst the officers near him. Raglan was hunched over a sabretache scribbling out an order, and a young aide was hurrying to fetch his horse from a collection of grooms standing below the crest of the hill. Nolan watched enviously as the messenger swung himself into the saddle and trotted back to the field marshal. The order was passed up to him and he set off at a canter down the path towards the floor of the north valley. Meanwhile a second messenger had been handed an order by General Airey, and he too rode off at speed, at a different angle to the first. Nolan caught the eye of an officer on the edge of the group, one of the few he liked and respected, and the man hobbled across to him, leaning heavily on a stick.

'What's going on, Leslie? What's Raglan's plan now?'

Captain Thomas Leslie came to a halt in front of Nolan, grimacing with pain. 'This damned leg! I'm so slow at the moment. But it's on the mend, and at least I can ride.' He flourished his stick at the Causeway Heights to their right. 'Lucan has been instructed to retake the ridge, now that the Russian cavalry have been dispersed. Infantry support is coming up from behind us, but it will take time to arrive. Lucan has been told to have the Light Brigade advance without waiting.'

'About time!' exclaimed Nolan. 'We can win back the redoubts and the control of the road, even though we've missed the chance to destroy their cavalry. What a shambles, but we might just win the day after all.'

'Steady, Louis, Raglan will hear you. You might be correct but keep your voice down. You'll do yourself no favours drawing attention to the mistakes.'

'But someone has to, Tom.' Nolan had the sense to speak more quietly. 'Raglan and Lucan barely talk to each other, and Cardigan ignores them both. Scarlett's Heavy Brigade did a fantastic job over there,' he gestured at the south valley, 'heaven knows how, but no thanks to Lucan, that's for sure. Anyway,' he took a deep breath, 'maybe he will redeem himself now. In the meantime, tell me about your leg. I've not been able to catch up with you for ages.'

'Oh, there's not much to tell,' replied Leslie, 'I took a musket ball in my thigh at Alma last month. The surgeon dug it out and sewed me up, and the wound's definitely healing, unlike some of the sawbones' patchwork. It hurts like fury, but I've been up and about for a week now.'

'Good, I wondered where you'd been. Hopefully you've come back in time to see what the Light Brigade can do when they are unleashed. The order should reach Lucan in a few minutes. Let's watch them go.'

The two men gazed down into the northern valley below, and quarter of an hour ticked by. Nolan fidgeted with impatience, checking his pocket watch repeatedly and huffing noisily after each inspection. 'What the deuce are they doing?' he burst out eventually. 'They must surely have received Raglan's messenger by now. Why on earth do they simply stand there?' Leslie had no answer, and another silence stretched out. 'Perhaps Lucan is waiting for the infantry,' he ventured after a further ten minutes.

'But I thought you said he'd been told not to wait for them. Didn't Raglan make that clear?' Nolan cast a glance laden with contempt at the field marshal, who was staring at the Causeway Heights through his spyglass and talking animatedly to the generals around him.

'That's what I heard him say, but I don't know what the precise order was. It looks as though he is as frustrated as you and me.'

'Well, at this rate, he'll need to send another man down. That idiot Lucan will sit there all day if he's allowed to decide for himself. It should be perfectly obvious what's expected of him.' Nolan stopped and gave Leslie a piercing glare. 'Tom, who is the next aide in line to deliver Raglan's instructions?'

Leslie answered without taking his eyes off the static scene in the valley below them. 'It could be me. In fact, it's time I went over to the field marshal, in case he does want to issue fresh orders.' He shifted his stick and turned towards the group of staff officers.

'Hold on,' urged Nolan, grasping him by the shoulder. 'Look at you, Tom, you can't ride at any pace with your leg like that. Let me go instead. I'm itching to join the Light Brigade when they charge.'

Leslie shook his head. 'There's no way I can do that, Louis. Raglan has his list of dispatch riders organised at the start of each day and he won't change it, whatever else happens. You can't butt in when it suits you.'

Nolan pressed his gloved hands to his face, almost in tears with exasperation. Then an idea occurred to him, and he peeled off a glove to delve into the tunic pocket harbouring his watch. 'Normally I would have to agree with you, Tom. But you know I'm the fastest man on horseback here, and any message needs to get to Lucan as quickly as possible.' He withdrew two dice from the bottom of the pocket and showed them to Leslie in an outstretched palm. 'Let us at least draw lots for it. If you win, I won't interfere, but if you lose, you will pass the order to me. That's fair game, isn't it?'

Tom Leslie hesitated, resting on his stick. He was well aware that his wound would slow him up and that Nolan's claim of superior horsemanship was reasonable, especially given the precipitous path down to the valley floor that would have to be followed. Moreover, he liked Nolan, a witty, energetic companion on what had been a demoralising campaign of errors so far. There was a faint risk he might be court-martialled if he disrupted Raglan's choice of aides, but the logic of having Nolan ride in his place seemed worthy of a consultation with the fates. 'All right,' he said, 'how about one dice each, higher score wins, the best of three throws,' and he lifted one of the small grey cubes out of Nolan's hand. 'We'll throw them onto that slab of rock.' He pointed to the ground beside them, then added, 'But you'll have to pick them up. I can't bend down that far.'

Nolan put his palm to his lips in a mock kiss, and then together they tossed the dice down onto the rock. 'Your five to my three,' said Nolan as he crouched to retrieve them. 'Round two, here we go.' They threw again, Nolan flipping his off a thumbnail in a jaunty attempt to hide his desperation. 'Your four to my six. All square. Come on, Lady Luck, one more for the road to the valley!' He gave one of the cubes to Leslie and let the other roll out of his hand. It bounced twice on the rough surface and came to rest before his opponent had thrown. Three black dots revealed themselves. He looked up at Leslie with a strained expression and watched as the second dice dropped onto the rock. 'One,' he declared triumphantly, his voice bubbling with relief. He restored both dice to his pocket and reached out to shake Leslie's hand. 'Thank you, Tom, I can't tell you how much this means to me. When he calls for you, take the message from Raglan and then I will grab it from you. That way you won't be blamed, and we can laugh about it over some brandy this evening.' Leslie nodded but said nothing and began to limp back to the field marshal.

Nolan continued to view the north valley from his solitary position on the hill. It stretched for over a mile, widening into an open plain defended by a mass of Russian artillery and the cavalry that had regrouped after their flight from the Heavy Brigade an hour earlier. Hemming the length of the valley to either side were the Causeway Heights on the right, and another ridge, the Fedioukine Heights, on the left. Both were occupied by Russian infantry, but the left-hand ridge was the lesser concern compared to Raglan's need to regain control of the supply road running along the Causeway Heights from Balaclava. Even from a cursory glance it was obvious that this should be the primary target.

A further fifteen minutes went by, and still Lucan's troops seemed rooted to the spot. Nolan was not alone in venting his irritation. The field marshal was holding a heated debate with his staff, and snippets of their conversation drifted to the cavalryman on the breeze. Why was Lord Lucan not following his orders? When would he understand the sense in attacking the redoubts on the heights without delay? The promised division of supporting infantry were on the march, but they would take another half hour to appear. How many more opportunities to crush the enemy would Lucan let slip through his fingers? Nolan decided the time had come to join the group, whatever the generals thought of him, and he hurried across the hill towards them.

As he arrived, his view diverted briefly to the groom tending his horse, a ripple of consternation ran through the assembled officers. All eyes were on the Causeway Heights, and he turned to follow them, raising the field glasses looped around his neck. 'They're taking our guns from the redoubts,' shouted one of the aides in horror, the first to absorb what they were seeing, and then other voices added to the clamour.

Nolan scanned the ridge and saw at once the implications of the Russians' activity. Loss of cannonry to the enemy was tantamount to defeat, whatever success had been achieved by the Heavy Brigade earlier in the day. It was imperative that the guns' removal be prevented. The problem would never have arisen if Lucan had done what he had been told half an hour ago, and Nolan watched with rising excitement as Raglan began to dictate a fresh message. General Airey scribbled it down in pencil, repeating it aloud as he wrote:

Lord Raglan wishes the cavalry to advance rapidly to the front – follow the enemy and try to prevent the enemy carrying away the guns. Troop Horse Artillery may accompany. French cavalry is on your left. Immediate.

'Thank you, Airey,' said Raglan, looking about him. 'Ah, there you are, Captain Leslie. Take this with all haste to Lord Lucan. We need those guns, without fail, d'you understand?'

'Yes, Field Marshal.' Tom Leslie took the written order from Airey and began shuffling across to the grooms.

Nolan sprinted past him, leapt up onto his horse and steered it round to the oncoming man. As they passed each other, Nolan leant down out of the saddle and snatched the piece of paper from Leslie's hand, whispering as he did so, 'The brandy's on me, Tom!' Then he rode on past the generals, calling out in explanation, 'Speed of delivery is critical, My Lord,' and spurred his mount into a canter.

Raglan made no effort to stop him, shouting merely, 'Tell Lord Lucan the cavalry is to attack immediately,' as Nolan clattered over the lip of the hill and vanished from sight.

The path into the north valley was a test for anyone on horseback, vertiginously steep and strewn with loose shale. Most riders would have approached it with trepidation and extreme care, but Nolan plunged down the seven hundred-foot escarpment as if the devil was at his heels. It demanded all his exceptional equestrian skills to stay in the saddle, and somehow the horse managed to keep its footing as it lurched towards the plain below. Once on the flat, and visible again to Raglan and his officers, there was a five hundred-pace dash to his destination, and Nolan was able to pick out his target with ease. Lord Lucan sat astride a splendid chestnut stallion, detached from his men, watching the aide with disdain as he caught his breath and wiped the sweat from his brow. Nolan passed the written order across in silence and waited as Lucan read it through.

'Advance to the front... prevent the enemy carrying away the guns? This means nothing to me.' The earl began to reread the message, slowly and deliberately, looking up halfway through to the valley ahead of him. 'It makes no sense,' he murmured, as if to himself, and Nolan could contain his impatience no longer.

'Lord Raglan's orders are that the cavalry are to attack immediately,' he burst out in frustration, against the usual etiquette of waiting to be invited to speak by a senior officer and oblivious to the justification for Lucan's bewilderment. If he had taken stock of the Light Brigade's surroundings, he would have realised that the field of vision down on the valley floor was very different to that of Raglan and his generals high above. A hillock rose out of the plain to the south-east, modest in size but enough to block out any glimpse of the redoubts on the Causeway Heights. From Lucan's position, there was no sign that the Russians were removing the British cannons from the ridge and nothing on the piece of paper to suggest that it was intended as a follow-up to the previous dispatch from Raglan.

A more enlightened commander might have taken time to describe his confusion but, goaded by his loathing of Nolan and the aide's offensive tone when addressing him, Lucan's temper boiled over and he could only bark, 'Attack, sir? Attack what? What guns, sir?'

Now should have been the moment for Nolan to appreciate Lucan's ignorance of the commotion on the Causeway Heights and to clarify in detail the purpose of the order. However, the younger man had seen the earl miss two opportunities to get the better of the enemy that morning, and he could scarcely believe the cavalry commander's hesitation in pursuing the latest instruction. Acutely alive to the disgrace of losing artillery, and seething with impatience, Nolan swept an arm out in the general direction of the valley's south-eastern flank and shouted in response, 'There, My Lord, is your enemy; there are your guns.'

Lucan looked again at the valley. Even without the use of field glasses he could see the enemy's gun battery at the far end of the mile-long stretch towards the east. To the north, Russian infantry were scrambling like ants across the Fedioukine Heights and he guessed, even though his view was obstructed, that the Causeway Heights would present a similar picture. He was being asked, no, ordered, to send his troops into a three-sided storm of cannonballs and rifle bullets. It was madness, but he had pressed the hateful Nolan on it, and unlike the previous order where he had assumed he was to wait for the arrival of the supporting infantry, he was required to act on this one immediately. So be it. Nolan's insolence did not deserve a reply and, turning his back on the aide, he walked his horse slowly over to the Light Brigade, drawn up in square with its commander, Lord Cardigan, at its head.

'Cardigan, we are instructed by Lord Raglan to attack the enemy's gun emplacements at the far end of the valley.' Lucan pointed due east. 'You will advance with the Light Brigade, and I will send General Scarlett to follow you with the Heavy Brigade. Is that clear?'

Cardigan raised his glasses and surveyed the valley with exaggerated care. Much as he disliked Lucan, the principle of following orders was deeply ingrained, especially those from the field marshal himself. Nonetheless, he could not resist challenging such an extraordinary request. 'Certainly, sir. But allow me to point out to you that the Russians have a battery in the valley on our front and batteries and riflemen on both sides.'

'I know it,' replied Lucan, 'but Lord Raglan will have it. We have no choice but to obey.' Cardigan gave him a long, penetrating stare, and then lifted his sword in speechless acknowledgement. As Lucan rode away, he could hear the order being relayed to the Light Brigade officers and the tightly grouped cavalrymen being moved into line for the charge. He studiously avoided eye contact as Nolan cantered by, intent on achieving the real aim of his escape from Raglan's hilltop station – permission from his friend Captain Morris of the 11th Lancers to join the assault.

Five minutes later, the Light Brigade began their advance, some 670 horsemen trotting with parade ground discipline down the valley. Lord Cardigan led the way, a few yards ahead of the three-line-deep attack formation, his back ramrod straight and his sword held aloft in readiness for the battle to come. Other than the scuff of hooves, the snorting of animal nostrils and the chinking of bridles, it was strangely quiet, and the officers had barely to raise their voices to remind the men following them, 'Steady now, keep your lines, keep your lines.' They had over a mile to run, and they knew the importance of keeping the brigade's shape for as long as possible, of sparing the horses in the early stages, before breaking into the final headlong race to decimate their enemy. To Lord Raglan and his staff, watching from their platform above the escarpment, it was a thing of beauty, a celebration of an army at the pinnacle of its military capability, and they waited for the moment when the brigade would wheel to the right and begin the attack on the Causeway Heights. And then the Russian guns began to fire.

The first cannonballs fell well short, throwing up great showers of earth but making no impression on the Light Brigade's methodical advance. The only disruption came from behind, as Louis Nolan abandoned his position next to Captain Morris in the first line to gallop past Cardigan, brandishing his sword and shouting at him. The noise of the gunfire was such that Cardigan could hear none of it, but he was incensed by Nolan's impertinence at taking the lead of the charge and he shook his own sword furiously in response. It mattered little, for by now the Russian gunners had found their range and the first accurate shell exploded directly in front of Nolan. Shredded by metal splinters, his horse turned, eyes rolling in pain and fear, and began to bolt back towards the British troops. Nolan himself had fared no better. A jagged piece of the shell's casement had smashed into his chest, shattering his ribcage and driving deep into his heart. His body remained upright in the saddle for several steps and then he toppled to the ground amongst the oncoming hooves of his fellow cavalry. He was the first man to die in the charge, but by no means the last.

*

The sun was at its zenith in the bright autumn sky when the last stragglers of the Light Brigade staggered into their starting point at the western end of the valley. Less than an hour had elapsed, but to all those observing the charge it had felt like a lifetime. No one had enjoyed a better view of it than Lieutenant Colonel Belikhov, not that anyone in their right mind, friend or foe, could have described the spectacle as a pleasure to witness. From his position on the Causeway Heights, Belikhov had followed Nolan's breathtaking descent towards the assembled British cavalry and had presumed that an attack was imminent. As the commanding officer of the Russian artillery occupying the redoubts on the heights, he had waited, like Raglan, for the cavalry's course to turn in his direction, until it finally became clear that he and his troops were not the target. It was hardly credible, but the British generals appeared instead to have deliberately launched a full mounted brigade into a death trap on the valley floor.

From that moment on, in a mixed state of relief and horror, Belikhov had watched the entire event, appalled at the destruction and awed by the riders' bravery. As Nolan's body was being trampled into the dust by the passing horses, the carnage had begun in earnest. Cannon-fire had rained down from the battery at the eastern end of the valley, while Russian riflemen on the ridges to the north and south had poured bullets into the mass of cavalry. Time and time again huge gaps had been gouged in the lines by exploding shells. Remarkably, with every breach, the neighbouring horsemen had been able to reform and, despite the chaos, the brigade's order had been maintained at no more than a tightly controlled trot until well over half the length of the valley had been covered. The leader, rigid and ferociously composed even to Belikhov's distant scrutiny, had seemed invincible as he rode on at the head of his men, shells bursting all around him and riderless beasts careering across his path. But at last there had come a stage where the casualties were so heavy the front line could be contained no longer. What was left of the brigade had broken into a frenzied gallop, every man for himself in a desperate rush to exact vengeance on his persecutors.

Those enemies, Belikhov's countrymen, had been swathed in the smoke of their heavy artillery, and after the three lines of

British cavalry had disappeared into the murk around them, there had been an ominous pause as the Russian guns fell silent. Unbeknown to Belikhov, the impetus of the charge had delivered the result intended. The soldiers manning the battery had been forced to flee and would have been ridden down if the Light Brigade's losses had been less severe. However, all structure had been lost and the men who had come this far had been in no condition to press their advantage. There were almost no officers to marshal them, and as the bloodlust receded, they had turned for home, emerging from the smoke to a scene from hell.

Littered across the valley's grass were hundreds of dead and dying men, some crushed by their horses, others broken into bloody pulp by the gunfire they had endured. Wounded animals ran wild amongst them, many trailing a fractured leg or stumbling blindly into their fallen brethren. Blood daubed every step of the long way back to the starting point, and the destruction was not finished. Belikhov had had to turn away as the Russian guns continued their grotesque work on the British retreat. A few of those fortunate enough still to be mounted had stopped to lift colleagues up behind them, making them easy targets for the sharpshooters on the ridges to each side. The rest had simply galloped helter-skelter towards safety, raked by bullets but more likely to survive than the walking wounded. It had taken over half an hour for the last remnants of the brigade to leave the killing field, and the toll had been truly terrible to behold. Belikhov could only guess at the numbers, but it seemed to him that over two thirds of the brigade had been lost in the insanity of the assault.

Sitting in the sun at the redoubt nearest the British lines, the Russian colonel's attention returned to the officer he had watched galloping out from the brigade's ranks at the beginning of the advance and shouting at his commander.

He could not be sure, but he thought it was the same soldier that had delivered the order to attack. What had he been trying to tell the leader? Had he realised the order had been misconstrued and been trying to redirect the brigade at the moment he was killed? Belikhov was an amateur historian, and he suspected that the British charge would go down as one of the most splendid, brave and shockingly foolhardy military actions of the century, if not the millennium. After the deliverance of escaping attack himself, and the gruesome sight of it unfolding below him, he wanted to learn more about the first man to die, and the best way to do that was to visit the corpse. It was clearly visible, easily identified by its isolation, and he knew he must act swiftly if he was to avoid meeting the surgeons and gravediggers that would soon be sent into the valley under a flag of truce. He called for a horse and began to make his way down the slope from the heights.

Other than from its location as the first fatality of the engagement, Nolan's body was barely recognisable. Bludgeoned by hooves, his dark, angular features were dreadfully disfigured, and the upper half of his torso was a gaping mess of blood and bone. However, the lower part of his tunic was intact and Belikhov noted a bulge in the pocket at the waistline. He knelt down and picked out a watch with a broken glass face, hands frozen at twelve minutes past eleven, and the initials LN engraved on its back. He tucked the ruined timepiece into the pocket again, and as he did so his fingers touched something else. He pulled out two small dice and examined them. A betting man, perhaps, or had the young officer merely used gaming as a means of passing the long hours of boredom that are a soldier's curse on campaign? The Russian searched the rest of the body for belongings, but could find nothing more, except the lancer's sabre lying clean and unblunted at his side. Then, hearing voices approaching, he looked up to see a group of stretcher bearers fifty yards away, unarmed and coming towards him. As a senior officer he had no wish to be accused of robbing the dead, but he remained curious about the dice and their owner. He curled his fingers into a fist and rose to gather his horse's reins. LN, whoever he might have been, could be buried in honour with his sword and his watch, and no one would miss a couple of ancient grey ivory cubes.

*

And then...

+ Colonel Belikhov is injured at the Battle of Inkerman in November 1854 and is repatriated from the Crimea to his hometown of Semipalatinsk in Kazakh Russia.

+ As he recuperates, he befriends the author Fyodor Dostoevsky, who is doing compulsory military service in Semipalatinsk after his release from a Siberian prison where he has spent a four-year sentence for distributing banned literature. In his spare time the author tutors schoolchildren of upper-class families, including that of Belikhov.

+ The two men gamble from time to time after the children's lessons are finished for the day, and Belikhov goes on to give Dostoevsky the dice as a wedding present on the author's marriage in 1857. Nine years later Dostoevsky bases a character – the General – on his Kazakh friend in his novel *The Gambler*.

+ At the height of his fame in early 1881 Dostoevsky agrees to an interview in St Petersburg by the English newspaper journalist William Stead, a long-standing champion of Anglo–Russian relations. The author dies just as Stead arrives in St Petersburg, and his widow gifts the dice to Stead in recognition of his wasted trip, explaining their link to Belikhov and the Crimean War.

*

Author's Note

The Charge of the Light Brigade was only one of several distinct actions during the Battle of Balaclava, and the battle was an early engagement in the wider Crimean War, which had broken out the previous year. Seeking territorial expansion to its south, Russia had invaded the region north of the Black Sea controlled by the Ottoman Empire and had begun to establish a naval fleet in the Crimean port of Sevastopol. The governments of Great Britain and France had seen this as a potential threat to their interests in the Mediterranean and beyond and had formed an alliance with the Turks to evict the Russian occupying forces. The war concluded in 1856 when Sevastopol was finally retrieved, technically a victory for the allies but in reality a catalogue of errors for the British in terms of planning, management of resources, battlefield tactics and communication amongst its senior officers.

In the hills above Balaclava on 25 October 1854, the Heavy Brigade's early success, the commanders' failure to capitalise on it, the subsequent events leading to the Light Brigade's mobilisation, Lord Lucan's fateful misinterpretation of his two orders and his verbal exchanges with both Captain Nolan and Lord Cardigan all took place as described. The written instruction snatched from Thomas Leslie by Nolan and carried to Lucan can still be found at the National Army Museum in London. While the order was imprecise and Lucan's readiness to interrogate it was short-lived, Nolan's excitable nature, his impatience with Lucan and his eagerness to see his favoured cavalry unit, the Light Brigade, launched into action were material contributors to the disaster that duly unfolded. His reason for galloping to the front of the charge and what he attempted to shout at Lord Cardigan went with him to his grave. For brevity, I have limited my account of the charge itself to the essentials, but the carnage amongst the 670 or so riders that set off was indeed terrible, with some 120 killed, 130 wounded, 60 taken prisoner and around 400 horses lost (records of the numbers vary). Lord Cardigan survived unscathed, as did the Heavy Brigade, which Lucan had intended to send in behind the Light Brigade but which he withheld as the scale of destruction became evident. The episode was immortalised six weeks later by the poet Alfred Tennyson – 'Theirs not to reason why, theirs but to do and die. Into the valley of Death rode the six hundred' – but was summed up more succinctly in the battle's aftermath by the French general Pierre Bosquet: 'C'est magnifique, mais ce n'est pas la guerre. C'est de la folie.' ('It is magnificent, but it is not war. It is madness.')

All the individuals named in the chapter besides Colonel Belikhov played the parts I have given them, although the wager between Leslie and Nolan is a fiction and Lord Raglan, whom for convenience I have termed Field Marshal, was not elevated to that title until November 1854. Belikhov's name surfaces only in connection with Dostoevsky, who tutored the colonel's children as set out in the 'And then' section after being introduced to him by Maria Isaeva, who Dostoevsky went on to marry in 1857. The author suffered from a mid-life gaming addiction and was reduced to penury by it on at least two occasions around the time that his novel on the subject, The Gambler, was published (1866). There is no indication that Dostoevsky knew William Stead, although Stead was a pioneer of interviews for newspaper publication and a Russophile who visited the country at least twice before the turn of the century.

The Sinking of the Titanic

14 April 1912 – The North Atlantic

Taking the steps down the carpeted staircase from the bridge two by two, in his usual brisk manner, Captain Edward Smith turned his attention to the guests that he was due to host on his table at dinner that night. He disliked leaving anything to chance and made a point of being briefed each evening on who he might find himself talking to. A veteran of the transatlantic route, he always tried to entertain as many as possible of his first-class passengers during the six-day crossing, and he had learnt from long experience their tendency to confuse excessive wealth with merit. They were apt to presume he would know all about them before sitting down to eat and, given the price they were paying to travel on his ship, he supposed it was not an unreasonable expectation.

It had been a long day already, with all the demands of captaincy that a vessel carrying over two thousand people generated, not to mention the added burdens of a maiden voyage and some exceptional sailing conditions. Although the sea and wind were as forgiving as Smith could have wished, the amount of ice in the water off the Newfoundland coast was much greater than usual for this late in the spring. Large floes, referred to as growlers in the maritime world, were visible from the *Titanic's* decks, and the wireless room had received several messages from ships tracking to her north warning of sizeable icebergs drifting southwards. In line with corporate policy, Smith had chosen neither to alter course nor reduce speed, but he had ensured that the lookout detail were fully alert to the berg risk, and he had emphasised the need for care to his team of senior officers. Ideally, he would have remained on the bridge himself, but it was manned by Second Officer Lightoller, a reliable deputy with whom the captain had sailed many times. He would check on Lightoller at the end of dinner, after performing what he liked to call his pastoral duties.

The chief purser, McElroy, usually organised a seating plan for him, but today Smith had intervened to mix some of the most illustrious names with a selection of lesser mortals at his table, in the hope that egos might be diluted, at least temporarily. One of his objectives on each voyage was to play Cupid with the younger men and women under his captaincy, by prising them away from their families and placing them next to each other. RMS *Titanic* offered the grandest, most sumptuous and most complete service on the high seas, so why not include a little matchmaking for free? It amused him to watch the reactions of the couples he threw together, even though, in all his twenty-five years commanding ocean liners for the White Star shipping enterprise, he had never heard of any marriages resulting from his efforts.

So, who was it tonight? He extracted a piece of paper from the inner breast pocket of his uniform and scanned it quickly to remind himself as he walked along the passageway. Ah yes, the middle-aged smelting magnate Benjamin Guggenheim and his young mistress, Madame Aubart – Mrs Guggenheim being safely out of the way in New York; then the redoubtable

Mrs Molly Brown, also middle-aged and enjoying a life of high society and philanthropy on the proceeds of her ex-husband's gold-mining success, without the inconvenience of his company; then William Stead, the celebrated English journalist and publisher who had let it be known he was heading to New York to attend a peace congress in the Carnegie Hall at the invitation of the US president, Mr Taft; then the Canadian property speculator Mark Fortune and his wife Mary, both in their sixties, and their eldest daughter Ethel – the captain had met Mr Fortune earlier in the voyage and had found him garrulous and overbearing, but they were a family of six, all in first class, and he had felt obliged to welcome at least three of them to his table; and finally his lovebirds, not that they knew it yet: Miss Margaret Hays and Mr Harry Widener, each in their mid-twenties, travelling with their parents and probably longing to be liberated from their supervision for an hour or two. He cleared his throat, nodded to the assistant stewards attending the double entrance doors and made his way into the vast saloon where the majority of the diners were already seated.

'Good evening, ladies and gentlemen, my apologies for not being here to greet you,' he said in a loud, genial voice, moving anticlockwise round the table to shake hands with each of his guests and glancing at the place cards to link names to faces before he took his own seat. 'I trust everyone has been introduced? Some of you will know each other by now, I am sure.' He turned to the ladies on either side of him, 'Mrs Fortune, Mrs Brown, it is a particular pleasure to meet you both.'

There was a minor pause, as napkins were arranged on laps and wine glasses were filled by the waiters. Then, as Smith had anticipated, Mr Fortune led the conversation for the entire table. 'Tell us, Captain, how are we doing for speed? There's been some discussion before you appeared about beating the record into New York. What d'you reckon?'

Smith had faced this topic at every one of the three dinners since leaving Queenstown in Ireland, the *Titanic's* final harbour-berth before venturing into the open seas of the Atlantic, and the standard starting gate for any measurement of steamships' journey time to New York. Passengers across all classes aboard the vessel were obsessed with speed and rarely stopped to consider the challenges associated with operating a seven-decked steel-clad monster almost nine hundred feet in length and 46,000 gross tonnage in weight.

'An excellent question, sir,' he replied diplomatically, 'and a matter that under my previous commands I would have regarded as a priority above all else. But here on the *Titanic*, we are focusing as much on comfort as time of arrival. The record across the Atlantic is held by RMS *Mauretania* at around four days, eleven hours, steaming west to east and averaging a fraction over twenty-six knots. A remarkable performance, I acknowledge, but with the help of current, wind and a good deal of discomfort, I daresay.' He chuckled at the absurdity of such an uninspired purpose. 'The *Titanic* is roughly 40% bigger than the *Mauretania*, and many times more lavish, and my officers' job is to grant our passengers the indulgence of the most magnificent ship afloat without rushing it. We will dock in New York in another two and a half days, that's six days in all, and I am confident that when you disembark you will agree it was worth every minute of the extra time spent.'

'Well, I'm in no hurry,' said Mrs Brown, 'I've come all the way from Egypt, and New York can definitely wait an extra day or two. The sea is like a millpond, so I don't have to fuss about feeling sick, and with food like this,' she waved a languid hand at the hors d'oeuvres now being delivered to the table,

'I could stay on board another week. My waistline might not thank me for it, though!' She peeled with laughter and the other guests all murmured their appreciation of the luxury they were enjoying.

'Speed and comfort are all very well, Captain,' Benjamin Guggenheim broke in, 'but what about safety?' A dapper blond-haired man, known throughout North America for his rigorous attention to detail in developing his business interests, he leant forward to labour the point. 'What about all this ice in the water? I've made this journey several times and I've never seen an iceberg before.'

After the day's wireless traffic, Smith had wondered whether this query would arise, and he had his response ready. 'That's just the scraps of the North Atlantic winter for you, Mr Guggenheim. What you are seeing around us are floes, not icebergs. They are small lumps of ice that have floated south from Greenland on the current. They lie on the surface without the undercarriage that bergs have, so ships can steer straight through them without any trouble. They won't make any difference to the voyage.'

'But what if full-blown icebergs are drifting down behind them?' Mrs Fortune argued timidly. She was a placid matron-like lady, used to operating in the shadow of her husband but always quick to worry about any threat to her four children, Smith guessed.

'Very unlikely,' he replied. 'We are a long way south for bergs to reach us, and even if one did, Mrs Fortune, they are not the evil giants the rumour-mongers would have you believe. We can steer round them, and if we were to hit one, well, there are various examples of ships striking them and not being severely damaged.'

'Is that so?' A dry voice spoke from the far side of the table, and the captain looked across at William Stead. 'I remember reading a book called *Futility* about fifteen years ago where a cross-Atlantic liner goes down after being holed by an iceberg in April and nearly all the passengers and crew die. It was by an American author, Robertson I think his name was, and the real cause of death was a lack of lifeboats on board.'

'The glorious world of fiction, Mr Stead.' Smith smiled cheerfully and went on before anyone else could take the conversation into even gloomier territory. 'Please, all of you, rest assured that we have men in the crow's nest twenty-four hours a day on the lookout for icebergs. We also have plenty of lifeboats, and most importantly, the ship is virtually unsinkable. Without going into all the detail, her hull has the best, most modern steel plating the industry has ever devised, and her internal construction is compartmentalised in such a way that, if we did take water on board in one area, it could not flood the rest of her. Now,' he turned deliberately to his right-hand neighbour, in order to break up the table-wide discussion, 'tell me about Winnipeg, Mrs Fortune. I'm told you live there, and it's not a place I've ever managed to visit.'

Their concerns dispelled, the diners settled into a series of paired conversations, and Smith began to relax. He had not lied about the ships that had survived berg strikes, but there were examples of others less fortunate, and the subject of sinking was not one to let passengers dwell on. He kept half an ear out for its revival, should it need to be quashed again, and listened to Mrs Fortune waxing lyrical on the attractions of life in the capital city of Manitoba. Hundreds of miles from the coast in every direction, it sounded too cold and isolated for him, but Mr Fortune had evidently built a thriving real estate empire there and his wife explained with pride that the family took regular vacations in Europe on the back of it. Smith asked politely which countries they had visited and, as the first course plates were removed and the main course served, Mrs Brown on his left-hand side could not resist joining in to tell them where she had been too.

Further round the table, Smith was aware of Mr Fortune, having been abandoned by Mrs Brown, regaling Madame Aubart with tales of his career, and Guggenheim, sitting opposite her, trying to interrupt the Canadian's self-inflated monologue. Beyond them sat Mr Stead and the three younger members, the Fortune daughter, the Hays girl and Mr Widener between them. Smith was gratified to see that a lively conversation had been struck up amongst the foursome, and he strained to hear what was being discussed.

'I suspect you must get given a hard time about your name, Miss Fortune,' said Harry Widener. 'Being called Widener is bad enough, but "Misfortune" is a tough draw. You ought to get married.'

'Is that a proposal, Mr Widener?' Aged twenty-eight, Ethel Fortune had heard all the jokes and was well used to batting them away. She shifted her gaze to look mischievously at Mr Stead and then caught the eye of Margaret Hays. They all laughed, and Widener turned faintly pink. Not wishing to extend his embarrassment, Ethel went on hastily. 'As it happens, I am engaged already, so you've missed your chance. I am swapping Miss Fortune for Mrs Gordon in the summer, but in a way I'll be sad to change my name, however silly it sounds sometimes.'

'That's nothing,' Miss Hays chipped in. 'My middle name is Bechstein, thanks to my dear parents. Imagine being named after a piano!'

'Well, I think that's superb,' said Widener. 'In fact, from now on I shall think of you as a grand piano.' He had the grace to grin sheepishly at his terrible pun, then continued. 'What about you, Mr Stead, are you saddled with an awkward middle name you'd rather go without?'

'If I was, young man, I certainly wouldn't admit it to you,' answered the Englishman. He smiled to take the sting out of his words. 'No, I have no middle name besides Thomas to worry about, but I confess I was known as in-Stead during my school years, which became very tedious after a time. Names are curious things, and as a journalist I have come across all sorts. Take our fellow travellers here on the *Titanic* as an example.' He gestured around the hall. 'I was talking to the chief steward yesterday, and he showed me a list of the passengers in first and second class. From the ones I can remember, we've got a Mr Salomon whose parents blessed him with the forenames Abraham and Lincoln.' He looked round his audience to ensure they had understood the reference to their late great US president. 'Then there are two men with the middle names Sleeper and Clinch, a family of three called Dodge, and a lady called Mrs Trout. All fine people, I'm sure, and neither they nor we should have any reason to feel ashamed of how we were baptised.'

Stead stopped speaking as waiters arrived behind each diner, ready to clear the main course and offer a selection of desserts. The threads of conversation had been broken all around the table and he decided it was an opportune moment to rescue Madame Aubart on his right from the attentions of the voluble Mr Fortune. 'I am intrigued, madame, by your necklace. It is very beautiful, but I am at a loss to know what I am admiring.'

Leontine Aubart turned towards Stead with an ill-concealed expression of relief, her fingers moving involuntarily to the pendant below her throat. A Parisian singer by training, some twenty years younger than Benjamin Guggenheim, she was unused to mixing in his elevated social circle and slightly overwhelmed by the grandeur of the *Titanic*'s first-class trappings. Conversing with Mr Fortune had been easy enough since she had been required to say little more than an occasional 'fascinating' or 'how clever'. But the Englishman on her other side seemed well meaning and she was delighted to be offered a topic on which she could talk with a degree of knowledge.

'Thank you, monsieur.' Her voice was soft, with a mild accent and the formality born of a foreign classroom. 'You are correct, it is highly unusual.' She reached behind her to unclip the gold necklace and held it up for Stead to examine more closely. The blue-black pendant hanging from a hoop at its base had a peculiar texture that he could not pinpoint, but its size was what had first drawn his attention. The length and breadth of a female hand, its exaggerated triangular shape reminded him of a tooth, despite its colour, although on a scale that was out of keeping with any beast he could picture.

'It is truly extraordinary,' he said after a few seconds, shrugging his shoulders in defeat, 'but I still have no idea what it is. You must put me out of my misery, madame. I would venture to suggest that it is a fossil of some long-forgotten animal, but I might be totally mistaken.'

'Pas mal!' the Frenchwoman exclaimed with glee. 'Well done, monsieur, you have guessed better than most. It is an ancient tooth, but not from an animal. It is from a fish called a megalodon, which was like a giant shark living in the sea millions of years ago. Mr Guggenheim has an interest in fossils, and he bought it for me as a present. Other girls might not be happy, I suppose, but for me, it is like treasure.' She clipped the necklace back into place and chose a dessert from the waiter hovering behind her.

'A unique item,' said Stead, nodding with approval, 'and there is surely no more personal gift than that.' He felt in a trouser pocket and set two small dice down on the tablecloth between them. Against the crisp snow-white linen, they had an exhausted grey pallor, and Stead was conscious of their sorrowful appearance by comparison to the huge tooth. 'This is *my* treasure. They don't look like much,' he added apologetically, 'but I have had them analysed by an expert who claims they are from a mammoth tusk, probably from Persia or northern India, and at least four thousand years old. How people figure that out, I cannot say. But the dice have had an unusual history, at least in the last sixty years or so that I know of, and I like to think they have played a part in many great events down the ages since they were first carved. I carry them everywhere, in case I am swept up in a great event myself.' He smiled at her to downplay any hint of pomposity and returned the dice to his pocket. 'Now, madame, tell me about your life in Paris. I expect it is most exotic.'

The conversation at the captain's table ran on for a further thirty minutes, as cheese and liqueurs were provided, until a man from the neighbouring group of diners rose to his feet, brandy in hand, and bellowed, 'A toast, to the mighty *Titanic*!' Smith hated this sort of excess but could hardly refuse to participate, so he stood and was joined by the majority of those in the hall. 'The *Titanic*,' they shouted and drained their glasses. As he waited for Mrs Fortune and Mrs Brown to resume their seats, he leant down to explain. 'The ship's surgeon, ladies. Dr O'Loughlin enjoys a celebration, and I hope you'll agree a vessel as splendid as this deserves to be saluted. But I must ask you to excuse me now. I need to check on the bridge and then get some sleep. The crew and I have a busy two days before we reach the American coast.' He moved round the table once again, wishing his guests a good evening, and turned for the door. It was close to nine o'clock and time to ensure there were no dramas brewing on Second Officer Lightoller's shift at the helm.

*

The logbook clock stood at twenty minutes past midnight when Thomas Andrews finished his briefing on the damage caused by the iceberg, a mere forty minutes since the collision itself, but in that time Captain Smith's faith in the might of the *Titanic* had evaporated. The shudder of the impact had awoken him, and he had flung his clothes on before racing to the bridge to learn what had happened. There, First Officer Murdoch, who had replaced Second Officer Lightoller for the night watch, had described how the berg had been spotted from the crow's nest too late for a meaningful change of path to be set. The berg appeared to have struck a glancing blow on the hull's forward starboard side, well below the surface, and stokers from the boiler rooms had reported that a significant volume of water was already being shipped. Smith had immediately instructed the engines to be turned off, ordered an emergency signal for assistance to be transmitted by wireless and called for Andrews to be summoned from his cabin.

A director of the Belfast ship-building firm Harland & Wolff, thirty-nine-year-old Thomas Andrews was the chief designer of the *Titanic* and had been invited by the White Star owners to travel on her maiden voyage as a tribute to his achievement. If anyone could provide an accurate assessment of the vessel's predicament, it was him, and Smith had listened with growing horror to his account. Andrews had made a swift but detailed inspection below decks and had provided a commendably concise appraisal, both of the damage done and the future in store. Yet Smith still struggled to absorb the full implications of what he was being told.

'So you are saying that there is nothing we can do to keep her afloat? I thought she was supposed to be almost unsinkable.'

Andrews looked intently at Smith, his eyes expressionless. 'As I explained, Captain, the *Titanic* was designed to withstand flooding in up to four of the hull's sixteen compartments, but there is evidence that six of them have been breached by the iceberg. The chance of that was considered highly unlikely when the blueprints for construction were being drafted. It will take a fair amount of time for those six compartments to be filled to the brim, but eventually the ship will sink. I estimate that we have around two hours from now to load up the lifeboats before she goes down. I recommend we start as soon as possible.'

'But... how can you be sure? Can we not wait for a vessel nearby to answer our distress call and then ferry passengers off?'

'You can take that risk, Captain, if you want. But you told me that there has been no response to your signal, and the time you have available for evacuation is simply a mathematical calculation. Two hours. No more.'

'My God,' muttered Smith, his face ashen. He too had performed some mental arithmetic, the outcome of which was too ghastly to put into words. The combined total of passengers and crew on board was just over 2,200, and the twenty lifeboats on the ship's decks had a maximum capacity of 1,178. At the very least, around one thousand would drown, and if there was any delay or inefficiency in loading the boats, the death toll would be even higher. Three and half hours ago, sitting in the luxury of the first-class dining saloon, eating and drinking the finest fare available in the world, chatting to some of the richest people in America, reassuring them of their safety amongst the ice, such an ending to the night had been unthinkable. He was one of those destined to die, it occurred to him belatedly, since he could not abandon command while others remained on board. My God, how had it come to this so fast?

He glanced around the bridge and realised that his officers were waiting expectantly for instructions. The time for information-gathering and deliberation was over and the necessary course of action was clear. He grasped the designer's hand and shook it firmly. 'Thank you, Mr Andrews. At least we know where we stand.' It would be pointless to mention the lifeboat problem, since there was nothing to be gained by doing so and, in any event, Andrews may well have worked it out for himself. Then he turned to First Officer Murdoch to issue the chain of orders for evacuation. Cabins must be emptied, lifebelts distributed, a controlled on-deck exodus arranged with women and children receiving priority and crew members allocated to release the lifeboats from their davits once loading was complete. Most important of all, panic must not be allowed to set in.

Twenty-five minutes later, an hour and five minutes after the collision, the first lifeboat was launched. The *Titanic*'s deck was a heaving mass of passengers and off-duty crew in varying states of undress, united in confusion after being roused from their beds and shepherded up companionways into the chilly starlit night. On arrival they were being marshalled into queues by officers equipped with megaphones, while junior crew members wrestled with ropes and fixings in preparation for lowering the remaining boats down the sides of the ship. The captain himself was going from queue to queue, urging everyone to remain calm, and in general they were proving remarkably amenable. His efforts, and those of his officers, were not helped by the deafening noise of steam venting through the four huge funnels from the vessel's boilers. Looking at the bustle of activity around him, however, Smith was aware that it could have been much worse, for although news that the ship had hit an iceberg was now common knowledge, the fact that she was definitely sinking and that only half of those aboard could be saved was not. There would be a moment, he knew, when the truth would become obvious and the boat-loading would degenerate into an ugly scramble for survival, but the longer it could be deferred, the more efficient the evacuation process would be.

The captain's judgement of the situation was in some respects misguided, though not in the manner he might have anticipated. Even after another half hour, despite water continuing to pour through the breached hull, the ship was still not listing to any material degree, and this together with the biting cold of the Atlantic night was enough to persuade many people to return to their cabins to await rescue. Half the lifeboats had now been launched, and hundreds of passengers were still queuing patiently on deck, a few (including Mr Guggenheim and Mrs Brown, Smith noticed with surprise) even assisting the crew in evacuating the women and children. For a perceptive handful, more familiar with the physics of flotation and having watched the number of available boats diminish, the reality of their plight had already dawned on them. William Stead had been surveying the scene for several minutes before he came to a reluctant conclusion. If he was to die, he would do so in the company of a good book, as befitting one of the great wordsmiths of his generation. He would fetch one from his cabin and retire to the first-class smoking room to read in peace.

At the foot of a stairwell leading up to the deck five minutes later, book in hand, Stead met Ethel Fortune hurrying down towards him, wrapped in a flimsy day coat over her nightdress. 'Miss Fortune,' he said in astonishment, 'what on earth are you doing down here?'

'I'm frozen,' she replied, taking the last step down into the passageway serving the first-class cabins. 'I've been standing up there for almost an hour and I'm so cold I can't bear it any longer. In any case, why bother? We don't seem to be sinking, and I heard one of the officers say there are other ships nearby that will come and help us. Why sit in an open lifeboat till then? I am going back to my nice, warm cabin.'

'But what about the rest of your family? They'll be anxious about you.'

'Oh, they know I'm down here. I was with my mother and sisters, and we had an argument about what to do. They're in a queue for the next boat to be launched. If someone else wants my seat, they're welcome to it.' A violent shiver ran through her, and she attempted to brush past Stead.

'Wait, Miss Ethel, please wait,' Stead spoke urgently. 'I appreciate you are cold, but listen to me for a minute. The ship really is sinking, I promise you. It may not appear that way, but quite soon the amount of water coming in will tip the bow below the surface and then we will go down very quickly.' His voice acquired a lower, harder edge. 'There aren't enough lifeboats for everyone still on board and when people finally realise that, there will be a massive scrummage for the few remaining places. You need to go back on deck and join your family while you can.'

'So why are you down here?'

'Because I am male, and the boats are reserved for women and children,' Stead looked at her evenly, 'and because I'm old; I've had a good life; and I have made my peace with what is about to happen.'

'Come now, Mr Stead, aren't you being rather melodramatic? We've stayed afloat now for over ninety minutes since hitting the iceberg. I'm not the only one deciding to return to my cabin.' She clenched her jaw to stop her teeth chattering and made another move to pass him, but he blocked her way.

'Miss Ethel, don't do this, I implore you. You must believe me when I say that many, many people are going to die here, but that does not have to include you.' Stead set his book down on the bottom step of the staircase with his left hand, the other balled into a loose fist, and spoke more gently. 'I much enjoyed meeting you at dinner this evening. You have a fiancé lucky enough to be waiting for you on land. Don't risk disappointing him by taking bad odds down here in your cabin. In fact, on that subject,' he opened his right hand, 'I have a wedding present for you.'

Ethel Fortune peered down at his palm in amazement. This was hardly the moment to be receiving marriage gifts. 'The dice I saw you showing Madame Aubart earlier?' she said doubtfully.

'Indeed,' replied Stead. 'Look, this may sound crazy in the circumstances, but I was taken by Mr Widener's comment about your name at dinner. Growing up as "Misfortune" struck me as very unfair on you. These are amongst my most favourite belongings. They have had a lengthy history, including being used in the Crimean War and being owned by a famous Russian author before they came to me. I'm not suggesting they will bring you luck, as such, but they do not belong in a shipwreck, so take them with my blessing for a long and happy marriage.' He pressed the dice into the girl's hand and bent to retrieve his book. 'Now, we must get you onto a lifeboat without delay; there's so little time before the chaos begins. Come on up to the deck, and let's find your family for you.' He ushered her up the staircase, unravelling a scarf from his neck as he went and draping it around her shoulders.

*

And then...

+ William Stead escorts Ethel Fortune to the lifeboat containing her mother and sisters, just in time for her to climb aboard as it is being lowered into the water. The boat is rowed away into the darkness and Stead takes refuge in the first-class smoking room where he finds Benjamin Guggenheim and his secretary Victor Giglio, dressed in white tie and tails, drinking brandy and smoking cigars. He joins them, and they wait for the inevitable.

+ At 2.20am on Monday, 15 April 1912, twenty minutes after the bow has begun to dip beneath the surface and fifteen minutes after the launch of the final lifeboat, RMS *Titanic* finally breaks in two and sinks to the ocean floor. Captain Smith, Thomas Andrews, William Stead and his drinking companions are among the fifteen hundred or more whose bodies are never recovered. The lifeboat passengers are rescued around 4am on the arrival of RMS *Carpathia* and are delivered to New York three days later.

+ Restored to her family home in Winnipeg, Ethel Fortune writes to William Stead's wife to express her gratitude for his kindness and receives a letter in response with information about the background of the dice and how Stead came to own them.

+ Ethel goes on to marry her fiancé Crawford Gordon in 1913 and lives for a further forty-eight years, dying in Toronto in 1961. After her death, much of her property is put up for sale at auction by her family. The dice are purchased by an unnamed British bidder attracted by the description of their association with the Charge of the Light Brigade.

*

Author's Note

The final hours of the Titanic's maiden voyage, and the causes of the tragedy, have been raked over by maritime analysts, journalists, authors and film-makers ever since she plunged to the seabed of the North Atlantic. My version of events, while seeking to portray the facts and timeline as reported in the aftermath, provides only a basic snapshot of the story, the principal fictional elements being the conversation at Captain Smith's dining table and the meeting between William Stead and Ethel Fortune as the lifeboats are being filled. The presence on board of all the characters referred to in the chapter, and their various fates, are accurately recorded, but no list of the captain's dinner guests survives, and there is no evidence that Stead met the Fortune family.

The calm conditions at the time of the collision meant that there were few waves splashing up against the iceberg, making it very difficult for the lookouts to spot in the moonless night sky. Unbeknown to the crew, icebergs originating in Greenland had drifted much further south than usual after the most severe winter for fifty years, and with the ship travelling at 21.5 knots, close to her top speed, First Officer Murdoch had barely thirty seconds to take evasive action. Within forty minutes, the Titanic's designer Thomas Andrews had assessed the damage as described in the chapter, and Captain Smith was faced with the bleak knowledge of certain doom for both the vessel herself and over a thousand of those aboard. Andrews' projection of the time it would take to sink was extraordinarily precise, and survivors' accounts of the lifeboat loading process indicate that it was performed with surprisingly little agitation or panic. One factor that I have not referred to, however, was the failure by the crew to make best use of the boats, many of them being launched well before they were full. As a result, far more people remained trapped on the Titanic as she went down than the captain had anticipated.

The exact figures for passengers and crew on board, split between fatalities and survivors, differ slightly amongst sources. The ship was built to accommodate over 3,500, but the number sailing on her maiden voyage was limited to just over 2,200, of which some 1,500 drowned. The seven hundred or so rowed to safety compares to the 1,178 maximum lifeboat capacity. Survival rates in the sub-freezing point seawater were minimal. Like many others, Ethel Fortune did return to her cabin but was persuaded by a steward to go back on deck where she joined her mother and two sisters as their lifeboat was being launched. Her father and her brother, Charles, did not survive. After helping women and children into the boats and recognising that there would be no escape for themselves, William Stead chose to read a book in the first-class smoking room, while Benjamin Guggenheim and Victor Giglio were last seen sitting in deckchairs, sipping brandy and smoking cigars, having gone to the trouble of donning formal evening wear for their demise.

By the time of the 1912 disaster, after a distinguished career in investigative journalism and publishing, William Stead had become a well-known campaigner for pacifism around the world. Memorial plaques to him can still be found in New York's Central Park and on the Thames Embankment in London. The novel Futility that he refers to at the dinner table did exist, written in 1898 by Morgan Robertson with a storyline about passengers aboard a British ship called Titan drowning in a manner uncannily similar to that of the Titanic. As for Stead's conversation with Madame Aubart about her jewellery, a golden necklace bearing what is thought to be a megalodon tooth was discovered amongst the Titanic's wreckage in 2022. The owner has not been identified, and the necklace remains undisturbed on the ocean floor, 12,500 feet below sea level, 370 nautical miles south-east of Canada's Newfoundland coast.

Epilogue

Fate's Finale

The summer solstice is always a popular moment on Mount Olympus, the highest peak in Greece and home to the twelve great gods of Greek mythology. Saturday, 21 June 1975 was no exception. Climbers eager to scale the mountain in a single day had flocked to the Spilios Agapitos refuge, a halfway mark between the village of Prionia and the bare, windswept limestone ridge above. There they milled around, swapping stories, checking rucksacks and replenishing water bottles as they gathered their strength for the more challenging hike ahead. After a three-hour trek to around 2,100 metres above sea level, some had decided the full expedition was too ambitious in the mid-year heat. They were content to aim instead for the Muses Plateau, a broad expanse of alpine tundra below the final rocky ascent providing unrivalled views of the 2,917-metre summit known as Zeus's throne.

The middle-aged Englishman sitting alone at one end of the refuge's balcony had already come far enough. He had underestimated both the stamina required for the climb and the number of people accompanying him. He sipped a cup of coffee and glanced at a guidebook he had brought with him on the bus from Thessaloniki. The boarding house he was staying in there was furnished with numerous useful items such as this, limiting the need to draw on his dwindling funds. Tall and imposing in stature, with a self-assured countenance and a sheaf of dark hair tucked under a floppy white cricketer's hat, he could have passed for the archetypal British gentleman, were it not for an ill-kempt beard and scruffy, badly fitting clothes. He paid little attention to the conversation around him, mostly in Greek, of which he had only a limited grasp, until suddenly a group of English-speaking voices broke through the babble. Two young couples had evidently met at the refuge and were comparing notes about their holidays.

'Yes, we've just arrived here, after hitchhiking across from Turkey. How about you?'

'We came out from London a week ago. A day to recover in Athens, then down into the Peloponnese, and now up here till we head home on Tuesday.'

'So what's the news from England? We haven't been there since the end of April.'

'Not a lot. All the usual stuff. West Ham won the FA Cup; we had the referendum about staying in Europe's Common Market; the weather went from really cold and wet at the beginning of the month to boiling hot as we were leaving. What else...?' The speaker looked at his partner for inspiration, before remembering, 'Oh, that guy in the papers who disappeared after the family's nanny was killed in November last year has been found guilty...'

The Englishman froze. Then he pulled his hat further down over his brow and shifted his chair to stare out across the ravine below the balcony's parapet, his back to his countrymen as they packed up their equipment and left to resume the hiking trail.

Although he had read out-of-date British newspapers brought to the Thessaloniki guest house by other travellers and knew that an inquest into the nanny's death was in course, he had not heard the outcome. But there it was, his fate now sealed, with neither his account of events nor his presence for the verdict considered worthy of concern. In the eyes of the law, as well as in the court of public opinion, Lord Lucan, old Etonian aristocrat, ex-military officer and merchant banker, professional gambler and father of three, was a murderer.

After ten minutes, with the balcony now empty besides a group of local men engrossed in discussion several tables away, Lucan lifted a canvas fishing bag from the paving onto his knees and extracted a small box from one of its front pouches. Opening the box, he picked out a pair of grey ivory dice. They had been almost his sole possession on his six-month journey to Thessaloniki, as he was passed like a ticking time bomb from friend to friend: over the English channel from Newhaven to Le Touquet, down through France to Nice and across the Mediterranean by yacht to northern Greece. He turned the dice over between his fingers, as if seeing the detail of their ancient, cracked surfaces for the first time, although it was an examination he had performed often in the preceding weeks while brooding in the guest house. The property of a nineteenth-century cavalryman killed at the Battle of Balaclava and then of a man drowned in the *Titanic* disaster, they seemed to have inflicted the same scourge of chance on him. They had been his companion ever since he had bought them in Canada fourteen years ago, and now he had only exile from massive gambling losses and a murder conviction to show for it. He wondered, as he had so often before, what the dice's history had been in ages past and whether they had somehow touched the destiny of his great-great-grandfather, the Lucan of the day that had ordered the Charge of the Light

Brigade. Whatever their story, his former life was over, and the time had come to be rid of them too.

He stood, abruptly, and flung the dice with all his strength out over the parapet towards the mountain's distant peak. They plunged into the ravine and were lost to sight as they tumbled down its rock-strewn side. The Englishman was not to know that he was standing on the terrace from which their fateful journey had begun many thousands of years previously. Now, at last, they had been restored to the Olympian lap of the gods.

*

Author's Note

At the inquest of Sandra Rivett's death in early June 1975, John Bingham, seventh Earl of Lucan, was found guilty by jury of her murder. Living in the family home as nanny to his children, Sandra had been killed seven months earlier in what is presumed to have been a mistaken assault intended instead for Lucan's wife Veronica, from whom he was estranged. Aside from the bitter breakdown of his marriage and loss of the children's custody, he had substantial gambling debts at the time. After the attack, Lucan drove to Newhaven on the coast of the English Channel, where he abandoned his car and disappeared. Despite numerous reported sightings around the world, he has never been caught, and my description of his journey to Greece is entirely fictional. In his absence he was declared legally dead in 1999, and a death certificate was finally issued in 2016.

Acknowledgements

A massive thank-you to all those who have supported my journey through the ages and pages of *Argentum* and now *Fortuna*. Your endurance is remarkable.